Blackwarren Books, LLC
112 Meadowbrook Circle
Fulton, NY 13069

www.blackwarrenbooks.com

Editing by Skye Sisk

Cover Art by Ivy Gladstone

First Blackwarren Books, LLC electronic publication: September 2023
First Blackwarren Books, LLC print publication: September 2023

CERTIFIED GOLD:
ON THE AIR

by David M. DeMar

DAVID M. DEMAR

For Lance

PROLOGUE

You would think that, as a Dragon, I wouldn't be fazed by being caught in a life-or-death struggle with an enemy that had been stalking me for months. Especially since I'm the last gold Dragon left in the world, next in line to be king, second in line only to the Ra'keth himself, praise be his name.

You could think that, but you'd be wrong.

Instead, I was in my human form, silvery blood streaming from a nasty gash across the left side of my face, trying desperately to not be stabbed to death by a Sidhe with a Dragonsbane-tipped rapier. This was same lunatic whose son had been making my life a living hell for the whole semester.

Of course, insulting him and his son over the radio – repeatedly – probably hadn't been the best idea I'd ever had.

I never shoulda taken that stupid accounting class, I thought wildly, remembering in a flash when this whole mess began.

CHAPTER ONE

"**S**o yes, this is exactly why cost accounting is so crucial to the managerial role. It considers all the input costs of your business and what it produces, and that means you need to pay attention to both your fixed costs and your variable ones."

I blinked up at the whiteboard as Professor Trevanche continued his lecture. I tried my best to pay attention, but the late morning sunlight was streaming in through the window on my right. A pair of black-capped chickadees were jumping through the branches of a hawthorn tree, picking at the berries.

"So, who can answer that question?" I tore my gaze from the window. A couple of students raised their hands, and he pointed. "Mister..." He looked down at his lectern. "Mr. Summers?"

I slumped as the impossibly handsome student in front of me dropped his hand. "Variable costs are tied to production levels," he said. He tucked an errant lock of platinum blond hair behind his left ear, which came to a graceful, upswept point.

As he spoke, the air around him seemed to shimmer like he had stepped into a spotlight. His voice, like many of his kind, was like honey. A blank, almost rapturous look fell across Trevanche's face as he listened, clearly entranced. "Like if a company has to keep up with demand for something they're making, they have to make more of it and that costs more."

The professor smiled dreamily, eyes half-lidded, before shaking himself slightly. He grinned, almost wildly. "That's right! What a great example. *Thank* you, Mr. Summers!" The student leaned back smugly, folding his arms across his chest. I rolled my eyes. *Leave it to Wyndham Summers to turn up the glamour on a professor*, I thought. Trevanche continued. "Yes, variable costs will fluctuate due to market conditions, whether a company decides to expand or contract their product line – there are any number of different things that could affect a company's variable costs."

Our professor droned on. I glanced up at the clock on the classroom wall, then back out the window. A larger bird, a gray one with white stripes on its wings, had landed in the hawthorn tree. The chickadees flapped away as it began picking through the berries.

"Mr. Konacsz?" I jerked back. Trevanche looked mildly annoyed. "Perhaps you could answer that?"

Shit. "Um. Could you.... c-could you r-repeat the question?"

There was an uncomfortable silence. Summers cleared his throat. The class tittered.

"Yes, I was asking if anyone could explain the core differences between cost accounting and financial accounting. Which you would know if you had been paying attention." He turned away. "Anyone want to provide him with the answer? Unless you have it yourself, Mr. Konacsz?"

"W-well, financial accounting is for... um, it's for p-providing information to external financial statement users, like, uh, creditors or investors, right? And it n-needs to be in a set, s-s-standardized format in order to meet generally accepted accounting principles. C-cuh-cost accounting..." I took a deep breath, slowing down my speech. "Cost accounting is more flexible. So it can adapt to meet management's needs. This means each company can have its own s-s-set of standards.

And even different departments of the same company can use different c-cost accounting standards."

Trevanche blinked. "Well, yes," he began slowly. "I'm sorry, Mr. Konacsz, you obviously were paying attention."

I shrugged. "My parents run their own business," I said.

The phone on Trevanche's lectern began to chime. He glanced down at it and tapped the screen. "All right, that's all the time we have for today," he said. Students began closing laptops and putting away notebooks. "We'll pick this back up on Thursday. Assignments are listed on the class portal."

Heart hammering in my ribcage, I got my own stuff together and slunk out the door into the hallway, losing myself in the crowd as students flooded out from other classrooms. When I got outside I beelined for the closest empty bench and sat down, trying to breathe. *Slow and steady, just like Miss Fremont taught you.* I closed my eyes and went over everything I had learned in speech therapy as a kid. "Okay," I breathed. "Okay."

My phone buzzed, and I jumped. I fished it from my pocket and looked down at the message notification. *How's your second week going?*

I unlocked my phone and tapped out a reply. *Hey, Dad - fine, busy with classes. GTG, next one starting in 10 mins*

I tapped Send. A few seconds later, a reply came in. *Good! Call Mom later, okay?*

I sent a thumbs-up emoji and stuffed the phone into my pocket, muttering to myself. I checked the time and did some mental math. *I should make it*, I thought, and set out across campus.

It was even nicer outside than it had looked through the window. The sun was bright and warm, and the old-growth maples lining the walkways were still fresh and full of leaves. The flower beds, loaded with snapdragons and with more than a few bumblebees bending their stems, stood out against meticulously placed deep red mulch. Even the looming neo-Gothic buildings on either side of me seemed less foreboding than they usually did. A shadow shifted and I looked up; one of the gargoyles on the Old Main Tower adjusted his position to catch a little more of the sun. *Must be nice*, I thought. *Do gargoyles have to go to college?*

I left the quad, passing under a wrought-iron arch with stone pillars. The landscaping continued to be impeccable, but the buildings here were closer to Mid-Century Modern and had a more lived-in look. Eventually, classrooms gave way to the dorms, and I walked up the steps to Coindre Hall.

The vestibule door was propped open, as was the inner door. I walked through into the lobby and saw why – a burly, blue-skinned Troll who had to be at least six and a half feet tall was wheeling a hand-truck to the vending machine. It was full of drink crates packed to the gills with heavy-looking glass bottles of iced coffee. Her work uniform had "Somerset Holdings" printed across the back. She set the hand truck down and picked up one of the crates easily with one hand. The bottles clinked almost musically.

I turned the corner and walked down the hallway. At the end, I pushed the door to the stairwell open, started climbing, and came out on the third floor. A short walk down the hallway past the bathrooms and showers and I came to a stop in front of room 314.

There was a sock on the doorknob. Again.

I stood there for a few seconds as a knot formed in my stomach. Finally, I reached up to knock, wincing away from the door like I was about to defuse a bomb. As I did so the door opened. I stepped back, startled, and a brown-haired student with his hair askew stepped out, a dumb grin on his face. "Oh, hi Ricky! We were just leaving." His shirt was on inside-out and backwards.

I moved aside to let him pass. Another student followed. He was shorter; his hair was a sandy blond. "Hi Ricky!"

I waved and moved to enter but had to dodge aside as a dark-skinned girl stepped into the hallway. "Hey, wait for me!" she called after the other two, racing down the corridor. She stuffed a pair of panties into her bag as she did so. "Bye, Ricky!"

I walked in. Niko was leaning back in a chair, his hooves up on his desk, wearing nothing but a dark red bathrobe that he hadn't bothered tying closed. Again. He grinned lazily at me. "Hey buddy! You just missed the squad!"

I dropped my bag on my bed and walked over to the window. "Jesus, it's stuffy in here," I said, pulling up the blinds and throwing open the window. Fresh air began pouring into the room.

Niko winced and turned his head to the side, shielding his eyes with the back of his forearm. "Oh, c'mon, man! I only just woke up!" He pushed his curly chestnut-brown hair out of his face and tucked it behind one of his curling ram's horns. "You know I need my beauty sleep!"

"You can't tell me you were just napping this whole time, were you?" I looked back at him and instantly regretted it. "Fuck's sake, could you close your robe?"

He laughed. "What's wrong, see something you like? You know you've got a standing invitation, buddy." He took his time pulling his robe closed, belting it. "The rest of the squad feels the same way."

I unzipped my bag and pulled out my accounting textbook. "You know I'm not really into any of that, Niko. I, uh, never have been, really?" I shrugged, putting the book on the shelf and pulling down a new one. The title read *Tonal Harmony: Basic Approaches to Music Theory*. "Besides, I've got my next class coming up – and this one I actually like." It slid into my bag, and I zipped it up. "I'll see you later."

CHAPTER TWO

I slipped out of my dorm, closing the door behind me. Two flights of stairs later and I was back on the ground floor, walking out the front door and into the sunlight.

Everything seemed better than it had been on my way to switch out my books. The sun felt warmer, the birdsong sweeter, and I found myself smiling even though I had to glimpse Niko's hairy Satyr balls for something like the twelfth time in the last two weeks. Other than that, he really wasn't that bad a roommate. *Could have been worse*, I thought. *Could've been a Sidhe.*

But even that dark idea couldn't affect my mood. I had gotten through another class of Cost Accounting Systems for Managerial Decisions, and I was on my way to my reward.

I reached the quad and turned left, skirting Old Main and taking a footpath towards a smaller, slightly less ornate building. I climbed up the short flight of worn stone steps and pulled the front door open, slipping inside.

A few students were wending through the hallways on the way to various classes. I joined the general flow of traffic, ducking aside the open door when I reached my own classroom. Professor Chen wasn't there yet, but a handful of other students were waiting. I found my usual desk, second row center, and pulled out my copy of *Tonal Harmony*, a pen, and a spiral notebook.

The clock chimed and Professor Chen bustled in, dressed as always in slacks and a tweed blazer over a rumpled graphic tee. I grinned when I saw it was the Bad Religion shirt that he had worn on the first day of classes last week. He waved, setting his messenger bag down at a table at the front of the class. "All right, guys, let's take attendance so we can get started."

Music Theory went all too fast. We had been in the middle of a discussion about the emotional impact of major versus minor keys when the clock chimed. "Okay, that's it for today! Listen, before you all leave, remember that the college radio station is still looking for students to staff up for the semester." He picked a sheaf of flyers off the table and waved them about. "And yes, that includes not being behind the mic or answering phones." Chen gave me a pointed look; I gave him a shrug in return. "Anyway, it's perfect if you want to learn more about audio engineering and day-to-day operations. It's filling up fast!"

I smiled at the professor on my way out and took one of the flyers, turning over the idea of working at the radio station in my head. I didn't put it in my bag; instead, I started reading through it as soon as I was back outside on the quad. I was so preoccupied I didn't realize what was about to happen until it was too late – in a flash, I collided with someone who had been walking the opposite direction, and I found myself painfully on my ass in the middle of the footpath.

"Watch it, fuckface—oh shit, look who it is." My blood ran cold at the voice. I looked up and my fears were confirmed – it was Summers, the honey-voiced Sidhe from my Business Management class. A retinue of hangers-on, all Sidhe like him, were clustered behind him. "You got some big old balls walking around by yourself in the middle of the day, you overgrown iguana." His face split in a mirthless grin that turned my stomach.

I clambered to my feet, still clutching the flyer I had grabbed from Professor Chen. Summers, impossibly handsome by human standards, laughed in my face. "You have no idea how lucky you are we're not allowed to just hunt you down on sight. Good thing, too – once I'd be done with you there would barely be enough left for a couple of collars for my hunting hounds."

My heart was hammering in my chest again. His leering followers were flanking him, forming a loose semicircle in front of me and blocking my path. "L-leave me alone," I said hoarsely. "I d-d-don't want any trouble, Wyndham, j-j-just let me by please."

Summers barked a short laugh. "What you got there, buddy?" He snatched the flyer from my hands. "The fuck is this? The radio station?" He looked back at me. "You wanna be a deejay, Ruh-ruh-Ricky?" He dropped the flyer and it fluttered to the ground. His cronies laughed. "Go back to your little pile of nickels before I mount your head on my wall, *Dragon*." He pushed past me, dropping his shoulder painfully into mine, and continued to jeer as he and his little court of fiends walked on.

Hands shaking, I scooped the flyer off the ground and walked unsteadily to a nearby bench, sinking down and listening to my pulse race through my temples. A few nearby people who had seen the exchange between me and Summers were shooting over some curious glances, but most were watching him leave, especially the humans. Even by Sidhe standards he was insanely good-looking, despite the perpetual sneer he seemed to like wearing – and that's all non-mythics saw.

He's right, I thought, looking down at the radio station flyer. *A DJ? I can't even talk to strangers*. Hands shaking, I balled up the flyer and went to toss it, but I didn't see a wastebasket anywhere. I stuffed it in a pocket instead, slumping back into the bench. *I should have stayed in Portland with Mom's side of the family*.

I sat there for a while, trying to stop shaking from embarrassment. I wasn't doing very well. Finally, I pulled out my phone and checked the time. *Shit.* I looked across the quad and checked again. *Nope, no way I'd make it now.* I sighed. *Fuck it, I'm in no mood anymore.* I stood up, knees still weak but mind made up, and set off.

CHAPTER THREE

"Ricky? Don't you usually have a class around now?" Naveen was behind the counter, looking at me quizzically.

"Yeah, I, uh... I wasn't feeling all that great." I shrugged, not about to get into it with a human about the Sidhe and the dim view they took of my kind. "I, uh, I thought I'd c-come by and check on that interlibrary loan I put in for a couple days ago?"

"Lemme check. Actually, hold on." He walked away from the counter, sticking his head through the office door behind him. "Hey Ellen, did Ricky's thing come in today?"

The answer was muffled. "Why, is he here?"

Naveen looked back at me and grinned. "Dirty blonde hair, light brown eyes? Really good tan for a New Englander? Who else could it be?"

I winced at his description, knowing what was coming next. Sure enough, Ellen came bursting out of the office behind the counter, clutching a mail basket nearly as big as she was. Only a tuft of dyed pink hair was visible over the edge of the basket until she set it down on the counter. "Hey Ricky!"

"Uh, hey?" I waved. "H-how—" I coughed. "How are you doing?"

"Better now that you're here!" She flashed me her million-watt smile. I shifted on my feet. "I think your stuff came in, let me see." She began rifling through the contents of the basket. "No, no... yeah, this is it. Wait... is this what I think it is?" She looked up at me, kohl-rimmed eyes wide.

For the second time in fifteen minutes, my heart crawled up into my throat – this time, for a different reason altogether. "If it's for me, that's exactly what it is."

Ellen pulled a sealed manila envelope from the basket. She read the label. "'Interlibrary loan, Frederick Konacsz, 314 Coindre Hall, Allora University. Contents one USB stick, four digital audio tracks.'" She looked back at me. "You lucky fucker."

Naveen cocked his head at Ellen, then looked at me. "What's the big deal?"

"It's... It's, uh, a digital copy of a kinda rare EP from the 1970s," I said. Ellen offered it to me, and I took it, carefully ignoring it when she brushed her fingers across my hand. "Been looking for this one forever. I can't believe Allora's library system had a copy."

"Huh. Well, that's cool, I guess. You wanna listen to it here? Audio lab should be open." Naveen pointed across the lobby. "Past the card catalog computers and to the left. There are headphones and everything."

"Thanks," I said, holding the envelope gingerly. "I'll, uh... I'll l-let you know how it is."

"Fuck that, Ricky, you give it to me next!" Ellen shook a fist at me and then turned to her co-worker. "*That's cool, I guess.* Naveen, you wouldn't know good music if it bit you on the ass."

"Oh my *God*, Ellen, I don't want to hear it again-"

The sounds of their argument faded as I walked through the lobby toward where Naveen had directed me. The rest of the ambient noise plummeted to almost zero after I walked into the audio lab, the door easing shut behind me.

Some of the tension in my shoulders left after seeing that I had the place to myself. The walls were lined with blue and gray anechoic foam wedges; two rows of cubicles with chairs ran down the length of the room. I chose one at random, laying the manila envelope on the desk and sinking into the chair.

The cubicle came equipped with an audio deck complete with a combination cassette/CD player, AUX input, and a USB port. A pair of over-the-ear headphones were hard-wired to the audio out jack, and I did my best in trying to position audio equipment designed for rounded ears over my pointed ones.

It took a while.

After finally finding a comfortable position, I broke the seal on the envelope and peered inside. It was a USB stick all right, stamped with ALLORA UNIVERSITY INTERLIBRARY LOAN on the front and DO NOT COPY on the back. I powered up the audio deck, tried to insert the USB stick, reversed it, reversed it again, and finally got it into the port the right way. A few moments later, a light on the deck lit up green and I pressed play.

A second went by, then another. Then there was a pop, a hiss, and -

Three, five, oh, one, two, five, go!

I grinned like an idiot as a driving guitar riff exploded in my ears, followed just moments later by a drum track. I closed my eyes and listened while Joy Division's "Warsaw" thundered through my head.

I was there in the back stage
When the light came around
I grew up like a changeling
To win the first time around
I can see all the weakness
I can pick all the faults
Well, I concede all the faith tests
Just to stick in your throats

I paused the playback, slightly overwhelmed. *This is the real thing*, I thought. I took a deep breath, let it out, and pressed play again, listening to the rest of the track and the other three nonstop. Then I listened to it all over again. It was grainy, and some of the warmth and depth of the original vinyl might have been lost due to it being copied digitally, but that sound was unmistakable. It was all there – Stephen Morris' drumming, Peter Hook's driving bassline, Bernard Sumner's growling guitar, and Ian Curtis' voice.

A part of me wanted desperately to find a way to smuggle it out of the library. I could probably get away with it, too. But as wonderful as getting to hear this was, it was still just a copy. Hell, you could find the same tracks on Spotify, if you wanted. Still not the same as an original pressing, of course. If I could ever track down the original vinyl, though….

Feeling considerably lighter, I left the audio lab and walked back to the front desk. Ellen took the envelope from me. "You have no idea," I said to her, grinning.

"I have some idea!" she said. "You look like a completely different person. I didn't want to say anything, but you really looked like shit when you walked in here—"

"Ellen! What the fuck?" Naveen snatched the envelope from her hands. She scowled at him, giving him the finger. Naveen filed the envelope somewhere beneath the counter. "Sorry, Ricky, you know what she's like. She's right though, you look like you're in a much better mood."

I shrugged. "Well, I am." I looked up at the wall clock behind them. "Listen, I better go. I'll see you guys. Thanks again." I waved and walked off. The last thing I heard before slipping outside was Naveen yelling at Ellen again. Ellen was yelling back.

I stepped outside into the now afternoon sunlight. *Mom should be home from work by now,* I thought. I tapped at my phone a few times; she picked up on the third ring.

"Ricky! Dad said you were gonna call. How's it going, honey?"

"Hey Mom, yeah I uh... okay I guess?" I started walking toward the dorms. "I just left the audio lab, my interlibrary loan came in."

"The Joy Division EP? Wait, did they have the actual vinyl?" I could practically hear her salivating at the other end of the line.

"Nah, I wish. It was a digital copy. But it was still amazing!"

"I'll bet, kid. Oh, I'm jealous. I told you I saw them live in '79, right?"

"Just about every time we talk about them, Mom." I looked up as some clouds scudded across the sun, temporarily plunging the campus into shadow. They blew by, and I lowered my gaze. "They opened for the Buzzcocks, right?"

"Oh, so you do pay attention, huh?" She laughed. *"Yep, your Uncle Lance hooked me up with tickets. He had seen them on New Year's Eve at the Swinging Apple in Liverpool in, uhh,'77 I wanna say? He told me that was when they started using their new name."* She paused. *"Shame about Ian, though. He was so young."*

"Yeah, but they were so influential, I mean the entire post-punk movement—whoops, sorry, hold on." I dodged around a small group of students who were talking in the middle of the paved path. "What was I saying?"

"You were about to tell me that New Order was just as good."

I scowled. "I was not! They deserve a place in history right along—listen. You know 'Blue Monday' is a masterpiece and you can't argue with that."

"I'll argue it all I want! Listen, when a cover by some nü-metal idiots from Los Angeles gets more play than the original, there's something wrong there. You couldn't turn on a radio without hearing it over and over and over." I fell silent. "Hey, Ricky you still there?"

"Huh? Oh, yeah, sorry Mom. I just..." I looked around, spotting an empty spot under a white oak next to the path. "You got a sec to talk?"

"Of course, hon. What's going on?"

I sat down heavily in the grass, the breath going out of me. "I... I ran into him again today."

"Who, that Sidhe fuckboy?" There was an instant edge to her voice. *"Tiamat's tits. Did he hurt you?"*

"No, no, I'm fine! It was in the quad in the middle of the day. Just his typical Summer Court bullshit. It's just..." I touched my pocket, feeling the lump of crumpled paper inside it. "I had just left Music Theory, and I had picked up a flyer for the radio station. I was thinking of going down there and volunteering to learn some audio engineering, but—"

"He saw it and gave you shit?"

I paused. "Yeah. It didn't help that I started stuttering as soon as he was in my face."

"Oh, Ricky." Her voice softened. *"Who the fuck cares about what that idiot thinks of you? He's so inbred he's practically a sandwich. I'm surprised he knows how to tie his fucking shoes without a team of Brownies to do it for him."*

My chest started feeling tight. "Yeah, but Mom, he's got a point. I mean who was I kidding, fantasizing about being a DJ?"

"Yeah but Ricky—"

"I mean it! I can barely talk to a single stranger without t-tripping over my tongue, how the hell w-would I be able to talk to hundreds or even thousands of s-s-strangers over the radio?" That tight feeling was getting worse, it was almost like a burning cold ember in my heart.

"Fidirikonaz." I froze. Years of only hearing your full name spoken by a parent when they were dead serious conditioned you pretty well. *"Stop it this instant. You are capable of anything*

you decide you want to do. You are destined for greatness. Have you forgotten who you are, my Ra'saar?"

"Mom, I... okay." I took a deep breath, trying to push down that knot of icy fire in my ribcage. "I'm sorry," I mumbled. "Listen, maybe I should go." I stood up and pulled the phone from my ear, ready to end the call.

"No." I paused. *"Ricky, you still there? Ricky?"*

"...Yeah."

"Don't let this Sidhe get under your skin. He's probably the youngest son of a minor earl who thinks he'll make his bones by harassing you. You? You're fucking royalty."

I stared down at my scuffed Chuck Taylors, rubbing the back of my head with my other hand. "Mom, do you really think I could work in radio?"

"Of course you can. Don't give up, Ricky, okay? What did The Great One always say?"

"You, uh, you miss a hundred percent of the shots you don't take?"

"That's right. Besides, think about how nice it would be to rub it in that asshole's face. Seriously, what's the worst that can happen? You go down there and it turns out they don't need your help?"

"Yeah, I guess. I mean, what could it hurt, right?"

"That's the spirit. Listen, I've gotta go, I'm waiting on an update from the Reykjavik office before end of day there. We'll talk later, okay?"

"Okay, Mom. And, uh... thanks."

"I'm proud of you, Ricky. Always remember that." I could hear the smile in her voice.

I stuffed the phone back in my pocket and fished out the crumpled piece of paper. I unfolded it, smoothed it out, and read it. *Student Union Building, 4th floor. Suite 416.*

There was a large, square concrete building across the way. A large sign near the front door read "The SUB". Students were streaming in and out of it at a steady pace.

I looked back down at the wrinkled flyer, then back up at the busy building. Finally, I took a deep breath and stood up. Dusting the dirt and grass off my clothes, I set off across the quad toward it.

CHAPTER FOUR

Before I knew it, I was standing in the SUB's fourth-floor hallway, pacing back and forth in front of the elevators, my stomach up in my throat and pulse throbbing in my temples. I walked down to the end of the corridor and stared at the wall for the fifth time. At a T-section there was a sign with the numbers "401-409" printed on it, accompanied by a left-facing arrow. Right under it was printed "410-418", with an arrow pointed right.

I glanced down the right hallway. The floor was carpeted in institutional brown, the walls painted a neutral tone of off-white. Turning my head in the other direction revealed much of the same. It was deathly quiet up here, and I hadn't seen another soul since stepping off the elevator almost five minutes ago.

This is a bad idea, I thought, turning around again. I looked down the short corridor to the relative safety of the elevator bank. *Maybe I should try tomorrow.* I took a few steps towards the elevators, a knot rising in my stomach, before pushing the call button.

An unbidden image of Wyndham Summers leapt into my mind, his face a cruel rictus of resentment and scorn. *"Go on, Ruh-ruh-Ricky. Run away like the little hatchling you are."* I snorted and looked away from the glowing button, shaking my head like I was trying to dislodge the image from my brain.

"Ignore that Sidhe fuckboy, Ricky!" Mom's voice rang in my

ears, like I was still on the phone with her. *"I didn't raise you to back down to fascist assholes. Get in there and take your shot, Gretzky."* I laughed despite myself, imagining each of them on my shoulders dressed in little cartoon angel and devil outfits.

The elevator dinged, and the doors slid open. I gazed into the empty compartment. My distorted reflection stared back at me from the polished stainless-steel wall: a tall, lanky kid with tousled dirty-blond hair, light brown eyes, tan skin, and dressed in college-chic denim shorts and a zip-up hoodie over a faded *Iggy and the Stooges* shirt.

Well, that's what I would have seen if I was human. Instead, my skin, covered in minuscule iridescent scales, shimmered where the light hit them. That, combined with my pointed ears and the slight hint of a vertically slit pupil was more than enough for other mythics to clock me as draconic. Lucky me – that was all the excuse Summers had needed to give me shit from the very first day of classes. At least he couldn't tell what color I was unless I was in my true form. *If he knew that...*

I bared my teeth at my own reflection, revealing a set of sharp upper and lower incisors. *No,* I said. *I'm not hiding. Not this time.* I glared at myself as the doors slid back closed, and then I turned around and walked down the corridor, turning right at the T-intersection.

I walked with purpose, knowing that if I slowed down, I'd lose my nerve immediately. The numbered doors continued climbing as I went, odd ones on the left, even ones on the right, and as I passed room 415 the walls began to be adorned with different framed posters of live music acts.

The next door loomed large ahead of me on the right. A large sign had "416 – Allora University Radio 96.7FM WPHX" printed in large letters. A line beneath it read "The Home of the Rising Firebirds." There was no window.

Taking a deep breath, I reached out and knocked. There was no response. Fighting the urge to cut and run, I knocked again, then waited. Finally, I reached out, grabbed the doorknob, and after a brief struggle with myself, went inside.

There was an office on the other side of the door. It was equipped with a beaten-up desk, its top and sides plastered with peeling band stickers. On the surface was a laptop, a phone, and several loose pieces of paper. There was a ratty-looking couch against the left wall with what looked like a crocheted blanket thrown over the back, and the walls were covered with more music posters and even some official-looking plaques. A small speaker installed in the far corner of the ceiling was softly playing some instrumental jazz. To the right of the desk was a doorway leading deeper into the studio, a lit "ON AIR" sign above it.

"Hello?" My voice sounded tiny, even in the small room. No answer. I fished the tattered flyer out of my pocket and clung to it like a talisman. I was drawn to one of the silver plaques on the wall. Peering closer, I read it aloud. "'The National Association of College Broadcasters' Radio Station of the Year 2021.' Huh."

"Yeah, not bad, right?"

I tried not to jump at the sound of another person's voice behind me. I like to think I didn't, even though I probably did. "Oh, uh…"

"Hi." What looked like an upperclassman, dressed casually in a pair of khakis and a tucked-in polo shirt, was leaning on the doorway, the expression on his dark-skinned face guarded. "Can I help you?"

"Oh, no, I mean yeah, uh…" I felt my ears go hot, but I took a second and steadied my breath. "Yeah my, uh, my Music Theory p-prof said you guys are luh-looking for help?" I waved the ragged flyer in my hand.

The student in the doorway relaxed a little. He nodded. "Oh, yeah, we're definitely still looking for people. You, uh, you don't seem like the type of person who feels comfortable behind the mic, though?" He paused. "Who do you have for Music Theory?"

"Um, Professor Chen?" I shifted uncomfortably. "I'm, uh, really interested in audio engineering. You know, b-board operation and stuff like that?"

"Hmm." He gave me an appraising look. "Yeah, let me check something real quick." He walked over to the desk and flipped open the laptop, leaning over it without sitting down, and ran his finger across the trackpad. "Well, we've actually got a couple of spots open for board ops, though most of the good slots are filled." He looked up at me. "How do you feel about a late-night shift on Friday? Hard to find people willing to come in during prime party hours so we're always hemorrhaging engineers."

"Uh, how late we talking?"

"Well, we don't have much coverage during the 2 to 4 AM slot. DJ's all right, bit of a flake as long as he's sober, but our engineer is looking to switch to an earlier slot. You could start training with them that night, shadow them for the broadcast, take notes, ask questions."

"Uh, yeah, I think I could do that. Strictly back-end stuff? You're right, I r-really don't feel comfortable talking on air." *That's putting it mildly.*

"Definitely, we're not about to drive off anybody who's willing to pull the graveyard shift. Why don't you come back Friday night, right around midnight? Might want to take a nap beforehand too – no drinks allowed when you're in the booth. That includes coffee."

"Right, yeah, okay, that's a good idea." I nodded. "I'll be there this Friday." I turned to go; my knees already felt like they were knocking together.

"Wait, my dude, I haven't gotten your name!"

I turned back, my ears feeling hotter than ever. "Right, sorry!" I said. "Just, uh... just a little excited, I guess?" He laughed, handing me a pen and a pink Post-It note. I wrote my name and my number as legibly as I could, hand shaking, and handed the note to him.

He read it. "Ricky... Kone...?"

"Konacsz."

He repeated it. "Cone-ax. Is that Eastern European?"

"Something like that. And, uh, I didn't get your name?"

"Right, I'm Byron. General manager." He held out his hand and I shook it. His grip was warm, professional, strong by human standards. "You probably won't see me Friday night, but I'll let your audio engineer know their newest trainee is coming. Welcome to Allora University Radio, Ricky."

CHAPTER FIVE

I rode the elevator down to the first floor in a daze. As soon as the doors opened, I rushed out into the crowd of students, weaving my way through the front door and down the steps. The late afternoon sunlight hit me square in the chest, and I took in great gulps of air like I had just come up from diving deep in the North Atlantic.

Holy shit. I thought. *Holy fucking shit. I did it.* I grinned, shaking my head in disbelief. *I can't believe I did it.*

I took out my phone and immediately tapped out a text to Mom.

I got the gig! Working the graveyard shift, training as a board operator. I START FRIDAY NIGHT

Barely thirty seconds went by before she wrote back.

Fuck yes Ricky! So proud of you!

I smiled, then blinked. Mom was sending more messages.

We need to talk playlists

What's ur target demo? U have freedom to choose artists?

You want to come pick up some of your vinyl at the apartment?

My eyes grew wide as Mom continued blowing up my phone. Finally, I got my wits together enough to type out a reply.

Mom, slow down, I'm just gonna be an audio engineer!

Another second, and her reply came through: *Yeah FOR NOW maybe*

Come for dinner tonight, Mack and Dags will be there, we can tell them the good news!

I winced. *I dunno mom I'm kinda busy, gotta study*

My phone dinged once more. *I'm making fiskeboller. Reykjavik sent it by courier earlier. Catch of the day – fresh haddock!*

There was no way I could say no to that. *OK, OK, I'll be there. PLEASE don't make a big deal out of it.* I got a thumbs-up emoji in response.

I stuffed my phone back into my pocket. *Better than cafeteria food for sure*, I thought.

I checked the time, did some quick calculations in my head, and set off toward the edge of campus. A few minutes of walking in the afternoon sunlight and I saw the UTA bus stop ahead of me. A small crowd of students, human and mythic alike, were waiting.

I joined the throng, craning my neck to look up the street. A few minutes later, a large commuter bus, already halfway full from the look of it, pulled to a stop. About a dozen people spilled out and went their separate ways; I waited my turn to step up and on, flashing my Allora University student ID at the bored-looking Dwarf driving the bus.

Most of the seats were taken, leaving just a few here and there with a half-occupied bench. I spied an empty spot, but the adjoining seat was filled by an otherworldly beautiful woman, her bag occupying the other seat. She had a delicately featured face, framed by a wild mane of sea-foam green hair. A series of long, horizontal slits started halfway down each side of her neck and disappeared beneath her shirt.

She was leaning back, her eyes closed, a pair of supremely

heavy-duty headphones with wood inlays over her ears, murmuring to herself along with the music. A palpable aura hung close to her, thrumming along with her voice. I grinned, watching her for a moment before reaching out and grabbing the handrail, just in time for the bus to lurch to a start. I looked away as Allora University slowly rolled out of sight.

Not much changed at first except most of the buildings became newer and more expensive-looking. We made good time across half a dozen stops as the bus followed the street northwest, with a handful of people getting off and on at each one. Eventually the woman in her musical trance opened her eyes, checked where we were, and stood up for the next stop, pulling her headphones down to around her neck.

I met her gaze. *"I see you, Sea-Sister,"* I said to her quietly, slipping into Sigil, the language of mythics. She blinked and looked at me curiously. *"Clan Snow wishes you calm seas and pleasant melodies."*

She beamed at me. Her smile lit up the entire space. *"May the oceans bring you bounty,"* she replied in turn, reaching out to steady herself on the handrail as the bus began to slow down.

"Are those a pair of GS 3000Xs?" I asked, switching back to English. I pointed to her headphones.

She grinned, her eyes sparkling. "Ah, you know your stuff!" she said. "They are. Just listening to something I've been working on. It needs some editing before it's ready. I DJ at the Palace on the weekends."

I let out a low whistle. "You make enough spinning records at the Palace to snag a pair of those? That's some serious cheddar."

She laughed. It sounded like a bubbling brook. "Oh, no, that's what I do for *fun.* I, uh, consult for a bunch of different recording studios in town. My ears are never wrong, and they all know it." She quirked an eyebrow at me. "But what are you doing riding the bus, shoal-serpent? You can't tell me you don't want to stretch your wings?"

I shrugged. "Trying to keep a low profile. My relatives all want a piece of me. You know how it goes."

"More snakes than a gorgon hair salon? I get that." The bus ground to a halt. "This is me. Always nice to see a friendly face from home." She waved and winked, sashaying past me, humming under her breath. I grinned at her as several humans turned at the sound like they had been hooked by the ears.

I took her seat, smiling. A few more moments and the bus was off again. Now, the buildings were getting lower, older, and more closely crowded together. Traffic increased, and soon the bus reached another stop. The digital marquee above the driver's head came to life, the words GRUNSTADT crawling from left to right.

I got up, brushed some dirt off my jeans, and hopped off the bus. It took me a second to get my bearings, but I was soon off in the right direction, walking through a neighborhood that had street names written in both English and German.

I walked for about two blocks and made a left, following the scent of fresh-baked bread that my sensitive nose had noticed as soon as I had gotten off the bus. I came to a stop at a small storefront under a green and white awning. The front plate glass window had HAELVIGDOTTIR'S BAKERY printed in large block letters in a semicircle. Beneath it, in smaller letters, read, "Established 1902."

I pulled the heavy wooden door open, causing a bell to tinkle. The smell intensified as I crossed the threshold. A large middle-aged human woman was behind the counter. She waved at me. "Hello!" she said. "How can I help you today?"

"Uh," I said. "Uh, yes. Do you..." I looked down at the glass counter she was standing behind. It was well-stocked with all sorts of cakes and pastries. "Do you have any *skyrterta* today?"

"Oh, you're in luck! Made fresh this morning. Topped with blueberries." She turned, bustling to a pie rack I hadn't seen when I walked in. She returned in a moment with a large round cake in a tin and set it on the counter.

"Looks good to me," I said, reaching for my wallet. "I'm, uh, h-heading to my parents' place for dinner and I wanted to bring something."

She nodded and pulled a box out from beneath the counter. "Not a problem! Is your family Icelandic?"

"My mother's side," I replied. "Been here since the... 1880s? Mom's a great cook but she's n-no good at desserts." I grinned. "She's making fresh *fiskeböller* tonight and I didn't want to show up empty-handed."

"Oh my goodness, you lucky boy!" She finished boxing up the cake. "Hope it's not far, that cake needs to stay cold." She dusted her hands off and I handed her my debit card.

"Nope, just a couple bus stops," I said. She ran the card and handed it back to me. I waved off the receipt, picking up the boxed cake carefully. "Thanks so much!"

"Come back anytime," she called after me. "Tell me how your mom liked the cake. Oh, and bring me back some *fiskeböller!*" I laughed, waved, and slipped out the door.

Back on the sidewalk I carefully pulled my phone out of my pocket, checking the time. I slipped it back in and turned around, picking up the pace as I retraced my steps.

This time, I crossed the street to the bus stop on the opposite side. A few minutes later, which I spent clutching the cake box as tightly as I dared, and another bus came grinding to a halt. I climbed up, carefully flashing my student ID, and found a seat.

The bus eased away from the sidewalk and trundled through Grunstadt, heading slowly southwest. The street names switched from German to Italian and then back to English by the time we stopped again. The lights on the marquee flashed "SOUTH BECKETSVILLE" as a few slightly haggard-looking humans climbed up the steps.

Looking out the window, I watched this new neighborhood slowly roll by. The age of the buildings here seemed about the same as in Grunstadt, but they certainly weren't quite as well-maintained in many places. Still, the streets and buildings had a sort of lived-in look that I found strangely comforting, even if it seemed like this neighborhood's best days might be behind it. This was only reinforced by the "CLOSED" sign on the marquee of what looked like had once been a good-sized performance venue. A dim, dusty neon sign, not lit, bore the name "The Roxy" in looping script. *I bet you that place was amazing back in the day*, I thought as the bus turned the corner.

We passed out of South Beckett, the bus winding its way closer to my parents' neighborhood in Allora. I got off at the closest stop. Another few minutes of walking in the afternoon sunlight, and I was in front of my parents' building. The RFID fob on my keychain granted me access; I walked inside, past the small but clean lobby where the mailboxes were, and pushed the call button on the elevator. It whirred to life, and a few moments later the doors slid open. There was no one inside.

I stepped in, turned around, and pressed the button for the third floor. A short ride later and I came out into the carpeted hallway, turned left, and walked down to the end. I could easily hear people talking from the other side of the door.

I took a big sigh, pushed a smile up onto my face that I didn't completely feel, and knocked.

CHAPTER SIX

"**O**h, that's probably Ricky!" The door opened, revealing my mother in her usual getup – ice-blue fauxhawk, sides freshly buzzed, two hoops in her left nostril, studs in both ears and a medium-sized spacer in her right earlobe. She was in well-worn ripped jeans and an open flannel over a black tee. Her shirt had the words "The Sex Pistols Always Sucked" stamped across the front. "Come on in, kid, you're the last one here!" She grinned at me and threw her arms wide, her pale skin catching the light from the foyer and causing her scales to glitter.

I smiled, more genuinely this time. "Hi, Mom!" I hugged her, careful not to crush the cake box. "I brought dessert!"

"Oh, Ricky, you shouldn't have!" She took the plain white cardboard box from me. "I'll set it with the others." She turned and walked into the kitchen. "Ricky's here, guys, dinner will be ready soon!"

I closed the door behind me and shrugged out of my hoodie, hanging it on the one last empty peg on the wall. The rest were filled: a lightweight longcoat, a battered vintage motorcycle jacket, a small, bright red jacket, and a suit jacket. On a coat hanger.

I trailed after my mother into the kitchen. She set the dessert box down next to two others on the counter, each one more ostentatious and expensive looking than the last, and turned back to the stove, where the *fiskeböller* were sautéing in a cast-iron pan and giving off their signature aroma.

I looked down at the largest and most ornate of the third boxes. The top was gold foil stamped with the name of the bakery and a Destry Bay address. A tag attached to the box read "From Mack."

I sighed, moving through the kitchen into the rest of the apartment. My father and brother were in the dining room, lazily setting the table and talking. Dad was in a faded Allora University sweatshirt, his salt-and-pepper beard trimmed impeccably to make up for the thinning mop on top of his head; Mack, who looked like a younger version of Dad with more hair on top but less on his chin, was in his shirtsleeves, a silver silk tie around his neck. The knot was loosened in a way I could only assume that my brother thought was "artful." They looked up when I walked in.

"Hey hey, there's the college boy!" My father's face split into a huge grin. He set down the plate in his hands and hugged me, harder than I was expecting. "How's the life of an undergrad?"

"Oof, hey Dad, yeah it's good! Busy, you know? Hey, Mack."

My brother waved to me over Dad's shoulder. "Golden Boy, late as usual! Nice of us to join us. When you getting a haircut, ya hippie?" He grinned, showing a little too much tooth.

I suppressed a shudder at the nickname and smiled back. "Same time you pull the stick outta your ass?" He laughed at that, a little too loud, his eyes flat.

Fighting a familiar feeling rising in my stomach, I turned back to my father. "Where's Dagmar?"

He hooked a thumb over his shoulder. "Your sister's in the living room."

I nodded and walked through the doorway, took a right down the short hall, and popped my head into the next room.

"Hey, Dags."

My sister was seated on the couch, her back to me, phone held high in hand and angled down at her. She soundlessly raised her other hand in greeting, holding up a finger, before casually running it through her pale, blue-streaked hair; I heard the faint sound of a phone camera shutter. She lowered her hand again.

"Hey, little brother. Sorry, sharing the link to Conny's crypto site like he asked me to." She craned her neck around, revealing features that mirrored my mother's closely, though she had chosen a cobalt blue undercut to Mom's ice-blue fauxhawk.

"Oh, gods, is he still trying to push that Lightning Coin garbage? And don't call me that, your egg hatched a whole three hours before me."

"It still counts." She slouched on the sofa, scrolling through her phone. "And it's Thundercoin, Ricky. He's ramping up to release some NFTs by Halloween." She rolled her eyes. "Lucky for him he gets free tech support from his girlfriend."

"Uh huh." I snorted. "Yeah, I'm sure your quarter of a million Insta followers don't hurt?"

"One point two mil now." She looked up at me with a grin. "And climbing."

My father called out from the dining room. "All right, come on guys, enough standing around! Dinner time!"

Dagmar sighed, threw up a peace sign, and took one last picture before getting off the couch. Stuffing the phone in the back pocket of what looked like designer jeans, she said, "Thank Bahamut you're here, by the way. If Dad and Mack went on for one more second about market capitalizations I was going to have to fly back to Portland with their blood all over me."

I trailed behind my sister on the way to the dining room. Mom had put a huge spread down on the table with the *fiskeböller* in pride of place. A couple of freshly opened bottles of wine stood within easy reach.

I pulled out a chair and sat down, picking up my napkin. "Cloth, Mom? Really? Is the Ra'keth coming to dinner?"

"Quiet, you!" She brandished a serving spoon at me. "I can't enjoy having my whole family under the same roof for a night? When's the last time this happened, huh?"

"Two weeks ago," Dad said, smirking at me. "Right before the fall semester started." He held out his plate to my mother, who filled it and handed it back to him. "Thank you, honey."

"And it's been a long two weeks without my hatchlings!" She gestured for my plate, and I handed it to her. She started ladling food onto it. A *lot* of food. "Who knows when we'll all be together again?" She handed me the heaping plate.

"Jeez, Mom, leave some for the rest of us," Dags said. She handed over her own plate. "You trying to fatten him up?"

"Well, he's so damn thin! Heroin chic went out with the 90s, Ricky, you gotta eat more." She handed back my sister's plate and gestured for Mack's.

"Yeah Ricky, maybe it's time to start hitting some weights or something? Maybe get on the protein?" My brother took it back from Mom and set it down. "We can't have our future Great Leader looking like the wendigo from those potato chips you like. What would Grandma Jutte say?" He leered at me.

I looked down at the huge plate of food in front of me. It smelled delicious and looked even better, but I suddenly wasn't very hungry. I picked up my fork and chased a fish ball around in the sauce for a second. "I mean I—"

"What your brother's *trying* to say, Ricky, is that he's just concerned for you. Right, Mack?" Dad shot my brother a look, who stopped mean mugging me and nodded, suddenly very interested in his own plate. "Besides, I can't say I'm not a little jealous. The last time I fit in skinny jeans was 1922." He grinned, leaning back, and patting his stomach. "Too much of Mom's *fiskeboller* and you won't fit on the throne!"

Oh Christ, I thought, forcing what I could only assume looked like a good-natured smile to my face. "Dad, you know I'm nowhere near old enough for that yet."

"You never know," Dags said, pouring herself a generous glass of wine. "Greatness thrust upon them or some shit like that." She looked up. "What? I read."

"Doomscrolling and Taylor Swift lyrics don't count." Mack speared a fish ball with his fork and jammed the whole thing in his mouth. His eyes rolled back. "Oh, my god. Mom, did you say this was fresh?"

"Flown in from the Reykjavik office this morning," she said, sipping from her own wine glass. "What, you think I was gonna just go down to Whole Foods and pick up a few pounds of the garbage they call 'fresh?' I wouldn't be caught dead there. Well, not without a couple of Molotovs."

And dinner wound on from there. My sister remained snarky, Mack barely kept his resentment in check, and Dad tried to keep the peace. Mom just looked happy. Finally, we finished; I stood up and helped clear the plates, trailing after my mother into the kitchen. Dad and my siblings stayed seated around the table, talking. Well, Mack talked.

I set the dishes down on the counter and took the top one off the stack, handing it to my mother. She turned, rinsed it off in the sink, and then placed it in the open dishwasher. "Sooooo. Spill it. The radio station."

I felt hot around my ears. "Oh, well, yeah, I'm starting Friday night. Uh, graveyard shift. The 2 to 4 AM slot. Just training as a board operator for now, going in a little early to get some hands-on experience. Their engineer wants to switch to an earlier slot, so I'd be… well I guess I'd be their replacement, eventually?"

"That sounds fucking exciting." She grinned as I handed her another plate. "This is how it starts, Ricky. First, you're running the board, next thing you know you're programming sets, recording promos, hell maybe you'll even start going out to shows and meeting local acts."

"Yeah, uhh, I dunno about that, I mean from what I've seen of the City so far the scene looks a little dead besides the Palace of Wisdom. I mean not that that's not an amazing venue, but isn't it the only game in town at this point?"

"Maybe. There used to be dozens of great little hole-in-the-wall places in this town, but most of them are gone."

"Yeah, I saw what was left of one today. The bus passed an old, run-down place in South Beckettsville on the way here after I stopped to pick up dessert. Looked like it was about twenty minutes from being knocked down and turned into another one of those gentrified coffee shops."

My mother paused. "South Beckett?" She cocked her head, not turning around. "You didn't catch the name, did you?"

I wrinkled my nose. "Uhh... I think it was Rock something. The Rockhouse? I don't really-"

"The Roxy," she said. "I know that place." She set the dish she had been rinsing down in the sink and turned around to face me, a bemused expression on her face. Her eyes were bright. "I can't believe it's still there."

"Well, it didn't look like it would be for much longer, Mom. The whole block seemed pretty much on the way out. Lots of 'for sale' signs."

"Ugh, tell me about it." She turned back to the sink, turning off the water and picking up the plate she had just set down. "Your brother's interning at this godsdamned real estate developer out in Destry Bay, they're buying up whole blocks in Beckettsville and Grunstadt so they can reno and flip them. Whole fucking city's getting gentrified. Like the Sidhe need more neighborhoods to stink up?"

She growled, slamming the dishwasher closed and turning around. "Listen, Ricky, you get a free afternoon, go back down there. You remember where it was?" I nodded, a little taken aback by how emphatic she was being. "About three doors down on the right there should be a little hole-in-the-wall record store. If it's still there, you better go in there and clear out whatever you can before the damn vultures show up and turn it into a gastropub where they use first pressings as placemats or some other bougie shit. Next chance you get, okay?"

"Um, o-okay." I blinked, but the words "record store" had certainly gotten my interest. "You think it's still there, though?"

"Oh, I've got a feeling," she said, reaching for the box with the *skyrterta*. "Come on, it's time for dessert."

CHAPTER SEVEN

T urns out what I had brought was a big hit. Even Mack had himself a second helping, though he was certainly less than enthusiastic that the very expensive-looking dessert he brought stayed wrapped up on the kitchen counter. It was getting late at that point, so I claimed that I needed to study and fled back to the relative safety of my dorm.

The next two days were a blur of typical freshman life. I fell into a steady rhythm that consisted of going to and from classes, catching meals of questionable provenance at the food court, and spending my downtime in the library studying or listening to music. Time wore on toward the end of the week, marked by steady texts from both my father ("*go get 'em champ*") and my mother ("*don't let them play any Top 40 garbage*"). By Friday I was ready for my first shift, though I wasn't sure if it was to show up or to throw up. Possibly both at the same time.

The SUB was deserted when I walked through the front doors that evening. I had to show my ID card and sign in with security at the front entrance, considering how late it was. The main floor hall, designed to accommodate large amounts of student foot traffic, seemed cavernous and liminal in its abandoned silence; the school bookstore was shuttered, and the doorway leading to the food court yawned darkly, leading to emptiness. My footsteps echoed weirdly in the empty space. The wait for the elevator seemed an eternity and the ride up to the fourth floor was even longer. The sound of the elevator cables was my only companion.

The doors opened, and I stepped out into dim after-hours lighting. I could hear, faintly, the canned sound of the radio station being piped in from the modest speakers mounted in the hallway. I followed it, turning right at the intersection, and arrived at the station. The door was propped open, light spilling dimly out into the hall beyond.

I took a deep breath, holding it in for a moment and conjuring an image of Gretzky's hockey jersey in my head. *Take the shot, number ninety-nine.* I breathed out and stepped over the threshold.

The main office was much as I remembered it from earlier that week, though there was a large backpack on the couch, a second laptop and several loose pieces of paper next to it. The speaker in the corner was playing the opening notes of "This Corrosion" from Sisters of Mercy. "Hello?" I called out. "Anyone home?"

"Yeah, one second!" It sounded like someone was rummaging around on the other side of the interior doorway, the one that led deeper into the station. "Shit, hold on... hey could you gimme a hand?"

"Uh, yeah, I... sure?" I stuck my head through the doorway and was almost knocked down by what looked like a stack of cardboard boxes with legs. I bumped into it, and it spoke: "Ah dammit, hey watch out! Grab the top box, would you? Put it down on the floor next to the couch."

I grabbed it, lifting it easily. As I did so, the person I had been talking to came clear, or at least their head and shoulders did: gracefully sweeping ram's horns almost lost in a tangle of curly, light brown hair and sparkling kohl-rimmed eyes, brows drawn together in effort. "Are you the new guy? Rick?"

"Ricky, yeah." I set down the box where the Satyr had

instructed. The other two boxes thumped down next to them. "Uh, Byron told me to come down tonight, said I could get some training on, uh… b-board operation?"

"Jesus, Rick, you're fucking tall. What they been feeding you?" The Satyr, who I had about a head and a half on in height, was looking up at me. An untucked, white button-down shirt, sleeves rolled up to the elbow, revealed intricately designed tribal tattoos flowing down their forearms. Below that was a black midi skirt. A pair of furry digitigrade legs ending in cloven hooves completed the ensemble.

I blinked, thrown off by the Satyr's appearance. "Uh—" Between the timbre of their voice and the way they were dressed, I was having a hard time pegging their gender.

The Satyr hadn't waited for an answer, thrusting out a hand in greeting. "Anagen. That's with a soft 'g", not a hard one." I shook it, carefully. "You ever work in radio before?"

"N-no," I said. "I mean, I want to. Uh, work in radio." *Jesus, Ricky, get it together.* I took a deep breath. "I mean, I like music?"

"Oh yeah? You and every other freshman that walks through that door." Anagen-with-a-soft-g turned away, skirt swishing. I tried to spot any physical sign that would let me figure them out. *I don't see any breasts*, I thought, immediately feeling like a jerk. Hell, they didn't smell anything like the other Satyrs I knew, that was for sure. "Whatever, if you're willing to spend your Friday nights holed up here then I guess beggars can't be choosers." They walked back through the open doorway, deeper into the radio station, leaving me in the office in stunned silence. A moment later, they called out, "Well, you coming or not, Rick?" I sighed, following.

The hallway was long and narrow, going back what seemed like 50 feet or so into the building. The right wall was plastered with music posters and band stickers; the left had several doors, some of which had glass windows. We passed by these, each revealing what looked like broadcast booths, complete with boom microphones, chairs and desks with computers, and engineering decks festooned with light-up buttons and graphic equalizer slides. There was what looked like a female student working in the first one, headphones on and dressed all in black, scowling as she flipped through a CD carry case.

She looked up, revealing pale, porcelain-like skin and burning red eyes. I caught her gaze and her scowl deepened. I waved tentatively, giving her a smile. Without missing a beat, she flipped me off and hissed at me, revealing razor-sharp fangs.

I jumped back, startled, colliding with the wall of the corridor behind me. "Uhhh, Anagen?"

"What?" The Satyr looked over their shoulder at me, then smirked. "Oh, I see you've met Soundra. She's the 12 to 2 slot. Don't worry, she's harmless. Well, mostly." Anagen grinned and continued down the hallway, continuing to talk a blue streak as we walked down it. "All right, so broadcast studios A and B are first, those are our bigger ones. Soundra was in A, that's her favorite. Studio C is usually used for prep work, though you can broadcast from there just as easily. We usually use it for the online feed, though." The corridor opened to the left, revealing a larger space. It was taken up with one of those bookshelf-on-rails systems, the kind with cranks on the side to open and close them like the ones in the school library's reference section.

"Here's the station library," Anagen said. "At least the physical one. A lot of our stuff is digital now, but we've still got shitloads of CDs, tapes, and vinyl." They motioned to each stack in turn; someone had applied strips of masking tape to label several of them. "If you can't find it in the library or in the database, you'll have to bring it in yourself. Or that's what we tell the DJs. You probably won't have to worry about that if you end up taking my engineering slot on Friday nights." Their voice got slightly fainter as they moved further down the hallway. "C'mon, Rick! Tour's not over yet!"

"Oh, r-right! Sorry!" Realizing I had been staring at the library, I tore my eyes away and walked through one last doorway into an even larger space, filled with older-looking audio equipment, a couch, a couple of mismatched easy chairs that were much rattier than the one in the front office, a large wooden wire spool that had been repurposed as a table, and a minifridge that was humming suspiciously loudly. Battens of anechoic foam were attached haphazardly to the walls.

Anagen stood in the center of the room, arms held out to the side. "And this," they intoned, "is the Garage." They spun on their heels, sweeping their arms wide. "General hangout-slash-meeting space. We also record live performances here, like if a band comes in for an interview and we have them play one of their tracks. It's not exactly the Regent, but it gets the job done." They dropped their hands, fishing a phone out from somewhere in the folds of their skirt to check the time. "All right, grab a seat and we'll start going over the basics. Then, I'll take you inside of one of the booths and show you how everything works."

I nodded, choosing the least soiled-looking easy chair. It sagged when I sat, its springs groaning. I wrinkled my nose.

"Yeah, you get used to the smell after a while. I think it had been left out in the rain before somebody picked it up and dragged it in here." They sat down on the couch and gave me an appraising look. "You're a draconic, aren't you?"

"Uh... yeah?" I flicked my eyes around the room. There was only way out – the same way I came in. "T-that's, uh, not gonna be a problem, is it?"

Anagen shook their head. "Worried the Sidhe are going to come in here and put your head on a spike? Not gonna happen." They flashed a grin that looked more like baring their teeth than smiling. "Soundra does *not* like them. Like, at all. The only thing she loathes more than Sidhe are poseurs." Anagen rolled their eyes. "You think those privileged Fae shitheads would get along with us Satyrs, but there's only one way we like to fuck humans, and that's not with fairy magic."

I laughed nervously. "Yeah, uh, my roommate's a Satyr, too."

"Oh, really? What's his name?"

"Niko. Do you know him?"

"Oh, because we all know each other, right?" They glared at me, then laughed. "Relax, Rick, I'm fucking with you. Yeah, I know Niko. Good guy, though he's got awful taste in music. I swear if I have to hear him talk about how *Be Here Now* is the—"

"The best Oasis album of all time? Yeah, he's obsessed." I smiled, feeling a little more at ease, though the image of Soundra bearing her fangs at me was seared into my memory. "I can't convince him otherwise."

"Oh my God, I *know*. It's embarrassing, isn't it?" Anagen laughed, clapping their hands. "Like he's got no idea of the context surrounding that album. All those music reviewers pushed it so hard when it came out, thinking it was gonna be the next big thing from the Gallaghers."

"Oh yeah, I remember that. They hyped it up like crazy!"

Anagen cocked their head at me. "You remember it? What the fuck, Rick. You're a freshman. You would have been like, what? Negative five when it came out?"

I blinked, realizing my mistake. "Uh, well I remember being told about it. I had an uncle that was big into the scene at the time, he was a photographer. I remember him telling me that Liam and Noel were just swimming in coke from like '96 to '97. He said they were completely out of their gourd most nights."

Anagen nodded. "Yeah, I heard they were fucked up pretty bad. No wonder the album sucked." I breathed an inward sigh as they dropped it. Last thing I needed to explain tonight was how Dragons aged so much more slowly than humans. "Anyway, I'll have you know not all Satyrs have shit taste in music like Niko."

They paused. "Okay, I've been meaning to ask this for a while now – you're like one of the only draconics I know of that isn't swooping over the Benedict looking for assholes to eat. What are you doing here, man? At Allora, I mean."

I grimaced. "Eh, well, my dad. He's an alumnus, wanted me to go as a legacy student. I kinda couldn't say no." I looked at them. "Can I ask you something, too?"

"Yeah, shoot."

"Um…" I bit my lip. "This is probably gonna sound really rude, but…" *How do I make this sound better?* "I don't think I've ever seen a Satyr wearing a skirt before…?"

Anagen looked down. "Oh shit, is this a skirt!?" They grabbed two handfuls of fabric in mock panic, then dropped them, grinning. "I'm enbie." I blinked. "En Bee? Non-binary?"

It clicked finally. "Oh. Oh! I'm sorry. Was that a sensitive question?"

"Relax, Rick. Yeah, most Satyrs identify as male, but plenty don't. I'm one of 'em." They looked at me. "You trying to figure out what to refer me as?" I nodded, my ears hot. "You can use they/them pronouns with me." They shot me an appraising look. "That okay with you?" I nodded again, still feeling like an idiot. "All right, now that we've got that out of the way, can I do any more emotional labor for you tonight or can we get on with the training?"

I smiled weakly. "Yeah, I, uh I guess we should?"

"Great. Come on, let's relocate to Studio C, it should be empty." They stood up. I did the same, following them down the corridor.

CHAPTER EIGHT

"Welcome... to Jurassic Park." Anagen threw the door open and bowed low, gesturing with their hand.

Studio C was smaller than the other booths. The furniture was a little older, with the desk sturdy but weathered; its office chair was similarly beaten-up. A small loveseat, an institutional-looking one like you could find throughout the common rooms in Allora University's residence halls, took up the wall to the right of the desk. A couple of battered filing cabinets, flanked by some metal folding chairs that had been stashed on either side, lined the back wall.

The equipment on the desk made my eyes water, though. A big boom mic on a metal armature looked like it had seen better days, thanks to the black paint flaking off the boom from several places. A ratty pair of over-the-ear headphones was resting on the tabletop, its cord patched in three different places (electrical tape, duct tape, and a Batmobile Band-Aid). The audio board looked like something from the 1970s, and the computer had one of those super-loud clickety-clackety keyboards, a beige two-button mouse without a scroll wheel, and an old-style square tube monitor. A set of battered-looking audio input equipment with a dual tape deck, a CD player, and an auxiliary input completed the ensemble.

I picked up the mouse and turned it over. It had a little

trackball underneath. "Well, now I see why Soundra likes Studio A. Pulling out all the stops in here, I see."

"It's not as bad as it looks. Come on, sit down." They gestured to the office chair. It creaked loudly as I eased myself into it. "See? Fits like a glove! Now let's start going over the board. You see all these little sliders? Each one labeled something different?"

They pointed. It looked like something from the control room of the Death Star's laser cannon. Still, I could see that at the top of each vertical slider's columns had been labeled with black Sharpie on masking tape. "Master, CD, Tape, Database, Aux, yeah... are these, uh, w-what do you call it? Volume controls?"

"Got it in one." They leaned down, their sleeve brushing against my shoulder, and tapped a translucent button at the bottom of the Headphones slider. It lit up. "When the light's on, line's open. If it's off, it's muted. DJ chooses their input for broadcast, fades it in and out manually, stuff like that. Board ops can do it remotely too when necessary, like from another studio." They tapped the button again, extinguishing the light. "And of course the master toggle controls volume for the whole board. If that's off, nothing's broadcasting, even if every other input is open." They leaned back, crossing their arms. "Make sense?"

I looked down at the board again. "It... seems simple? I mean... I wouldn't be adjusting anything, uh, live on the air, right?"

Anagen smirked. "No, but you need to know how to operate the board for doing things like setting up station identifications, PSAs, and shit like that. We don't really run commercials, especially on overnights, but if a local event is scheduled to happen soon, like that *Secret McQueen* sneak preview happening on Halloween, you'd need to know how to queue it up so the DJ can access it through the computer." They patted the giant tube monitor. It wobbled.

I looked around the room. I didn't see any music shelves. "So, what, all the audio can be pulled from the computer or something?"

"Yup." They turned the monitor on. I winced at the sound. Anagen shot me a quizzical look. "What, you heard something?"

I rubbed my temples for a minute. "Yeah, uh… We've got pretty good hearing. Dad's Clan Argent, but I take after my mom. She's Clan Snow. Really good hearing, even for a, uh, a draconic." The high-pitched whine began to fade.

"Clan Snow… which one is that?"

"Uh, I guess you'd call them white Dragons? Semi-aquatic, so kind of specialized for swimming. Mom's side of the family can hold their breath for hours." I grinned. "She likes to say she could hear a sturgeon fart at a thousand fathoms during a Nor'easter."

Anagen wrinkled their nose, looking at me. Then, they burst into laughter. "Your mom sounds pretty cool, Rick." They shook their head and pointed at the screen. A small window was in the center, the words "ENTER YOUR LOGIN AND PASSWORD" in block letters. "This is Spinitron, it's the database program we use. I'm sure Byron hasn't put you in the system yet so let me log us in for now." They leaned over me again to tap the keyboard.

The screen cleared, revealing a complex-looking menu. "All right, this is the main database. It's connected to the station's server where all our digital audio lives. Not just songs but pre-recorded PSAs and station idents, too. It also runs our streaming station." They handed me the headphones. "Here, put these on, I'll show you how to play one. Let me just turn them on…" They tapped the corresponding button on the board. "… and the feed from the database." They tapped another.

I slipped the headphones on, inexpertly trying to fit them over my ears. "Okay," I said. "Now what?"

Anagen grabbed the mouse, navigating through the

database. "Let's play a station ident."

"Ah, shit!" I winced as the headphones came to life. **"YOU'RE LISTENING TO 96.7 FM WPHX, ALLORA UNIVERSITY RADIO, THE HOME OF THE RISING FIREBIRDS!"** I yanked the headphones from my ears. "Fuck, that's loud, man!"

"Oh, shit, sorry, sorry, I didn't – God dammit. The last idiot in here left the volume slider up too high. Who the fuck... let me check." Anagen turned around, opened the top drawer of the left-most filing cabinet, and pulled out a clipboard. "Let's see who's the asshole... yup. Fucking Chauncey."

I rubbed at my ears, squinting up at Anagen. "Who's that?"

"That, my friend, is the shit stain that has the 2 to 4 AM DJ slot on Fridays." They sighed, tossing the clipboard back into the open drawer. "He's the reason I'm looking to switch slots."

"What, because he doesn't take care of the equipment?"

"No, because he 'accidentally' misgenders me every chance he gets. He's a fucking cum fart of a person and if I have to put up with him one more semester, I'm going to end up on America's Most Wanted." They sighed, pushing the drawer closed with enough force to make it slam.

"The 2 to 4 slot... wait, isn't that the one I'm supposed to replace you on?"

"Oh, don't worry. He's a typical cis het dudebro, shouldn't give you any shit. Just say you're into crypto, or not discussing your emotions or something." They looked up at the wall clock above the door. "In fact, he should actually be here soon, supposed to be in an hour before shift to start prep. Hold on." Anagen took out their phone. "I'll text him. I swear he better not have gone off on one of his ketamine benders again."

I blinked. "Are you serious? Isn't that, like, a horse tranquilizer or something?"

"He swears up and down it's for his depression." They

tapped their phone again and then stuffed it back, somewhere in their skirt. "I think he just likes a little Special K for breakfast, lunch, and dinner, that's all. Anyway, let me show you how to put a set list together using Spinitron. It's all drag-and-drop, like building a Spotify playlist."

Anagen took another few minutes putting me through the paces, letting me get some hands-on experience on going through the database to find audio files and slotting them into the playlist. It was a lot less complicated than I thought it would be, especially after staring at the board and all its sliders and buttons – the audio player showed runtime for each track, the entire playlist, and –

"What do these mean?" I pointed at a time readout on each track that preceded the runtime. Each one was different, but they were usually anywhere from a few seconds to almost half a minute.

"Oh, those are cues." Anagen started playing one of the tracks. The first readout began to tick down while the overall runtime started ticking up to the track time. "When the first number hits zero, the lyrics kick in. Here, like this." They turned on the audio. I heard an instrumental track until the cue ran out – then someone started singing. "This way, the DJ knows how much time he has to hit the post."

"The post?"

"Yeah, you know how you're listening to the radio and the DJ seems to know exactly how long they can keep talking before the next song starts up? That's called hitting the post. Used to be DJs just had to know each song they were playing, but now everything is keyed so you can see exactly how much time you have if you're, like, introing a song or something. Feels like cheating if you ask me."

I watched the runtime tick down as the track kept playing. "Huh. I did not know that."

There was a knock at the door. Anagen and I looked around as it opened, revealing Soundra standing there. "I'm out of here for the night, Anagen," she said, eyeing me warily. "Rest of my set is scheduled to run through till 2."

The Satyr looked up at the wall clock, then back. "All right, hon. Say hello to Amy for me? I'll be back at the Palace in a couple hours."

Soundra nodded, not taking her eyes off me. "Hey, you. New kid. Behave, or I'll eat you." She curled her lip to flash her fangs again, then laughed, turning to go. "See you later, sweetie."

Anagen laughed as well, shaking their head. "Vampires," she said. "Don't worry, she's not serious. At least I hope not." They stopped the playback and logged out of the database. "All right, if Soundra's leaving now, Chauncey should be here any minute. She hates being around when he shows up. Let's get out of here and I'll walk you through the prep process." They checked the time again. "Actually, he shoulda been here by now. I don't think he texted me back, though." They pulled out their phone. "Cutting it close, man, we've got barely 20 minutes before he's on the air."

Anagen began showing me what it took to set up for a broadcast, pointing out what felt like a dozen different things a second. I tried to keep up, but a lot of it was pretty esoteric. I was about to ask them - again - for clarification on something when a crash came from the front office, making me jump. "The fuck? Chauncey?" Anagen walked out of Studio C. I got up and stood in the doorway, looking down the hall. "Chauncey, you're really late, what the fuck- oh, shit. God damn it." They sounded suddenly very tired. "Rick, come here!"

I hurried down the hallway, stopping short behind Anagen. A blonde-haired human student dressed in a rumpled red hockey jersey and tan cargo shorts was sprawled face-first on the carpet, ass in the air. A weather-beaten Teva sandal was hanging from one foot. The other was missing. "Reporting fer duty, ma'am," he slurred, flailing one arm in what I could only imagine was meant to be a salute.

Anagen sighed. "Oh for fuck's sake, not again!"

CHAPTER NINE

Anagen kneeled down and pushed, rolling Chauncey over. He protested, flailing halfheartedly. The front of his jersey was emblazoned with the words ARGENT CITY CORGIS, along with a large black paw print in the center. It was also wet, stained, and smelled strongly of cinnamon and vomit. "Dammit, man, Fireball? I told you that shit's gonna kill you." They looked up at the clock on the wall and cursed, floridly, in what sounded like Greek. "Rick, help me get this malákas up on the couch."

"Uh, r-right..." I bent down, wrinkling my nose, and hooked my arms under his armpits. Anagen grabbed his ankles. We heaved on the count of three and easily got him up, his head lolling back at an awkward angle.

Anagen grabbed a plastic wastepaper basket and put it on the floor close to Chauncey's head. "Well, we're fucked," they said. "We've got... less than fifteen minutes until we've got to be on the air. He better have a set list picked out." They strode over to the desk, leaning over it to flip the laptop open. A few clicks later and they scowled. "Godsdammit. Nope. Now we've got to come up with 2 hours of music in... eleven and a half minutes? Shit!"

I started backing up. "Uhh... maybe I should go? You look like you're... going to be... really, uh, busy...?"

"Yeah, I sure fucking am, godsdamned—" Anagen looked

up at me, their eyes like sharp, shining flints. "Wait. That's it. Rick, you got a music player on your phone?"

"Uh, yeah, but w-what does that…" My heart skipped a beat. "Oh. Oh, no. N-no no no, you don't want *me* to pick a playlist, do you?"

"You're here. And I can't do it, you don't know enough to run the board for a live broadcast yet." They pulled open a desk drawer, rummaging through it. "You don't have a login for the database, but we can route your phone output to the aux pickup. If I can just find the… right!" They pulled out a battered looking male-to-male audio cable, holding it aloft like a carnival prize. "Please tell me your phone has an audio jack."

I blinked several times. "I don't… I mean, yeah, it does, but no, y-you can't just—" I took a deep breath. "Anagen, I'm supposed to be behind the *board*, not the mic! Can't you do both? Or, uh, call Soundra back? She can't have gotten far!" I fought to keep the pitch of my voice from going up through my throat. I wasn't doing well.

"No, not with… eight minutes to get everything organized." They walked over and grabbed my elbow. "Come on, it'll be fine. Just pick a song, intro it, and use the run time to keep building a playlist from whatever you can think of. I'll handle the rest."

I tried to pull away, but Anagen's grip was like faesteel. They led me back into the station hallway, practically shoving me into Studio C as my heart hammered in my chest.

"Come on, gimme your phone and put on the headphones! I'll get the board set up." They pulled one of the folding chairs from the wall and flipped it open, plunking it down in front of the computer. I unlocked my handset; Anagen grabbed it, stabbing one end of the cord into the headphone jack and handing it back to me. They jammed the other end into the aux port on the audio deck. "Pick our first song."

I stared down at my phone. The icons on the screen might as well have been Sumerian. "But—"

"Rick! Now is *not* the time!" Anagen glanced up at the wall clock. "We have *six minutes.* Come on, choose something, anything!" They dashed out of the studio, shouting, "I'll be right back!"

My face was hot, blood rushing in my ears. My stomach felt like it was being squeezed in an icy, electric vice grip. Knees weak, I sank into the office chair, staring at my phone screen. All I could hear was the wall clock, each slow tick like a jotun's footfall.

I thumbed my music player icon. A moment later, it sprung up, showing the last track I played. Anagen stuck their head back through the doorway, making me jump. I might have even whimpered. "Hey, I'll be in Studio B, the equipment's better in there. I've slaved the board in here to it." I opened my mouth and pointed to my phone. "You found something? Great! You'll hear me in your headphones. All you need to do is tap play on your phone when I tell you." They were gone before I could say anything.

I checked the time. Two minutes fifteen. Then, I looked down at my playlist. The first song was...

Oh boy. The last thing I had been listening to had been the *AKIRA* movie soundtrack.

I heard Anagen's voice in my ears. *"Okay, we're set up here."* I winced, turning the volume slider down a little. *"Make sure your mic is close to your face, it's directional."*

I pulled it over and fumbled for the button that turned it on. "Can... can you hear me?" I heard the slightest echo of my own voice coming back through the headphones.

"Yep, loud and clear. Okay, a minute twenty. I'll drop a station ident, then you can hit play after seven seconds."

"What? Why? What's—"

"Seven second delay! Standard for radio! All right, hold on Rick, don't freak out." The lights on the board in front of me flickered for a moment. Then, the sliders on the mixer began to move on their own.

"Uhhhhh Anagen? Is that supposed to—"

"Yes, I told you I'm controlling it from the next studio. Get ready, station ident coming up!"

The ON AIR sign lit up. A digital display underneath it began to count seconds. My headphones were flooded with sound.

"UP ALL NIGHT?" An audio clip of a howling wolf played. "YOU'RE LISTENING TO ALLORA UNIVERSITY RADIO, 96.7 FM!"

Four seconds, five, six...

I pressed play, jamming my thumb hard on the screen. The track started with a peal of rolling thunder, followed a few seconds later by Japanese taiko drums. *Shit, this is mostly instrumental, should I say something?* I opened my mouth as the drumbeat swelled. My throat was so dry.

"Uh. Hel-lo Allora Y-yuh-university." The xylophones on the track kicked in. "Your, uh, regular DJ isn't... isn't here tonight. So I..." I took a breath, trying to get my hands from shaking. "I'm... Ricky? Here's, uh, 'Kaneda'? From the *AKIRA* m-movie soundtrack?"

I slapped the button that muted the mic, feeling like I had just played Frogger in traffic with cars driven by angry Sidhe. The music washed over me hypnotically as the track grew more layered.

Anagen stuck their head back through the doorway. I jumped. Again. "Okay, you're on it. Wouldn't have pegged you for a weeb, but it'll get the job done. What's your next song?"

"Next song?" I stared at them, wide-eyed.

"Yes, your next song! This track can't be more than three,

four minutes long, right? Get it queued up." They disappeared before I could say anything.

I grabbed my phone, scrolling through my playlists feverishly. *Need something different. C'mon Ricky, think.* I had another minute and ten seconds before the first track ended.

Wait, what was that? I scrolled back up to a folder labeled "New Wave/Post-Punk Weirdness" and tapped it, opening it up. *Talking Heads, Dead Kennedys, Joy Division... yeah this will work.* I swallowed, wishing I had some water.

The first track was winding up. I knew the next track had a few seconds before the lyrics started, so I put my hand on the mic button and waited. *Gods, what was it called? Hitting the post?*

The track began to fade out, and I thumbed the mic button. "T-that was–" my voice cracked. I leaned my head to the left, away from the mic, and coughed. "That was 'Kaneda', from the *AKIRA* m-motion picture soundtrack, by Geinoh Yama–" I squinted at the screen. "Ya-ma-shi-ro-gumi." I pressed play on the next track. "Up next, w-w-we've got 'Cities' from Talking Heads, off their *Fear of Music* album." I paused, listening to the next track begin to fade in. *Need to buy myself some more time. I don't have to intro every song, do I?* "After that, 'Holiday in Cambodia' f-from the Dead Kennedys. You're... you're listening to Allora University R-radio." I set my phone down and muted the mic again.

Anagen chimed in over my headphones. "Okay, I'm getting it. Not bad so far, let's keep it up! Better than the shit Chauncey would play every Friday night." The relief in their voice was plain. "We got this, you and me, Rick. Just another hour, fifty-six minutes, and fifteen seconds to go."

A wave of nausea washed over me. I pushed it down. "Okay," I whispered to myself, picking up my phone. "Let's do this."

CHAPTER TEN

I don't even know what time I got back to my room that morning. I really don't remember the rest of my set very well, to be honest. What I did know is that I woke up at around 10:30, feeling like I'd been dropped off a building with my wings pinned.

Groaning, I sat up in bed, looking around blearily. I was the only one there. "Huh." I pulled my phone from the nightstand, unplugged it, and squinted down at the screen. There was a text from Niko.

Out for the weekend with The Squad. No sexy parties without me! jk lol

I put my phone on silent and lay back down with a sigh. I closed my eyes and just breathed. After a minute, my stomach gurgled. *Dammit,* I thought.

I got up, threw on my bathrobe, and slipped into my shower sandals before grabbing a towel and the rest of what I needed.

I had the communal showers to myself this morning so I took my time, just standing under the water for a few minutes while trying to process last night. It was mostly a blur, but, well... looking back on it, it had been at least a little fun. Kinda. *Not enough to do that again, though. I guess the radio station was a bad idea after all.*

When I got back from my shower, it was close to 11. *Shit, I missed breakfast.* I started rummaging through my closet for the snacks I had stashed there but only came up with an empty cardboard box. "The hell?"

There was a teal Post-It note stuck to it. "We got real hungry last night. We'll get you back after the weekend! –Niko." Grinding my teeth, I grabbed my phone and looked up the food court hours on the university website. Lunch didn't start until 12:30. I sighed. *Well, there's always the diner...?* I winced at the idea.

The thought of otherwise having to wait an hour and a half to eat what was barely a step above prison food motivated me. Just 20 minutes on the UTA and I could get whatever I wanted. *But the price,* I thought. *There's always a price.*

A little less than half an hour later, I got off the bus in front of the K Street Diner in all its squalid glory. I hesitated to walk up the steps, my resolve fading, until my stomach rumbled again. *Ugh, fine,* I thought.

The bell tinkled when I walked in. It hadn't changed a bit since the last time. Same stool-lined countertop, same worn yellow booths... same waitresses.

"Hi, is it just you t—oh! Ricky! That you?" A middle-aged human woman dressed in a well-worn waitress uniform smiled at me. "Look at you! Hannah, come look, it's Ricky! You here to see Dave?"

I tried not to wince. "Oh, uh, hi Sharon. Is he – is he on today?"

Sharon grinned at me. "You know he can't afford to hire any other cooks. Surprised he's still got us on the payroll." She rolled her eyes. "I'll get you your usual booth. You need a menu, or you know what you want?"

"N-no, actually, can I get it to go? I got, uh, studying to do."

"Sure thing, Ricky." She pulled a pen and her guest check

pad from her apron pocket. "What'll it be, then?"

"Umm… the ham and cheddar omelet, rye toast, and hash browns please."

"Coming right up." She pulled a pad out of her apron and scribbled on it. "I'll put this in right now." She smiled. "It's good to see you again, Ricky." I watched her slip back behind the counter and stick the check in the carousel.

I leaned back against the hostess stand and just people-watched for a few. It was the regular crowd for a late Saturday morning, about an equal mix of humans and mythics. There was even a particularly hung-over looking pair of werewolves in the farthest corner. From the looks of it, they had two bloody steaks each. They weren't using any silverware.

I turned to look out the window, watching the traffic crawl by for a few moments and losing myself in thoughts about last night's trial by fire. I must have zoned out slightly because I jumped when a large brown paper bag was plunked down in front of me on the hostess stand.

"Here you go, Ricky. Good to see you, by the way." Hannah, the other waitress, dusted her hands off.

"Hey! Y-yeah, it's been forever since I had the chance to stop in. Things have been crazy with school." I cocked my head, noticing that the shoulder seam on her waitress uniform was slightly torn. "Hey, what happened there?" I asked, pointing.

"Hm? Oh, yeah." She sighed, placing the guest check on the counter next to the to-go bag. "A couple of Sluagh were in here late last night, thought they would start some of their spooky shit. I gave them a taste of The Great Huntress and they bolted, but I didn't have a spare uniform with me. I had to borrow one from the back." She hooked a thumb over her shoulder. Barely visible through the pass-through was a large cardboard box. The words "Fort Werelion" in Sigil were scrawled across the front with black Sharpie. Someone had cut out an image of Nala from

The Lion King and taped it to the side.

I winced. "Sorry, Hannah. Well at least they won't come back any time soon, right?"

She grinned, growling deep in her throat. Her pupils turned into slits for a moment. "I almost hope they do. Dave says it's okay if I eat a few unruly customers time and again. Keeps the rest of them in line."

I laughed and pulled out my wallet to pay for breakfast. Despite myself, I was looking forward to digging in as soon as I got back to my dorm - my uncle had been doing this long enough that the K Street Diner had a reputation for pretty decent food. Which was good, because nobody came here for the ambiance.

Hannah handed me the receipt and I signed it, then pulled some bills from my wallet and stuffed them in the tip jar on the counter. "Ricky!" Hannah scowled. "What are you doing? Put that back right now-"

"Oh, no you don't," I said, waving her off. "I know what my uncle pays you guys. Take Bank out for a night on the town or something."

Hannah grinned toothily, shaking her head. "You're a pain in the ass, Ricky, but you're a good kid. Say hi to your folks for me, okay?" She reached out and ruffled my hair.

"Aw, jeez, Hannah!" I winced, dancing out of her reach. "I'm not a hatchling anymore!" She smirked, relenting, and turned to greet a pair of humans that had just walked through the door. Thinking I was in the clear, I grabbed my to-go bag and turned, ready to slip out the door.

"Heyyy Ricky! Ricky, that you, kid?"

I froze in my tracks, cursing under my breath for a second. Then I turned around. My uncle had stuck his head, all glittering silver scales, through the pass-through. He waved, an offset spatula in his hand. "Hey, come 'round back before you leave!"

No avoiding it now. "Okay, I'll be right there!" Hannah gave me an apologetic look as I made my way around the counter, clutching my bag of food.

I stepped through the doors to the kitchen. "Hey, Uncle Da —huh?" I looked around but there was no sign of him. *Where the hell is he?* "Uncle Dave?"

His familiar voice rang out from the recesses of the kitchen. "Back here, kid!" I craned my neck, noticing the fire door along the back wall had been propped open. A scaly hand waved me over and I obliged.

My uncle was there on the loading dock leaning against the outside wall of the diner, the bottom of one foot braced against it in his best Anthony Bourdain pose. He grinned at me. "Nice to see ya, kid! How's the fam?"

"They're okay." I shrugged. "Mack's doing his corporate thing, Dags has her nose buried in her phone, Mom's plotting the overthrow of the government, and Dad's trying to keep all the plates in the air. You know, the usual."

Dave pulled an unlit cigarette from behind his pointy ear. He screwed it into the corner of his mouth, no mean feat considering he was half-transformed as always, and then cocked his head, using a finger to close one nostril. He shot a short jet of flame out of the other, lighting the end of the smoke. "Yeah, that sounds like Chad." He took a deep drag, plucked the cigarette from his mouth, and exhaled.

I wrinkled my nose at the smell. "That's... that's not tobacco, is it?"

"Nope." Dave grinned at me. "What, you think I'm out here raw-dogging reality? The hell with that. We all have our vices, Ricky. Besides, I'm out of Virginia Slims." He took another drag. "So, this is your first semester at Allora, right? How you liking it so far?"

I shrugged. "Okay, I guess? Just a couple weeks in, so I'm

still feeling things out. Classes are… interesting?"

"Yeah, I'll bet. Your dad told me you joined the college radio station, too. Actually, he wouldn't shut up about it. He's proud as hell, Ricky."

"It was *one* night, Uncle Dave. And I was just pitching in because the overnight DJ literally pissed himself in the front room and the engineer needed help choosing two hours' worth of tracks."

"Hey, you gotta start somewhere, right?" Dave took another long drag, then pulled it from his mouth, the butt pinched between his scaly thumb and forefinger. He pursed his lips, directing a pencil-thin gout of flame to char the stub to ash. "So, you know what I'm gonna ask you –"

"No, I didn't play any."

"Oh, come *on*, Ricky! You know they're one of the best bands in the history of hard rock! Why you gotta do them like that?"

"Oh my gods, Uncle Dave. Yeah, masters of what? Dressing up in a schoolboy uniform and duck-walking across the stage for 50 years? They're butt rock, and you know it!"

"Hey, don't you disrespect them." He mock-glared at me. "They're iconic! C'mon, you couldn't have at least played *one* track? They've got so many hits to choose from. I mean you can't tell me the opening to 'Thunderstruck' isn't one of the most recognizable riffs of all time."

"Yes, that's because it's been used in like a billion commercials for a billion years."

"You say that like it's a *bad* thing! Jeez, Ricky, you gotta play at least one track next time."

"Oh no, that was a one-time thing, I swear." I ran a palm slowly down my face. "Besides, the whole ordeal was exhausting, man. I had about 30 seconds of prep time and I was pulling songs out of my cloaca left and right. It was terrifying. I thought I was going to die. I must have been crazy to agree to do it but I couldn't deal with the prospect of two hours of dead air, even at 2 in the morning. At least now they have time to get a permanent replacement DJ and I can stick to working the board, which was what I was *supposed* to be doing that night!"

My uncle laughed. "If it was such hell, Ricky, why do you sound like you kind of enjoyed it?" He grinned. A desk bell chimed, inside, and he then stuck his head back through the open doorway. "Whoops, looks like break time's over," he said, dusting his hands off on his apron before clapping me on the shoulder. "Don't be a stranger, okay, Ricky? And play a little AC/DC next time." He winked and disappeared back into the kitchen.

I rolled my eyes. "Not if my life depended on it!" I called after him. I walked down the back loading dock steps and slipped through the alley leading out to K Street, retracing my steps to the UTA station. I tried not to salivate too badly at the smell of my late breakfast coming from the bag. Instead, I dug my phone out from my pocket to check the time.

I had something like five or six text notifications, all from the same number across about a period of three hours. I unlocked my phone and brought them up.

Hey it's Anagen, Byron gave me ur number. Call/text me back

Hey Rick, where r u? Gotta talk real quick

OMG answer ur fuckign phone, nerd

WE NEED 2 TALK, CALL NOW

Swearing, I tapped the "call now" button on my screen and held the phone up to my ear. I could hear my heart ratcheting up in my chest while the line rang.

The line clicked. *"Rick? It's about fucking time, where the hell were you all morning?"*

"What the hell is going on? My ringer was off, what's the

big—"

"Shut up and listen to me, Rick." I clammed up. *"You're a hit."*

My mind went blank. "W... what? What are you talking about?"

"Your set last night. You're a fucking hit!"

CHAPTER ELEVEN

"**A**nagen, w-what the hell are you talking about?"

"The station got three emails and a dozen Twitter mentions last night, all good ones. During your set. The hashtag 'WhoIsRicky' was trending. You've gotta come back!"

The bottom of my stomach dropped out. "Oh, no. No no no. *Fuck* no. I thought I was gonna *die* up there." I cast my gaze left and right like a gazelle looking for an escape route while being chased by a hungry lion. "No, you... you gotta find someone else, you've got p-plenty of time to find a replacement DJ. What about Soundra, or s-someone else—"

"Not for this time slot." Anagen laughed mirthlessly. *"The 2 to 4? Nobody else wants it. Soundra included."*

"What about Chauncey?"

"Chauncey is out, man! Byron bounced him for this last little stunt. Can you believe that drunk fuck tried to bribe Byron with crypto to let him back in? Stormcoin or something-"

I groaned. "Thundercoin," I said.

"Whatever. You know it took me half an hour to get the smell out of the couch after he pissed himself? I'm not doing that ever again, and Byron agreed. Rather have you in the hot seat than MC Pee Pants."

"Yeah, well I almost peed my *own* pants last night!" My voice cracked. "I want to be *behind* the scenes, not in the spotlight! You gotta find someone else, I'm not cut out for this. Why don't you do it?"

"*Because I've got my own shit going on, Rick. That's why Byron signed you on to train as my replacement in the first place!*" They sighed. "*Listen, Ricky, I know part of you liked it. Go on, check the radio station Twitter feed. I gotta go, we'll talk about this later, okay? This isn't over!*" The line went dead.

My knees gave out; I sat down heavily on the bench at the bus stop and stared down at my phone screen, breakfast forgotten. A couple of other people who were already there pointedly ignored me.

They've got to be fucking with me. I pulled up Twitter and scrolled, tapping on the radio station's timeline. *Please tell me they're fucking with me.* I started scrolling.

Yo this new DJ is so much better than the last one, where you been hiding him? #WhoIsRicky

#NightNest is KILLING it with the post-punk tonight! Keep it up!

I don't know #WhoIsRicky but he's got some good taste in music

Chauncey can suck the sweat off my balls. #MoreRickyPlease

#WhoIsRicky? He sounds cute in a real first-season-of-The-Big-Bang-Theory kinda way

#NightNest playing some BANGERS for once #StevieWonder #Superstition #WhoIsRicky

The notifications kept going. I kept reading, perplexed.

My heart was beating so hard it felt like it was going to explode out of my chest. I couldn't just sit there anymore – I needed to go calm the fuck down.

There was only really one place I could think of. I looked

across the street at the entrance to the UTA rail station, but I couldn't bear sitting still for another minute. Instead, I set out on foot and began walking crosstown, to the east, my to-go bag in tow. Moving my feet seemed to me the only thing I could reasonably do now. I didn't trust myself to text or call anyone, and I sure as hell wasn't showing up at my parents' place. *Both Mom and Dad would send me right back to the radio station*, I thought, shaking my head, as I continued east.

The City was a big place, easy to get lost in if you didn't know your way. Once you've seen it from the sky, though, it's much less difficult to navigate, even if you're doing it the old-fashioned way. It took me a lot longer than if I had taken the train, as I had to weave through Grunstadt so I didn't end up walking through Little Kingston. Bank was cool with me, but the rest of the Anansi would see me as a walking wallet, and I really didn't need that right now. So, I went out of my way, skirting through Kitsune territory. I knew that if I kept my mouth shut and didn't bother anyone it was unlikely that they would pay me any attention – outside of getting stared at and hearing the words *gaijin no ryu* while walking through little Tokyo.

I knew I was getting closer when an easterly wind brought with the tang of saltwater with it, the faint cry of seagulls, and the unmistakable smell of the high-test boat fuel used by the yachts down at the wharf. I knew I was in the right place when I crested a small hill and saw the early afternoon sun glittering on Destry Bay.

You would think that the Grunstadt Seaport would be hopping on a clear, warm Saturday in late September, and you would be right. The entire wharf was hopping with tourists and upper-middle-class locals shopping in bougie stores lined up on the boardwalk. It was an idyllic scene if you didn't mind all the gentrification.

I snaked my way through the good-sized crowds, getting a few curious glances from humans and mythics much better dressed than I was, ultimately reaching the edge of the wharf. I came up against the worn wooden railing that cordoned off the marina from the boardwalk and put my elbows on it. Leaning out over the edge, I closed my eyes and breathed deep, filling my lungs with sea air. The gulls wheeled and dived around me.

After a moment, I opened my eyes again and just stared ahead, past the breakers and out to the endless gray expanse of the Atlantic. A few boats were traversing the bay, trailing their wakes behind them like fading memories.

A gull swooped down and perched on the railing a few feet away. It cocked its head at me, clacking its beak expectantly. It was eyeing my to-go bag.

"Sorry buddy," I said. "Nothing for you." I jerked my head to the left. "Go fuck with some tourists." The bird squawked, lifted its tailfeathers, and left a runny shit on the boardwalk before taking off.

"Yeah, you and me both," I muttered. I looked away from where the gull had left its critique of the waterfront, my gaze wandering down the length of the marina. About 30 yards from me there was a short flight of steps, leading to a service gate for accessing an old culvert that fed into the bay.

I walked closer, the sound of rushing water growing stronger as I approached. The path down to the culvert was clear, but the service gate had a DO NOT ENTER sign on it, along with a padlock.

The lock was dusted with the kind of oxidation you only get from being exposed to salt air for years. I grabbed it with one hand to steady it and slid a finger between the shackle and the hasp. A good, hard tug – harder than any human could pull off – and the shackle popped, flakes of rust raining down to the ground.

The grate creaked when I pulled it open, making my heart jump in my chest. I slipped through clumsily and pulled it shut behind me, praying no one had heard the racket. It took me a good minute to ease my panicked breathing as I clung to the inside bars of the grate, but after it became clear no one was going to come investigate I finally caught my breath and turned around.

I felt my pupils dilate inhumanly wide as my vision adjusted to the low light inside the culvert. The diameter was large enough for an average human to stand upright. There was a central sluice and a narrow raised concrete path on either side. The water passing through seemed to be a couple of feet deep; the pipe itself angled gently downward to a spillway about ten yards downhill from me. Another grate blocked off the exit. This one was locked too, but the padlock on this one was in even worse shape than the one above. It gave out immediately and the grate swung open with a halting groan.

I stuck my head out the end. I was directly under the raised pier, completely isolated from the crowds above. Below me, a short rocky slope led to a shore strewn with trash and seaweed. I looked back and saw the high-water mark halfway up the side of the culvert's opening.

The Atlantic was right there, lapping against the wet, rocky shore. It was dark and comforting, and for the first time in what felt like forever I felt like the iron band around my chest had loosened slightly when I leaned down and dipped my hand in the water.

I swept my gaze up and down the shore. There were no signs of habitation, human or mythic, for as far as I could see. This was the closest I would get to having some peace and quiet before the tide rolled back in, so I pulled off my shoes and socks, hiked up my jeans a little, and walked out into the bay.

North Atlantic beaches, even the best of them that had been basking in full sunlight, could be kind of cold by late September. Well, for a human, at least. When you grew up as a hatchling and spent your winters diving in Casco Bay for fresh haddock and Atlantic Bluefin, dangling your feet in early autumn water was like stepping into a warm bath.

I sighed, lost in thought, as I dug my toes into the wet sand. A moment later my phone buzzed, shocking me out of my reverie. I fished it out and unlocked it to see another message from Anagen.

Hey I know I came on strong before, but you gotta understand – this is the most attention ive ever seen the 2 to 4 slot ever get and ive been doing this for FIVE SEMESTERS now

Take some time. Think about it. Get back to me and we'll figure out what to do next. You've got free rein in choosing tracks, if it's not in the station library bring in your own shit. If you really cant do it then well find an alternative, just don't leave me on read, k?

That iron band around my chest had returned. *What am I supposed to say to that?*

Last night had been fucking terrifying. It was bad enough knowing that my voice had been going out over the airwaves, blanketing the city and beyond for, what? 30 miles? 40? That meant people out in the suburbs could have been listening to me spin those tracks. And apparently there *were* people listening, even at 2 in the morning on a Friday night. Or early Saturday morning, if you wanted to be pedantic about it.

The idea of going through that even one more time was enough to tie my stomach up in knots. This kind of attention was exactly what I didn't want. Hell, I didn't want *any* attention, but I knew avoiding that forever would be impossible, being who I was and what I'd have to do someday. *So why rush it?* I thought.

Still… there had been a lot of people talking about my set last night. People that seemed to care about music quite a bit. People that, apparently, I had something in common with that weren't related to me. I had to admit - a small, secret part of me kinda liked that.

I shook my head, fighting off a sudden chill. "No," I

muttered, "that's fucking crazy." This was just chasing a high, right? Some stupid thrill? Just because a bunch of strangers liked what I played last night doesn't mean I should do it again. Not with how absolutely horrifying that spotlight was.

At the same time, I had seemed to have found something that I was sorta good at. And how much of my anxiety was from being thrown to the sharks without warning? Maybe if I went into it with some time to prepare properly. You know, record intros and station breaks in advance so I could get them right. Just once more, until Anagen could find a suitable replacement?

I looked down at my phone. I had been ruminating for so long that the screen had shut off on its own. I turned it back on, unlocked it, and tapped out a reply.

OK listen maybe I'm willing to do this once more. ONCE MORE

This is temporary. Just until you find a replacement

But I'm gonna need more than 5 minutes of prep time, I'm not fucking Batman

My phone was silent for about thirty seconds. Then, a reply: an animated .gif of David from *Schitt's Creek,* wearing a black shirt with the letters I'M STUPID printed across them. He was jumping up and down and clapping. The caption underneath it simply read: "THANK YOU!"

I sighed, placing my head in my hands. *I'm the stupid one,* I thought.

CHAPTER TWELVE

I might have been experiencing the draconic equivalent of shitting bricks in fear at the thought of putting my neck out there again, but I was pretty much the only one. My parents were immediately thrilled, and even Dags expressed her approval in her own way, though I had to insist that just because I had a second gig didn't mean I'd start taking requests from her. I figured that my listening audience – whoever in the world these strange creatures actually were – might be a lot of things, but Taylor Swift fans they were not.

Uncle Dave was even worse. He began a coordinated campaign to get me to play a few AC/DC tracks, bombarding my father with texts and emails that Dad dutifully forwarded to me. Well, until they got into an argument about their own musical tastes. Apparently when my uncle found out that his brother listened to The Panda ("107.6 FM, WPND! The Argent City's home for Adult Contemporary Music!") there was an issue. Something about "Easy Listening with a fig leaf." Thankfully, I wasn't privy to the details.

With a whole week in advance, though, I had plenty of time to prepare an actual setlist that I didn't have to pull out of thin air. Plus, I had Anagen in my corner – well, kind of.

"Are you telling me that you're not going to do *any* live PSAs or station idents? Come *on*, Rick!"

It was Thursday night, and Anagen had asked me to come

to the studio for some prep work and training. I was already agitated by the time I made it up to the 4th floor - I had stepped into the SUB and had been waiting for the elevator only to come face-to-face with Summers and his miniature confederacy of dunces when the doors opened.

"Oh, look, everyone, the court jester is here!" The Sidhe grinned at me maleveolently. "Going up, Ruh-ruh-Ricky? Room for one more." His friends tittered.

I jerked back from the open doors. "Uhhh, yeah, n-no thanks, Wyndham. I'll, uh, I'll take the n-next one."

"You sure?" he said, his voice dripping sarcasm. A few humans pushed past me and stepped inside the waiting elevator doors. They began to close. "Oh well, next time, Ricky. I'm sure we'll... run into each other again soon."

It took me a while before I could muster the courage to get up to the 4th floor after that. When I did, the Satyr waiting for me was more than a little miffed. I might have been a little short with them as a result, something I immediately regretted. "Anagen, I had a 49-and-a-half-hour panic attack after last Friday night. You want me to intro songs and try to hit posts? Fine. But you gotta give me *some* way to get a little relief. Can't we just pre-record them so I d-don't have to f-f-freak out by trying to do them live?"

They sighed, running a hand through their hair and tugging on one of their horns. "All right," they said finally, "I should give you some more board time anyway, I guess. Let's head to Studio C and we'll get you set up. But just the station idents, okay? PSAs change too often to justify pre-recording them."

A wave of relief washed over me. "Oh thank Bahamut," I said. "I cuh-can deal with that I guess. What kinds of PSAs do we usually have?"

They stood up, gathering their things. I followed suit.

"Well, like I said, they change pretty regularly. Most of them have to do with events on or near campus. Sports events, concerts, art exhibitions, you know."

We walked down the hallway towards Studio C. Anagen pushed the door open while looking through their notes. "Here's a good example. From now until the end of October, we're supposed to plug that *Secret McQueen* live premiere on Halloween night." They gestured to the beaten-up office chair and I sat. "It's not a campus event but it's right in North Allora. Tickets are going like crazy, there's even scalpers selling them at a huge markup." They turned to grab one of the folding chairs leaning against the wall.

"Wait, what? I thought tickets were free."

"They are. Or were, anyway. Until someone figured out they could resell theirs to make a quick buck. Classic psychology, right?"

Over the next hour Anagen tutored me on how to run the board during a broadcast. It was less complex than my Intro to Management Accounting class and a hell of a lot more interesting, though Summers's little threat in the elevator was still interfering with my ability to concentrate. Not only that, but screwing up an accounting quiz wasn't nearly as mortifying as doing the same during a radio broadcast, even if it was going out at 2 in the morning.

I tried not to think about that too much.

After that, Anagen gave me some time to pre-record some of the station idents and even gave me an opportunity to practice introing songs and hitting posts. That went even worse.

"Fucking dammit," I said, pausing the recording and pulling my headphones off. "H-how the hell am I gonna do this if I keep t-tripping over my own godsdamned words?"

Anagen was leaning back in their chair and scrolling through their phone, hooves up on the table. "Hey, take it easy, man. You just need practice. I'll admit last week was a real trial by fire, but you got through it, didn't you?"

"Yeah, barely! I don't even remember most of it." I glared at the mixing deck, thinking hard. "Actually... wait, I have an idea. Is there a way to have what I'm saying into the mic fed back to the headphones live? Like, without the 7-second delay?"

"Huh?" Anagen looked up from their phone. "Yeah, that's easy enough. But why?"

"An old trick from Ms. Fremont, my speech therapist from grade school." I looked down at the board. "She made me practice speaking on the phone, calling up businesses and asking them when they were open, stuff like that. It was called... shit what was it? D-duh-delayed auditory feedback. Something about hearing your own voice while you're speaking short-circuits your brain, helps you c-control your stutter."

"No shit, really? Damn, Rick, I never woulda thought of that." They leaned forward, smacking my hands away from the board. "Stop, let me show you before you fuckin' break something. This dial here..."

It took a little tweaking, but eventually we got it – I could hear my voice in my ears, just like when I was using the phone when I was younger. It was both easier and harder than back then, as I wasn't waiting for a response from some bored retail clerk wondering while some kid was calling them on the phone. Instead, I was preparing to literally broadcast my voice across the City.

I ran through some more station idents with the new settings, finally pulling the headphones off in relief. "Damn," I said softly.

"Not bad, Rick." Anagen was still on their phone, but I could see the hint of a smile on their lips. "Sounds like you're ready for tomorrow night, huh?"

I blinked. "Yeah, I.... well, I guess I am." I laughed lightly, shaking my head. "Can't believe that worked." My own phone buzzed in my pocket, so I fished it out to see a message from my mother.

Hey hon! I know you've got your next show tomorrow night (SO EXCITED 4 U!) but can you come by Saturday and keep an eye on the apartment? Dad and I are going out of town and your brother and sister said they're busy

I tapped out a reply. *Beats smelling satyr musk all weekend. Sat to Sun? I have class early Monday morning*

"What's up?" Anagen rose from their chair, flipping it closed with a clank. They craned their neck over my shoulder.

"Huh? Oh, my folks want me to keep an eye on their place this weekend while they're away." My phone dinged again:

Yup, thanks kiddo! Help urself to anything in the fridge. EXCEPT THE ICE CREAM, you know the rules. Love you!

"Aww. Guarding the treasure cave, huh?"

I stood up, stuffing my phone back in my pocket. "If you mean a third-floor apartment in West Allora, sure I guess. So is there anything else we need to go over tonight? Figure we'd finish on a high note."

Anagen checked their notes again. "Hmm, no I think we're good. As long as you've got your music picked out for tomorrow night, you're free to go. Seeya then, Rick."

I left the studio and took the elevator back down to the ground floor, head swimming with everything I'd just gone over at the station.

Campus was busy. I had learned quickly that most students arrange their schedules so that they didn't have any Friday classes, letting their weekend start a day early. No one had told me as an incoming freshman, of course, so I still had classes the next day. Everyone else, though, was gearing up for a night out on the town; there was a steady stream of students moving generally in off-campus directions. With any luck, Niko and the rest of the crew would be out doing something tonight, giving me a few hours of peace and quiet.

Coindre Hall was about as busy as you'd expect at that time of night. Most students who had plans to go out had likely already left. There were a couple of people hanging out in the lounge near the front door, mostly reading or doomscrolling on their phones.

Before I went up to my room, I stopped at the bank of mailboxes to check if there was anything waiting for me. With Mom and Dad right in West Allora, I didn't really get "letters from home," but I liked to keep my mailbox free of flyers and stuff like that. As I expected, I fished some notices about upcoming campus events from my box. I closed it and started flipping through them, sorting them for the recycling bin in the lobby, when I came across a small green index card.

I took a closer look. It had "YOU HAVE A PACKAGE" printed on the front in large block letters. A line underneath it, in a slightly smaller font, instructed me to pick it up at the RA office next to the mailboxes.

Puzzled, I turned around and walked over to the office counter. Ibrahim, the RA on duty, was in there, looking bored as he played on his phone. "Hey," I said. He looked up and I waved the card at him. "This says, uh, that I have a package?"

The RA nodded, sliding his feet off the desk and standing up. "Yup," he said. "What room are you in?" He reached out for the card.

"314." I handed it to him and he took it, putting it on the desk. Then, he leaned down to rummage in a mail basket. A moment later and he pulled out a small cardboard box. He turned it over in his hands, checking the shipping label, and then handed it to me. "Here you go," he said.

"Thanks." I looked down at it, more than a little confused.

I waved goodbye and made my way upstairs, hefting the box easily with one hand. It wasn't particularly heavy, but there was something inside; I could hear it thumping slightly whenever I moved the box.

I was relieved to see there was no sock on the doorknob when I got to my room. Knowing I had at least a little time, I let myself in and sat down on my bed, taking a closer look at the package.

It was plain cardboard, maybe the size of a shoebox or something smaller. The address label was just a square piece of paper that had been taped to the box. My name and address were written there in block letters. There was no return address. In fact, there weren't even any stamps or anything else that showed it had gone through the mail to get to me.

Oh boy, I thought. *I hope Ellen didn't decide to send me something again.* It had been hard enough avoiding her advances in person whenever I went to the library, but if she had begun dropping little presents off for me? *I'm gonna have to find a way to tell her I'm not interested.*

I flexed my right hand. My index finger elongated slightly, the nail turning sharp and pointed, and I used the partially transformed digit to slit the packing tape on the box. I shook my hand out as it regained its human form with a tingle.

I opened the top flap. There was a smaller box inside the first. I pulled it out and examined it, my nose twitching from a curious smell that started wafting up from the open package. The small box had been decorated with some tasteful wrapping paper. It was even festooned with a bow. A handwritten note was taped to the front. It read, "I can't wait until our next meeting! Until then, here's a little something to remind you that I'm thinking about you."

I didn't recognize it, but the handwriting matched that on the address label. I tore open the wrapping paper, revealing a small, rectangular plastic box with a lid. The strange smell became stronger as I fiddled with the box top. Pausing, I took another sniff, becoming increasingly perplexed. The scent reminded me of something, but I couldn't quite put my finger on it. Finally, I pried the lid loose and pulled it up.

The interior of the box had been lined with what looked like red silk. Nestled in the center, placed there with what looked like love and attention, was an ornate book, bound in finely tooled leather that had been dyed a deep, rich green. The title had been inlaid in gold leaf: RECOLLECTIONS OF A FOX-HUNTER. It had been the aroma of an antique book that I had been smelling. Completely perplexed, I pulled the book from the box and turned it over in my hands.

I opened the book to the first page; the publication date was 1861. As I did so, something fluttered from between the pages and onto the floor. I picked it up, seeing clearly that it was a note, written on heavy, expensive-looking paper in an elegant hand. The words were in Sigil.

To the esteemed neophyte of the bardic arts, Ricky Konacsz,

Our chance meeting today was a delight for all. That you chose not to share a moment in Prince Leopold's conveyance was near wounding, as we have much to discuss in private. I took the liberty with furnishing you this small token of my esteem in the hopes that someday you would join us for a hunt at your earliest convenience, at which you would be our guest of highest honor. It would be our exquisite pleasure to show you the hospitality for which the Sidhe of the Summer Court are renowned, and most certainly give you the thrill of your young life. For one, I would absolutely love to introduce you to my hounds!

See you in class.

With esteem,

Wyndham Summers, Scion of the Earl of Elmwood

I stared at the note, my hands shaking and my stomach doing flip-flops. Sure, it looked like the kind of letter a privileged asshole like Summers would send to one of one of his friends, but I knew better. The only way a Sidhe would invite a Dragon to a "fox hunt" would to be the fox.

The one thing that had me more scared than anything else, though? This had been delivered to my dorm. *How in the Nine Hells does he know where I live?*

CHAPTER THIRTEEN

Friday night went surprisingly well even though Summers had sent me a little love note the night before. Naturally, I hadn't gotten even a moment of sleep – not after the "gift" he so generously bestowed upon me – but I was too rattled to do or say anything about it. Instead, I put that stupid book and his impeccably polite death threat and stuffed them back in the box they came in, sliding it under my bed.

I was an even bigger nervous wreck than usual when I showed up at the radio station that evening. "Jumping at shadows" doesn't even begin to describe it. It was a huge relief when I stepped over the threshold into the station interior; it was comfort knowing that not only were there witnesses, but they were a no-nonsense Satyr and a very spicy Vampire, even if Soundra low-key terrified me. At least she didn't hiss at me this time when I came in.

It took me a while to get into a decent headspace, once I settled in, but eventually I was able to put all the insanity of the night before aside. The new audio settings we had figured out helped me control my stutter to the point where, while I wasn't exactly less awkward on the air, at least I wasn't tripping over my own words as much. All in all, it went well enough that I didn't look over my shoulder more than twice on my way back to the dorm after my shift. I woke up Saturday morning to my phone blowing up from another glowing report from Anagen.

Rick I don't know what you did to Byron but he's got a hard-on with a cheeseburger at the end of it for the show, said engagement was even higher this time around

He wants to rebroadcast it Saturday nights from 8 to 10 instead of repeating the NPR broadcast from that morning. Chauncey is A N G E R Y, you better watch out or he might pee on you in retaliation lol

I shook my head, barely comprehending what I was reading. *That's great,* I tapped back. *BRB refilling my propranolol prescription.*

I got an animated .gif of Squirtle from the *Pokémon* cartoon in return. He was putting on a pair of sunglasses. The caption read "deal with it."

I can't handle this on an empty stomach, I thought. It was early enough to catch breakfast on campus this time, so I got dressed and headed out. After that, I came back, showered, and threw a few things in a bag before heading to my parents' place. I fretted the entire time, though I was less worried about running into cryptobros in hockey jerseys around every corner than I was getting dragged off to "participate" in a fox hunt.

When I got in, I shot off a quick text to my mother, kicked my shoes off, and made myself at home, seriously in need of some self-soothing time. Before long I was reclined on the couch, a pen behind my ear and a spiral notebook in my lap. A fresh mug of cocoa was on the coffee table. It was resting next to my phone, which was streaming music to my earbuds as I listened and took notes on some of the tracks that I was thinking of using for my next broadcast. Late afternoon sunlight was streaming in through the window, which I had opened slightly open to bring in a cool autumn breeze. I had the whole apartment to myself.

Much better, I thought, reaching for my cocoa. *I could get used to this.*

The door banged open violently. I tumbled from the couch in a panic, scrambling to my feet in time to see my sister come storming in and slam the door behind her. Cracks spiderwebbed through the frame.

"FUCK!" she screamed, making a beeline for the kitchen. I heard the fridge door open as she rummaged around. "God dammit, where's the Rocky Road?"

"Dags! What the hell? You scared the crap out of me!" I dusted myself off, checking to make sure I hadn't gotten any hot cocoa on my vintage shirt.

"Ricky?" The fridge door slammed, and she walked out into the living room holding a pint of ice cream. "Where's Mom and Dad?"

"They went back up to Portland for the weekend, work stuff, you lunatic. They asked me to house sit. Said they asked you and Mack but neither of you were around?"

"Did they?" She looked lost for a moment. "I guess they did. Yeah, that was back when I had plans for the weekend." She sank down onto the couch, clutching the pint of Rocky Road in one hand. She popped the top off the container with the other and tossed it on the coffee table.

I looked at her. "Uhh, you want a spoon or something?"

"Nope." An imperceptible, almost electric hum ran through the room as my sister snapped her fingers. In moments they morphed as she transformed partially, the digits lengthening into wicked claws. "Don't need it." She scooped a massive chunk of ice cream from the pint and popped in her mouth, now an elongated, scaly muzzle lined with razor-sharp teeth.

She chewed contentedly for a moment before looking back down at the rest of the ice cream in her hands. "Fuck it," she growled. Opening her jaws wide, she stuffed the entire pint in her mouth, container and all, swallowing it whole.

I blinked. "Jesus, Dags. What the fuck is going on with you? I haven't seen you do that since they discontinued Netscape Navigator."

She glared out the window, slowly returning to her human form. "Conny and I broke up." She crossed her arms, but her voice quavered. "Well... no, that's not true. He fucking dumped my ass again. Over Instagram." She handed her phone to me. "Take a look."

I took it from her, looking down.

A half-transformed blue Dragon in a shirt with a popped collar and sunglasses halfway down his muzzle was leering into the camera. Another blue, a female in a low-cut top, was pressed up against him, kissing his cheek. The caption read: "Me and the new girlfriend! #sexualnapalm #droppingoutoflife #devotingmypassiontofuckingher #respectthehustle"

I handed the phone back to her, my eyes wide. "What the actual fuck? Are you kidding me?"

"Nope." She stuffed her phone in her pocket violently. "Turns out he was never interested in me as a person. He had just been looking for an SEO bump for his stupid fucking crypto website."

I winced. "Oh god, is this the Thundercoin guy? The one who thinks he looks like John Mayer?"

"Confurziliaz? Yeah. The stupid shit thinks he's so goddamn tech savvy but he didn't even know how to create a cascading style sheet. For fuck's sake, their site uses Drupal, Ricky. *Drupal*." She sniffled, wiping her nose on her sleeve. "Suits me fucking right for not seeing the signs."

"What the hell? Isn't that what you had to use for that web programming class in high school?"

"Yeah, the one where I ended up biting the laptop in half." Her eyes flashed. "I can still remember the sound the LCD screen made. It was so crunchy." She looked out the window. "God, how could I have been so stupid! Soon as I link his ugly-ass site to my followers, he pulls this shit. And then to top it all off...” Her lip quivered, scrolling on her phone again. “... he did *this*.”

She held the screen up to me. It was an animated .gif of Michael Scott from *The Office,* making his patented “disgust” face. The caption read: “when the new Taylor Swift album drops.” It was bracketed by poop emojis on either side.

I winced. She pulled the phone back. “I’m fine with him needing help for his dumbfuck cryptocoin. Whatever. I could make a picture of dog shit trend if I wanted to. I can even deal with him dumping me again, this wouldn’t be the first time. But you. *Do not.* Come for Tay Tay.” Her eyes flashed menacingly.

“Hey, no argument here, I swear.” I held my hands up, trying to make myself look as non-threatening as possible. She turned back to look out the window, exuding a literally palpable aura of frost in her rage. Ice was forming on the glass. “Listen, Dags, I’m sorry. I... I really don’t know what to say beyond that. I mean, I know this has to suck, but—”

“Ricky, thank you, but no thanks.” She looked back over her shoulder at me. “I’m not taking love advice from someone who couldn’t find his dick with both hands and a Sherpa.”

I scowled. “What the fuck, Dags? I’m just trying to... you know what? Forget it. Deal with it yourself.” I stood, picking my mug off the coffee table, and stomped off to the kitchen.

“Oh, dammit – Ricky! Ricky, wait, I’m sorry.” I stopped, turning around. My sister had stood up as well, a pained expression on her face. “That was really shitty of me. I didn’t mean it.”

I sighed. “Okay, but just because I know your emotions have you all messed up right now.” I took my mug to the sink and started rinsing it out. “Let me guess... you were listening to *Folklore* on the way over here?”

“Nooo.” She looked away.

"What, then, *Evermore*?" She nodded silently.

"Shit." I turned off the faucet and placed the mug, upside down, in the drying rack. "You haven't put 'No Body No Crime' on repeat yet, have you? ...Dags?" She shifted, her back still to me. "Dagmarikinniaz, you tell me the goddamn truth. Do we have to call the Elder Council?"

"What? No! This isn't like when I almost dropped John Mayer's car off Victory Tower. And don't call me that, you sound like Mom." She paused, her back still to me. "I was listening to 'Tolerate It.'" She turned around, eyes brimming with tears once more.

Oh boy. "Okay, hey, take it easy." I walked over to her and hugged her in the only way I knew how – awkwardly. She was stiff as a board at first, but after a moment she let out a strangled cry, lowering her face onto my shoulder. She began letting out massive, gut-wrenching sobs.

We stood there for a minute, me holding her and feeling helpless in the face of her pain while she continued to wail. A few moments later, she pulled away, wiping her cheeks with the sleeves of her hoodie. "Sorry," she said, sniffling. "I just... I really thought he was the one, you know?" She looked up and laughed suddenly. "Oh God, uh... I kind of slimed your t-shirt."

I looked down, stepping back. There was a damp spot. "Ugh, is that snot? Thanks a lot!" I shivered and whipped a hand towel off the oven handle. "This is vintage!" I rubbed at the suspiciously tacky stain.

"Oh, shit. Hey, I said I was sorry!" She began backpedaling.

"Yeah, for freaking out, not for snotting all over my 'Death to the Pixies' shirt!" I lunged at her. She shrieked, turning tail and running into the living room, giggling the entire way.

"Hey, get back here you little shit!"

We spent the next thirty seconds chasing each other around the couch before collapsing on it, laughing like idiots.

Dags put her head on my shoulder, catching her breath. "You're a goddamn weirdo, but this helped. Thanks. You're a good little brother."

I wrinkled my nose and pushed her off me. "Hey! Only by like three hours!"

She laughed. "It still counts!" She rearranged herself on the couch and sighed. "Still, I can't believe he fucking dumped me. And over Insta."

"At least it wasn't TikTok. Could you imagine him doing a dance routine to that stupid-ass Justin Bieber song?" I started singing it as loudly and off-key as I could. "*I do the same thing, I told you that you never would—*"

I took a pillow to the face. "All right, all right," I sputtered, pushing it off me. "I deserved that! Just showing you, it could have been worse! You remember the time we were playing Dungeons and Dragons with Uncle Dave and I ate the last slice of pizza?"

My sister snickered. "Uh huh."

"And how you never told me the house rule where the person who brings it gets last rights?"

She grinned wider. "Uhhh huhhhh."

I narrowed my eyes at her. "And how you just *neglected to mention* to me that both you and Mack already knew that the guy playing 'Radcliffe the Wizard,' the guy who had brought the pizza..."

Dags was turning red with glee. "... was actually the Ra'Keth, praise be his name?"

"Uhhh huhhh." I snorted. "The two of you. And Uncle Dave. Letting me make an ass of myself in front of the fucking Lighting Rod. And you wonder why I have anxiety."

"Serves you right." She was grinning. "Still, I wish there was some way to get back at that shitbird Conny." I shot her a warning look. "No, I'm not talking about anything serious, calm down. I mean, like... telling the world what an asshole he is. You know, so the next girl he decides to pick up at the Apple Genius Bar knows what to look out for."

"Hm." I scratched my cheek absently. "Wait, that gives me an idea." I sat up, grabbing my phone from the coffee table. "I think maybe I can use my powers for good. Just this once, anyway."

She leaned forward, looking over my shoulder. "The hell are you doing?"

"Hey!" I turned away from her. "I'll show you in a second! Chill."

She sighed and leaned back onto the couch with a huff. "This better be worth it."

"It will be." I was tapping and scrolling furiously. "Just be patient for once in your life."

"Ugh, you sanctimonious little shit, I swear if you weren't the—"

"Yeah, yeah, shut up. Here. Look at this." I handed her my phone.

She took it, looking down at the screen quizzically. She began scrolling through it. "Carrie Underwood, Pussycat Dolls, Justin Timberlake... Ariana Grande?" She looked up at me. "Ricky, what in the holy hell is this?"

I took the phone back from her. "The beginning of my newest playlist for The Night Nest."

Her eyes went wide, and then she laughed. "Are you serious?"

"As a heart attack." I stuffed my phone back in my pocket. "We're putting him on blast."

She shook her head. "Ricky, I love you, but playing a couple of breakup songs during the 2 to 4 AM slot isn't exactly high-vis."

"Oh, didn't I tell you?" I grinned, showing more teeth than I usually did. "They're syndicating the show. Rebroadcast Saturday evenings from 8 to 10 PM. Drop the link to the online feed in your socials, and..."

"Instant karma." My sister's eyes were wide, then narrowed. A predatory grin slipped across her face. "You'd really do this for me?"

"Why the hell not?" I shrugged. "I never liked the guy anyway."

She literally rubbed her hands together like a supervillain. "Oh, I can't wait to plug this show. He's gonna be drowning in mentions. One request, though – can the last song of the set be 'Goodbye Earl' by the Chicks?"

I grinned. "A classic. You got it, sis."

CHAPTER FOURTEEN

A couple of days later, it finally dawned on me what I had done. I spent the usual Thursday afternoon prep meeting with Anagen breathing into a paper bag and wishing I had the human physiology to take that Propranolol after all.

"Oh, come on, Rick." They threw up their hands. "Even with 'Goodbye Earl' at the end it's just an hour of angry breakup songs, you've got plenty of airtime to play your usual stuff. You know, those ultra-rare B-sides that nobody besides you has ever heard of? The ones you bought off eBay after someone dug a crate of discarded LPs out of a Dumpster behind Abbey Road Studios in 1978?"

I glared at them. "Hey just because your idea of 'good music' is Zamfir, master of the pan flute doesn't mean—" They were scowling at me. I trailed off.

"That's Romanian," they said.

"What?"

"Zamfir. He plays Romanian music, you Eurotrash idiot." They shook their head at me. "Besides, this is a huge opportunity! I thought you'd be happy about the exposure. I know Byron is going to be ready to slob your knob for hours if we get a nice little bump in engagement from this. And think about how mad *Chauncey* will be—"

I shook my head. "Y-you don't understand. She's an *influencer.* Her follower count is *huge.* Yeah, it'll put her ex in the spotlight but..." I made a pained face. "That's a lot of people. A *lot* of people. Even r-ruh-rebroadcasted. What the hell did I agree to?"

Anagen pulled their phone out. "It can't be that bad. What's her socials? I wanna see something."

I covered my face with my hands. "It's @DagsToRiches," I said, my voice muffled.

"All right, let's see here. Influencer my ass, what does she have, like—" Anagen choked and sputtered. I whimpered behind my hands. "Is that one point five *million*?"

"Oh god, it went *up?*" I pulled my hands away from my face to meet Anagen's gaze. Their eyes were as wide as my own. "Is it too late to fake my own death, move to Newfoundland, and join a grade-A whale shit adult hockey team?"

Anagen was scrolling through my sister's social feed. "This is incredible. And she'll plug us for the rebroadcast Saturday evening? Shit, if even one percent of her followers click that link that's like... what, fifteen thousand people?"

"I know!" I wailed. "Do you see now why I'm freaking out!?" I ran my hands through my hair, tugging on it. "I'm not even supposed to *be* on the air! I just wanted a nice behind-the-scenes job!"

"Oh for the love of – Rick, you *malákas.* What, you want to work at the Quick Stop your whole life?"

"That's not what I mean, you know I—" I paused, looking at them wildly. "Wait, w-was that... was that a *Clerks* reference?"

"If the Mooby's uniform fits."

I stared at them for a moment, then laughed despite myself. "Fuck you, man."

"Not a man, remember?" They grinned at me. "Now get

the hell over yourself. You made a commitment to your sister, didn't you?"

I sighed. "Yeah… yeah, I did. I just—"

"Yeah, I know. Look, nothing bad is gonna happen to you. You don't even have to do any station idents live. We pre-recorded a bunch of them last week, remember? And with your reverb audio trick—"

"D-delayed audio feedback."

"Whatever. It works, right? You'll be able to hit those posts and do those PSAs no problem, just like you practiced. Remember, we've got to plug that *Secret McQueen* thing in North Allora next week."

"Shit, I forgot about that." I breathed for a minute. "Are there even any tickets left that haven't been scalped?"

"I dunno, but we gotta warn people to be on the lookout for legit tickets. Man, thank the gods we're not broadcasting live *that* night, right? Could you imagine?"

Friday night came and went. The next morning dawned early, and I blearily left my dorm room before the tangle of arms, legs, and hooves under the covers of Niko's bed had begun to stir. The only thing on campus open that early was the coffee shop, so I had dragged myself across the quad to the SUB and gotten myself a hot cocoa and a cinnamon roll, which I was trying to eat without getting it all over me. Until Anagen had sat down across from me, that is.

"We're broadcasting live Halloween night."

I dropped my fork with a clatter. "What."

They reached over, picking at my breakfast. "Are you wearing diapers? Cuz you're about to soil yourself like Chauncey after a Corgis game." They plucked a piece off my cinnamon roll, popped it in their mouth and chewed thoughtfully. "Jesus, that's sweet."

I glared at them blearily. "Anagen. I've been up all night, trying to block out the sounds of my roommate getting every orifice he has violated repeatedly by half the university co-ed water polo team. I'm running on approximately 14 minutes of sleep. What the hell are you talking about?"

"I'm talking about how your sister came through for us yesterday. Byron called me this morning after he got into the studio. *Called* me, Rick. Over the phone. He didn't even bother using his white voice, either."

"His *what?*"

Anagen shook their head. "Jesus, Rick, it's called code switching. Google it later. Point is he went over the metrics from last night and the streaming server almost fucking crashed. Twice. Byron is losing his shit, and in a *good* way. He wants us to broadcast live on Halloween night for the two hours leading up to the *Secret McQueen* premiere!"

"I don't… what—" My phone buzzed. I looked down at it in a daze; my sister had messaged me. *Conny deactivated his account last night*

like a billion people linked him the radio stream

when he blocked the URL they started spamming him with links to the music video for Goodbye Earl

that'll teach him to DISRESPECT MY TAY TAY

The next message was an animated .gif of Louise Belcher from *Bob's Burgers* in front of a flaming background. She was cackling, the words "REVENGE" under her.

I turned the phone around and showed Anagen. They grinned. "See? You performed a public service. And probably put the station in the running for another award this year. Nothing succeeds like success."

I sighed, putting my phone down on the table. "Are you serious about the live broadcast on Halloween, though?"

"Look for yourself if you don't believe me." They pulled their own phone out and flipped it around, showing me the screen. It was an email from Byron.

"That's… that's a lot of exclamation points," I said.

"Told you. Here, let me perform a dramatic reading." They cleared their throat. "This is my favorite part: 'I dunno where this white boy came from, but we're getting him on the air that night because he's solid gold. In fact, that's his new DJ name – Ricky Gold. I'm raiding the station budget and printing up stickers for next week's show.' Oh, delightful, you've got your first DJ name! They grow up so fast."

I groaned. "This can't be *happening*," I wailed.

"Oh, it's happening, Mister Gold. Now listen, we've only got a few days to get this organized, but luckily, it's not much actual work. Byron wants us to hit some specific PSAs during the broadcast, most of them having to do with the *Secret McQueen* event, but he also wants the set to be themed."

I stared at them. "Are you… are you for real? Why, because it's Halloween? What does he want me to do, play the fucking Monster Mash?"

Anagen grinned. "He left it up to us. As long as we've got a few spooky songs in there, he'll be happy. Yeah, I know, it's cheesy, but weren't you telling me about that band from the seventies, the one that wrote a song about someone getting body parts donated by a serial killer after he was executed? What were they called, The Commercials or something?"

"What? Oh, uh, no, the Adverts. It's called 'Gary Gilmore's Eyes.'" The wheels in my head started spinning. "So, you're telling me we just need to spin some tracks like that, hit some new PSAs, and Byron will stay off our backs?"

"You tell me." They pulled another piece off my cinnamon roll. "Think you can handle that without losing your shit? It'll be live, and there'll be people actually listening this time, judging on how well the rebroadcast went. You can thank your sister for that." They popped it in their mouth. "You know, these aren't that bad once you get used to the taste."

"Are they? I wouldn't know, someone keeps interrupting me."

"Aww, poor widdle Rick." They patted my cheek. "You eat your numnums and get to work on a new setlist…. Mister Gold." They stood up, licking some frosting off their fingers, and sauntered off.

CHAPTER FIFTEEN

Despite my apprehension, the idea did appeal to me. Could I create a Halloween-themed setlist, but do it my way? Breakfast forgotten, I picked up my phone. "Gary Gilmore's Eyes" is a great start, but there's got to be more…

I began scrolling. *All right, Dead Kennedys for sure. I mean it's even* named *Halloween, for Bahamut's sake.* I looked up and out through the window. *The Ramones? I mean Johnny was a real right-wing asshole, but Joey was a good guy. All right, "Pet Sematary" is in. Now, what else?*

It turned out to be pretty easy in the end. Before long I had almost a whole two-hour set, leaving room for PSAs and station idents. It made me feel better about this new gig coming up, though the words "live broadcast" made me want to climb out of my scales.

That feeling only got worse as the week passed, the date inexorably approaching. Anagen wasn't helping; it was like they were reveling in my discomfort, constantly sending me stupid memes and animated .gifs. And as much as Niko really was a pretty good roommate, I could do without him constantly trying to get me to join him and his polycule in their "extracurricular activities." At least I had an excuse when they asked me out to a party Halloween night.

It was barely even 6 PM when I stopped pacing in my room and went down to the SUB. Night had already fallen and the skies were clear, making it look like a fantastic evening was in the making. The quad was crawling with humans in costumes and mythics walking around without having to conceal themselves. There's a reason why this is often a favorite holiday for the non-humans in the City, after all – though I could do without the ghouls hanging around the corners of Old Main and trying to bum cigarettes off the zombies.

We were the only ones broadcasting live tonight, as the rest of the feed was set up to be automated for the holiday. As a result, the halls up on the 4th floor felt sepulchral and deserted. Well, almost. There was someone waiting for me in the hallway outside the station – a student dressed in a Corgis jersey. The front was suspiciously stained.

"Hey," he said. "You this Ricky dude?"

Oh, for the love of Bahamut. "Y-yeah," I said slowly, walking towards him. "And you're, uh, you're Chauncey, right?"

"That's right." He puffed his chest out and gave me the "upnod," jerking his chin at me. "I hear you disrespected my bro Conny last week."

I blinked at him. Well, blinked down, anyway. He was about a head shorter than me. "I... what?"

"Yeah, you heard me." He walked over and jammed a finger in my chest. I stepped backward in complete surprise, my back up against the wall. Chauncey grinned, obviously thinking I was frightened. "You wanna take my radio show? Fine. Whatever. Fuck if I care. But you come for my boy and all. Bets. Are. Off." He punctuated each word with another poke.

I gaped down at him. "Wait, you're a friend of *Conny's?*"

"Ride or die, bro!" He raised his arms, gesturing wildly. "My boy's gonna hook me up with tons of Thundercunt–"

"Thundercoin."

"S'what I said. So, you better keep his name out yo' fuckin

mouf, ya hear?"

I shook my head at the absurdity of being threatened by a non-mythic. "Yeah, uhh… okay, Chauncey. Whatever you say." I put my hands up, palms out, in the universal "I've got no beef with you" pose.

"Hmph." He stepped off, brushing imaginary dust off his arms. "That's right, bitch. So, you gonna apologize on the air tonight, then?"

I let out an explosive, nervous laugh before clapping a hand over my mouth. "Are you… are you fucking serious?"

Chauncey looked up at me. A funny noise came out of his throat.

I cocked my head at him. "Are you… *growling* at me, man?"

He narrowed his eyes. "You were warned." Turning on his heel, he stomped off, pulling out his phone. He put it to his ear as he walked around the corner. "Yeah," I heard him faintly say, "yeah no, he's not gonna—"

The elevator doors dinged, cutting him off.

What the fuck just happened? I shook my head, completely lost, trying to regain my bearings and shift back into broadcast mode.

Only Anagen had the key to the station, so I leaned up against the wall to wait. Still completely confused over being "confronted" by Chauncey, I pulled my phone out and went over my playlist for what felt like the thirteenth time in the last hour. I had settled on "The Creeps" by Social Distortion, "Eve of Destruction" from The Dickies, "Dig Up Her Bones" from the Misfits, the Dead Kennedys, Adverts, and Ramones tracks I'd initially chosen, and about a dozen others. By then I had completely forgotten about Chauncey's little tantrum, though I did make a mental note to talk to my sister about why his ex was messing with mortals for his crypto scheme like some fucking Coyote.

Before long, I heard the elevator ding once more from far down the hallway. A few moments later, there was the muffled sound of Anagen's hooves on the carpet. They came around the corner, dressed in a black tank top and pants, a wide, studded black leather belt, and a massive ankh necklace. Elaborate eye makeup and black lipstick completed the ensemble.

"Enbie Endless?" I said as they came closer.

"Hey, look at that, Rick reads Gaiman. Or did you just watch the Netflix show?" They pulled a bristling keyring from their pocket and unlocked the door to the station.

"Hey, I've got a signed first edition of *American Gods* at home, thank you very much."

Setup for the live show was deceptively simple. It felt like any other night with the station so empty, which helped me not think about how I'd be broadcasting to an actual live audience. Instead, I loaded my playlist into the system and began picking when my breaks for idents and PSAs would be.

Before I knew it, it was five minutes to broadcast time. I did my best to ignore the piece of flaming ice that had settled in the pit of my stomach. It didn't work very well. Instead, I slipped on my headphones in Studio C, checking my levels and setting them to give me the audio feedback I needed to help with my stutter.

The lights flickered for a moment. A far-off rumble high above made me look up at the ceiling, as if I could peer through the roof to the sky above. "Hey, did you hear that?"

"Hear what?" Anagen stuck their head in the studio. "All I saw was the lights kinda flicker for a second."

"You didn't hear the thunder just now? It was faint, but it was definitely there."

"You're losing it, Rick. Skies were clear when we came in. Come on, stop stalling." They disappeared from the doorway.

I sighed, turning back to the console, watching the last few seconds tick down. Anagen's voice came over the headset. *"Seven second delay starting in three... two... one."* I took a deep breath and pressed play as the ON AIR light flicked on.

"Good evening, Allora University!" *Geez, dial it down a notch, Ricky.* "This is, uh, a very special live broadcast of the Night Nest. I'm your h-host, Ricky Gold. Thanks for joining me tonight." The first track began to play, a simple bass beat establishing a driving tempo. "Halloween is upon us, and so is the *Secret McQueen* world premiere event, right h-here in North Allora. Hope you got your t-tickets, 'cuz this one's sold out for sure. In the meantime, let's get a little spooky tonight. First up is 'Psycho Killer' from the Talking Heads. Hold on to your butts!"

CHAPTER SIXTEEN

Despite my anxieties, the rest of the set began to unfold without incident. My audio trick kept the worst of my stutter at bay, and the tracks seemed to be flowing well from one to the other. A little over halfway through, though, and I heard what sounded like thunder again.

I checked the runtime left on the current track. I had about a minute forty-five, so I muted my mic, pulled off my headset, and set the next two tracks to play uninterrupted. Then, I went next door to Studio B where Anagen was monitoring the broadcast. "Tell me you heard it this time."

"Heard what? Thunder? Come on Rick, those ears of yours are playing tricks on you." They had their hooves up on the console, playing idly with the chain of their ankh with one hand while using the other to tweak the board.

"I dunno, I mean-" A stronger peal of thunder interrupted me, and the lights flickered again. "Okay, I'm not going fucking crazy. You noticed *that*, right?"

"Yeah, I did." They pulled their hooves down and sat up in the chair, wheeling over to their laptop. "Weather says clear skies for Allora tonight. In fact... okay, that's weird."

I leaned over their shoulder. The live satellite feed was showing a small but angry-looking dot growing over a map of the City. "What the hell is that? Freak thunderstorm?"

"Looks like it." Thunder crashed again, louder this time, and the lights flickered once more. "Don't worry, the station's well insulated. We've even got backup batteries in the case of a blackout. They won't last forever but—" A massive peal of thunder rumbled overhead, loud enough to shake the entire station. "Okay, that's a little concerning. But even though—"

The loudest clap of thunder I'd ever heard split the sudden silence. I doubled over, my ears ringing, as the studio was plunged into darkness. The emergency lights came on. Only they and the lights of the console equipment running off the battery backups illuminated the room.

"Shit!" Anagen was standing, leaning over the board. "That was a ground strike. Pretty sure it hit the SUB – the radio antenna's the tallest thing on campus. We've gotta go to the roof." They pushed past me.

"Wait, what?" I followed Anagen out of the studio and into the hallway, struggling to keep up. They were practically galloping on their hooves. "What do you mean, we've got to go to the roof?"

Another peal of thunder shook the building. Anagen didn't even look back. "That first strike likely fried the lightning arrestor. It needs to be replaced, without it another hit would cook the transmitter. We'd be off the air for weeks."

"*Weeks*? Isn't there a backup?" We rushed out of the station and into the 4th floor corridor, taking a right and rounding the corner; the hallway dead-ended at a plain utility door. We pushed through it, revealing a short set of stairs that led up to another door. This one was labeled "Roof Access."

"There is a backup transmitter, but it can only be operated from the doghouse." Anagen pulled out their keyring again. "We have to switch to the backup while we replace the lightning arrestor anyway, so we'd have to go up there either way." They fumbled with the keys, flipping through them frantically. "Fuck, where is it... godsdammit Byron, I told you to *label* these pieces of shit... fuck!"

Another massive peal of thunder split the sky, shaking the entire building. Anagen let loose a string of Greek curses. "We're running out of time, dammit!"

"Move over," I said.

"What? This isn't the time, Rick—"

"Jeez, Anagen, just fucking trust me, okay? Now move. Over."

They shifted to their left, giving me access to the door. "If this is some macho bullshit, I don't know what you think you're gonna—"

I stepped forward and grabbed the knob. I took a deep breath, and my hand flexed, fingers lengthening to claws as the scales covering my skin grew larger, thicker, and more iridescent. I twisted, hard, and pushed.

The door to the roof popped open violently, and I winced against the sudden onslaught of the wind and rain. My nictitating membranes slid into place reflexively, my hand returning to human form.

"Damn, Rick, I take it back." Anagen pushed past me out into the storm and pointed. "Come on, it's right ahead!" About halfway across the roof, through what looked like a maze of HVAC vents and air conditioning units, stood an FM dipole antenna, mounted on what looked like a 40- or 50-foot-tall mast. At the bottom was a small, windowless shed. A single bare emergency bulb was burning above the door.

I followed them out into the torrential rain. Thunder split the skies again, this time accompanied almost immediately by a cloud-to-cloud lighting strike that illuminated the entire night and laid bare the clouds above.

I blinked, the hairs on the back of my neck standing

straight up. "Anagen!" I raced after them. "There's something wrong about this storm," I yelled, pointing. "It doesn't feel natural. Look at the clouds!"

"What are you talking abou— what the *fuck*?"

The storm was raging directly above us, thick thunderheads swirling – but nowhere else. We were in the center of a self-contained storm cell only a few hundred feet across. The rest of the night was starry and clear.

Anagen pushed open the door to the shed. I followed, the door slamming shut behind me. The sound of the storm lessened, save for the steady drumming of rain on the corrugated steel roof. The interior was cramped, dominated by a beaten-up desk with an ancient-looking audio deck, mixing board, and microphone. Power and data cables connected the deck to a nearby server rack. A trunk line ran from the other side of the rack and out the wall.

Anagen bustled past me, looking through a shelf loaded with banker boxes. "You ever seen anything like that before?"

"Uh, what? That? Out there? I don't know, I mean maybe someone picked a fight with the Ra'keth or something?"

"On Halloween night? Talk about stupid." They pulled a box out, rummaging around inside. "Please tell me there's one… yes, got it!" They pulled out a metal tube almost the entire length of their forearm. It had coaxial connections on either end. "Here it is."

"Great, so where do we plug it in?"

They set the lightning arrestor down on the table. "Not so fast. We gotta switch over to the backup transmitter first. Then, someone's gotta go outside and replace the fried one with this new one."

"Outside? Where, like on the side of the shed?" They remained silent. "Anagen?"

"Uh, think... higher."

Another peal of thunder struck, shaking the shed. "Higher... like on the antenna?" The bottom dropped out of my stomach.

"Yup. And I can't do it, I've gotta work down in the doghouse to do the switchover. Plus, we're still on the air, I've gotta keep your broadcast up." They picked up the arrestor. "Gotta be you, Rick." They tossed it at me.

I caught it, staring at them. "W-wait. You've gotta be fuckin' *kidding* me, right?"

"Nope." They turned away, reaching into another box and pulling out two pairs of lightweight wireless headsets. They fiddled with them for a second, then nodded. "Good, they're charged. Here, put this on so we can keep in contact while you're outside."

The headset got dumped into my hands atop the lightning arrestor. "Anagen, this isn't—"

"Rick, we don't have time for this. Without the arrestor, the next time lightning hits the antenna there'll be nothing there to ground the charge. The whole station will be fried."

I swallowed. "But I can't fly up there, not if you want me to install this thing! I need human-sized hands for that. I'd have to *climb up* the antenna!" I started breathing heavily. "C-can't we get someone else to do it?"

"You think I'd let you go out there if I had another choice!?" Anagen glared at me, eyes blazing. "We're the only ones here, the rest of the godsdamned world is out at that *Secret McQueen* premiere. There is no help coming – it's us or nothing."

A screech split the skies, silencing us both. Anagen's eyebrows shot up as they looked up at the roof. "That's... that's not thunder," they said slowly. They looked down and blinked. "Jeez, Rick, what is it? You're white as a sheet."

I shook my head mutely. It took a second for my mouth to start working again. "Th-that's a Dragon call," I said hoarsely.

"*What?*"

I nodded. "B-blue Dragon. The lightning, the rain – they're causing it." I swallowed, thinking of my sister's ex and how he had to turn off his socials after we put him on blast last week. "And I'm pretty sure it's my fault."

CHAPTER SEVENTEEN

"Rick, what the fuck are you even talk—you know what? Tell me on the way up. We're almost back from that last song." They plunked the headset down over my ears and pushed the lightning arrestor into my hands. "Get up there and switch it out before your buddy fries the whole place."

They pushed me out into the howling rain and slammed the shed door closed. A second later, I heard Anagen's voice in my ear. *"All right, check one two. You getting this?"* I could hear my playlist being piped in over the headphones in the background.

I nodded, dumbly. "Uh, yeah, I mean yes I can hear you-"

"Great, fantastic. Stick the thing in your pants pocket or something and climb the fucking antenna already."

I looked up at the station mast. I wasn't afraid of heights – not exactly, anyway; you don't get far as a Dragon if you aren't at ease spreading your wings – but I wasn't enthused at the prospect of climbing 50-feet of steel during a Dragon-controlled lightning storm while in human form.

"This is insane," I shouted into the wind, the rain pelting me from what felt like all sides. I stuffed the lightning arrestor in my waistband and reached out, grabbing the access ladder that ran up the side of the radio mast.

"Yeah, well, Satyrs aren't fireproof," Anagen said, their voice

breaking up slightly when another thunderbolt shot across the sky. The next part of their response was lost in a crackle of static. "—*have built-in parachutes either, so you're it.*"

I began my climb, white knuckling the ladder rungs and cursing under my breath. The supernatural storm thundered around me as I rose higher, causing the mast to sway back and forth. My hand slipped from one of the rungs about 20 or 30 feet up, causing me to scramble and shriek. Not my proudest moment.

Thunder and lightning split the sky again. My headset crackled. "—*nearly over,*" Anagen said.

"What was that?" I winced as an errant tree branch flew by me, missing my face by inches.

"*I said the last song you had queued up is nearly over!*" They sounded faint and garbled. "*What do you want me to play next?*"

Even with my ears it took me a moment to understand what they had said. "Are you... are you kidding?" I shouted over the din. "Just anything!"

"*Anything?*"

"Yes, please, put anything on!" Thunder split the sky yet again. "Uh, anything but 'Thunderstruck'—" Lightning leapt from cloud to cloud, and then flashed down right next to the SUB, hitting a street lamp and sending a shower of sparks across the quad.

The headset fuzzed out again. "—*you sure?*"

"Yes, absolutely!" I checked the lightning arrestor to make sure it was still there. "Listen, I'm almost all the way up, just gimme a little more time!"

"*All right, the link is at the base of the antenna, at the top of the mast.*" I heard a clatter over the other end. "*Tell me when you're there, I'll play the next song. Hurry up!*"

The current track began to fade out. I gritted my teeth and

went back to climbing as the new one started, a single hi-hat accompanying a fast-paced guitar riff. I wondered, wildly, what Anagen had chosen.

The riff continued for a few seconds, something about it tickling the back of my mind. The song seemed awfully familiar. Then the chanting started. *Wait, is this…. This isn't—*

"Anagen!" I howled over the storm. My sister's ex-boyfriend shot across the sky above me, firing wickedly forked lightning from his gaping mouth and deep into the still-thickening cloudbank. "Anagen, what did you choose—"

THUNDER! The toms joined the hi-hat as the chant and the riff continued.

THUNDER! The bassline kicked in, driving the beat forward further.

Son of a bitch. "Anagen! Damn it, are you playing what I think you're playing?"

"*You told me to play 'Thunderstruck!'*"

"I said *ANYTHING BUT* 'Thunderstruck', Anagen! **ANYTHING BUT!**"

"*I'm sorry, the lightning cut off—*" As if on cue, the link erupted in static again as another blast of electricity ripped across the sky.

"I can't fucking believe this," I muttered, pulling myself up hand-over-hand as Brian Johnson began screaming at the top of his lungs the only way he knew how.

I was caught in the middle of a railroad track (**thunder**)

I looked 'round and I knew there was no turning back (**thunder**)

"Of all the stupid, overblown – fuck!" My hand slipped as I reached for another rung. A chill ran up my spine as I grabbed empty air, my balance faltering.

"No, no, nononono—" I felt myself falling backwards, away from the service ladder, arms flailing.

I closed my eyes, taking a deep breath as I began to fall. My body thrummed with a surge of power; in a flash, my limbs elongated. The subtle scales on my arms and legs growing larger and tougher, splitting my sleeves to the elbow and the legs of my pants to the knee. My fingers transformed into sharp claws, as did my feet, which burst through my All-Stars like they were made of rice paper.

In a flash my eyesight sharpened, my pupils dilating far beyond human capabilities. My hearing intensified as my ears grew into even finer points, as did my sense of smell as my mouth transformed into a muzzle of razor-sharp fangs.

The back of my soaked hoodie flexed and ripped as a pair of leathery wings, tipped with wicked spikes on the joints, unfolded from my back and snapped open in the gale, buffeting me and slowing my fall. A thick, scaly prehensile tail sprung from my backside. I swung it around me, instinctively using it to grasp the side of the radio mast, arresting my fall completely and giving me the time I needed to grab the ladder once more.

I folded my wings down against my back to keep them out of the wind and looked down at my transformed hands, now covered with golden scales that glittered with each lightning strike. "Fucking hell," I growled, surprised as always at how pitched down my voice had become.

Well, it'll be easier to get to the top of the mast now at least, I thought.

"Rick? Rick you still there?"

Somehow, the headset had survived my partial transformation. "Yeah," I said tersely. "Just nearly slipped. Caught myself." I looked up; I could clearly see the place at the top of the mast where the antenna was connected to a junction box. "I'm almost there, I'll swap out the... oh, shit."

I looked down. The replacement lightning arrestor was pinned between the badly stretched waistband of my jeans and my newly transformed body. Without the friction of human skin, the pressure being exerted on it was making it slide slowly across my now-scaly waist.

"Shit, no, come on..." I reached down for it. The replacement arrestor slipped even more, now being held by just a rapidly fraying scrap of denim. I froze, not wanting to shift it even more. "Uhh, Anagen, do we have any more of these things-" Thunder clapped again, and I jumped. The sudden movement sent the lightning arrestor tumbling from my ruined waistband. "Oh come *on!*"

I lunged for it with one hand, just barely missing it as it fell from my grasp. It began to fall; in a flash, I unwound my tail from the radio mast and whipped it out, snagging the lightning arrestor and wrapping around it tightly.

I let out a breath I didn't even know I was holding. Brian Johnson was still screaming.

And I was shaking at the knees - could I come again, please?

"*Any more lightning arrestors?*" Anagen barked over the headset. "*No, why?*"

I set my jaw, keeping a strong grip around the arrestor. "Uhhh, no reason! Gimme another few seconds!"

Climbing was much easier in this form. My hands was stronger, the scales on the pads of my fingers textured for better grip, and I could swing my tail from side to side to alter my center of gravity. In no time at all I had reached the junction box.

"Okay, I'm here, Anagen! Walk me through this!"

"*All right, open the cover carefully. There should be something in there that looks like the thing you've got in your hands.*"

I hooked one arm around the ladder and reached out, popping open the junction box. The hinges snapped, and the cover got snatched away in the wind. "Uh... no problem!" I looked in the box. "Okay, I see it – looks like a giant spark plug. It's all charred!"

"Yeah, I knew it! Pull it out and slot the new one in its place. It'll interrupt the feed so do it as quick as you can."

"All right," I said. I reached inside the junction box and grabbed the ruined lightning arrestor as there was another thunderclap. I looked up; Dags' ex seemed to be finally starting to lose some steam. The lightning bolts had begun to strike a little less frequently, the flashes a little less blinding. *Can't keep it up, Conny? Maybe you should have thought of that before fucking over my sister.*

With as fluid a motion I could, I yanked the old arrestor out of its socket. The audio feed to my headset cut off. Immediately I slotted the other one in with my tail, unwinding it and seating it in place with the tip. The station roared back to life.

Yeah, it's alright, we're doin' fine, fine, fine

Thunderstruck, *yeah, yeah, yeah* **thunderstruck**

I slumped against the radio mast. "It's done," I said. "Coming back down."

Anagen let out a war whoop that nearly split my head in two, followed by a string of excited Greek. They kept it up until my back claws left the last rung and landed back on the roof. In that moment, with the adrenaline draining from my system, I flopped down on my back, reverting to my human form, the lessening rain pattering down around me.

"All right, Rick, that's it. You wanna say anything to your listeners? I can patch you into the live feed."

I laughed, wheezing. "Sure," I said. There was a tone in my ear as the song began to fade. "That last one... that last one goes out to my Uncle Dave, down at the K Street Diner. 'Thunderstruck,' by AC/DC, off their 1990 album *The Razor's*

Edge." I palmed the mic on the headset and coughed. "This is Ricky Gold for the Night Nest, only on 96.7 WPHX, Allora University Radio. Happy Halloween, everyone, and enjoy the show."

CHAPTER EIGHTEEN

"**S**o let me get this straight. The two of you forced your way out onto the roof, broke into the station's utility shed, conducted an unauthorized transmission transfer, and then climbed the mast to change a burned-out lighting arrestor in the middle of a freak thunderstorm? Do you have any idea how many different university rules, OSHA regulations, and municipal laws you broke!?" Byron didn't seem very amused.

Anagen and I shared a glance. "T-to be fair," I said, "I was the one that climbed the antenna mast—"

"It was *my* idea, Byron, he was just following my lead—"

"—was completely *my* choice, I could have said no—"

"—was the one who forced the door open, not him—"

"—and besides, we kept the station running—"

"*Enough!*" We fell silent. "The two of you are absolute fucking idiots. What do you think would have been worse? Dead air or dead DJs?" I opened my mouth. "That was rhetorical!" he barked. I closed my mouth.

Byron started pacing back and forth across the Garage, dodging the beaten-up furniture that just a few weeks ago I had been sitting in when Anagen and I had met. "Word of this gets out and you two would be expelled in a heartbeat. The radio station would be shut down, possibly permanently, and at the very least anyone involved even tangentially would end up with a massive black mark on their records."

He stopped, his back to us. "People would lose scholarships, jeopardize their entire futures, all because you both had your heads up each other's asses." He turned around. "I've got an interview with NPR in two weeks. You think they're gonna hire someone who got his entire station shuttered and saw one of his fastest-growing DJ kicked out of school? Fuck that. We're not gonna breathe a goddamn word of this to anyone. *Anyone.* You hear me? It never happened."

We both nodded silently.

"Good." Byron tucked his Polo shirt back in and brushed some nonexistent dust off his forearms. "You're back on overnights, starting this week. We'll keep rebroadcasting on Saturdays but for now you two need to keep a *low profile*. Can you two manage that?"

"Y-yeah. Uh, sorry."

"Yeah, Byron, message received."

"Fine, great. Now get the fuck out of here before I change my mind." He raised his voice. "And any of y'all hearing this *better keep your damn mouths shut*, you hear me?" A burst of sudden activity in the hallway beyond was the only answer.

Anagen and I left together, walking past about a half-dozen students that pointedly ignored us. We remained silent all the way to the elevator bank. I pressed the call button; the doors opened, and we stepped inside.

It wasn't until the doors closed that we spoke. "Holy *shit*," I said.

"Yeah, not what I expected." Anagen pushed the hair out of their face and tugged on one of their ram's horns. "At least we're not shit-canned, right?"

I sighed, slumping against the wall behind me. "Would

CERTIFIED GOLD: ON THE AIR

have been a lot easier if we coulda told him what caused the storm," I said.

"Oh, yeah, that would've gone over great." Anagen snorted. "'Hey, sorry boss, but a rogue blue Dragon tried to take us off the air. Good thing the *next king of the Dragons* was there to put a stop to it.'" They punched the Emergency Stop button and leaned over at me, glowering. The elevator stopped as an alarm started going off. "Were you ever gonna tell me, 'Your Majesty?'"

"Fucking hell, Anagen, it's not like it's gonna just come up in casual conversation!" I slapped the Emergency Stop button myself, silencing the alarm and causing the elevator to begin moving again. "And I don't *want* to be the Ra'saar, okay? It was a goddamn freak circumstance. Chosen by the fucking Fates, or some shit."

"Fine, whatever." The Satyr leaned back, folding their arms across their chest. The barest hint of a smile played across their features. "You're lucky you've got good taste in music. And that Niko vouches for you." The elevator stopped, doors opening with a ding. "I'll see you next time, Rick." They walked out into the first-floor foyer, raising a hand in farewell.

I sighed, watching them disappear into the crowd. I exited the elevator myself, slipping by students getting on, and made my way out into the early November air. *Well, at least things should be getting back to normal around here.*

I walked across the quad, fallen leaves crunching beneath my feet as I made my way back to Coindre Hall. A student with an empty campus mail bag was leaving as I walked in, so I stopped to check my mailbox, though I was half expecting Summers to have left me a dead pigeon or something. I pulled out a packet of flyers, which I began leafing through on the way to my room.

Besides the usual crop of notices about campus events, there was one thing in the stack that was different. A bona fide letter, in an envelope, addressed to "Ricky Gold" in ornate hand-lettered calligraphy. Puzzled, I slit it open, pulling out a piece of embellished stationery printed on gilded cardstock. The message was written in Sigil:

Dear Mr. Gold,

Upon review of your continued performance as a disc jockey on 96.7FM WPHX, we are delighted to inform you that you have been selected to present a curated playlist live at The Palace of Wisdom.   Please contact the Lady Amelia at your earliest convenience.

I flipped the card over. There it was, clear as day: the official crest of the Palace of Wisdom, the mythic-run nightclub that was the cultural heartbeat of the Argent City. And they wanted me to play a set.

What the hell have I gotten myself into? I looked back down at my phone and began scrolling through my contacts. *I'm gonna need a lot more music.*

CHAPTER NINETEEN

It was early afternoon by the time I put my phone away and made my way back out of Coindre Hall, judging from the angle of the sun. My ears were still ringing from the call I had just made.

"What did I fucking tell you, Ricky? Our people are out there. It's just up to us to find them! You absolutely cannot quit."

"Mom, please! I don't know the first thing about putting together a live set for a dance hall, let alone the Palace! If I show up there with a crate of Ramones records they'll cover me in honey and stake me out next to a colony of fire ants."

"You're not gonna get the same sound from digital, you know that. Do you need me to have the rest of your collection flown in from Portland?"

"What? No, I didn't mean literally—" I sighed, pinching the bridge of my nose. "I mean can't I just, uh, decline the offer?"

"DECLINE?" I pulled the phone away from my ear with a wince. Between my hearing and my mother's lung capacity, it didn't help much.

I put the phone back up to my ear when she wound down. "Okay, okay! Jeez Mom, so what do you want me to do? I can't just play Darude's 'Sandstorm' on repeat."

"So do your research, kid! The Blues didn't help invent the internet so you could sit around crying about not knowing

downtempo from dubtronica."

"From what to what?"

"Fuck's sake, Ricky. Go to the experts!"

I rubbed at my face. "What experts? It's not like I can go to the mall, the last Tower Records in the City closed like 15 years ago." I paused, grasping at straws. "Hey, what about that record store you were telling me about? The one in South Beckett?"

"The one three doors down from The Roxy? Yeah, that'll do it. It'll have exactly what you're looking for, trust me. And don't worry about the folks working there. If any of 'em gives you shit, you give it right back, you hear?"

"Uhh..."

"Ricky. Do you trust me?"

Something in her voice gave me pause, like when she had mentioned it that night at dinner. "Y-yeah. Of course, Mom."

"Then go now. Just don't spend too much time down there, days are getting shorter. And for fuck's sake, stay out of Tolon Park on your way home." Her voice softened. *"You won't regret it. Oh, Ricky, I'm so proud of you! I mean I'm always proud of you, but this is just amazing. Wait until I tell everyone!"* Her voice faded for a moment. *"Chad? Chad, come here, you're not gonna believe this—"* The call dropped.

I checked my phone again. It was barely 2, which meant I should be able to get down to South Beckett and back to Allora with plenty of time to spare. *The hell was she so worried about Tolon Park, anyway?*

True to my estimations, it only took around half an hour for me to ride the line to where I got off the other day to pick up dessert. Another 15 minutes on foot through progressively shabbier blocks brought me to the corner where I had seen The Roxy and its sad-looking marquee.

It hadn't gotten any better. The sign was still just as

grungy looking, its beautifully curved neon dim and dusty. The windows of the will call were caked with grime, and an errant gust of wind set the trash that had accumulated in the alcove swirling in a miniature dust devil for a moment before dying down. Leaves and other detritus fluttered back to the broken pavement, like a dying animal giving its last breath.

I cupped my hands on either side of my head and tried to peer in through the glass. I concentrated and my pupils dilated wide. The inside sprung into focus, revealing a foyer covered in threadbare, dingy carpet, walls with chipped paint, and high ceilings adorned with faded Art Deco scrollwork. Three sets of ornate double doors with round inset portals and tarnished brass handles were against the back wall, doubtlessly leading to the stage. Sweeping staircases led up into darkness on the far left and right. Motes of dust danced in the scant light filtering in from the windows.

I stepped back, blinking as my eyes re-adjusted to the afternoon sunlight. *Shame*, I thought, shaking my head. *I can only imagine what it would have looked like even just a few decades ago.* I dusted my hands off, wiped them on the back of my pants, and turned to look down the street. *Now where did Mom say the place was? Three doors down?*

I walked the short block past The Roxy, checking building façades as I went. A boarded-up bar and grill, a run-down brownstone with graffiti across the front door… finally, I came across the storefront I was looking for.

Or at least I thought I had found it. It was a bare sliver of a thing sandwiched between the brownstone and a corner store, a bodega that looked like the only business that was still up and running on the block. The storefront was barely wide enough for a glass door plastered with old music posters that had been taped up from the inside. A small display window that was crowded with a drum kit and a pair of ancient-looking amplifiers took up the rest of the space. It didn't even have a business name across the awning. The only thing betraying the fact that it wasn't a long-shuttered pawn shop was a small cardboard sign in the front window where the words "I ASSURE YOU WERE OPEN" were scrawled in black Sharpie. The apostrophe was missing.

I tried to peer through the cluttered windows to see inside. No dice – I was getting glimpses of a dimly lit interior but that was about it. *What the hell is she getting me into?*

My heart started beating harder in my chest. *I don't like this. This is a bad idea.* I looked back down the street, mostly deserted except for a steady trickle of people going into and out of the bodega. I looked up at the sky, judging the time by the height of the sun. *Well, I'll just… I'll just duck my head in and leave after five minutes. That way I can tell Mom I did it.*

I grabbed the door handle and pulled. A bell attached to the top of the door frame let out a muffled ring as I stepped across the threshold.

The place was bigger than it looked like from the outside. It wasn't much wider than the storefront let on, but it went back deep surprisingly far, and I could see several rows of shelves and bins packed with LPs, cassettes, and CDs. There were handwritten signs taped up everywhere with music genres written on them: "Motown A-Z", "Jazz A-F", "R&B A-L", and others.

Directly to my left was an ancient, tan-colored cash register perched on a high counter. It had a huge tube monitor resting on a flat desktop unit that had half a dozen power cables protruding from the back. I peered closer at the long rectangular label on the back. It had the words "TANDY 1000 RSX" printed on it, along with its model and serial number.

"Damn, this thing is almost as old as I am," I muttered.

"Probably older."

I'd like to say I didn't jump at the voice. I'd like to. I can't, though.

The woman standing behind me looked to be in her early-to-mid-sixties with a close-cropped pixie cut and a prominent ring in her left nostril. She was dressed in black distressed jeans and a dingy green cardigan, worn open over a white graphic tee with the words "CORPORATE MAGAZINES STILL SUCK" printed on it. She was wearing scuffed work boots.

She arched an eyebrow at me. "Take a picture, it'll last longer."

"Oh, shit. Uh, sorry?" I winced. "I mean, uh, I just... I didn't ex... I didn't realize there was anyone here."

"Door's unlocked and lights are on, aren't they?" She made a sweeping gesture. "Welcome to Morrigan's Music." She pointed at herself, then motioned to the shelving units behind her. "I'm Morrigan. Here's our music. Records, cassettes, and CDs. You wander in here by mistake, kid?"

"What? Uh, no, I h-heard about this place." I swallowed hard. *Don't be weird, don't be weird.* "There's no other record store three doors down from the Roxy, right?"

"Nope, we're the one and only." She cocked her head at me. "Where'd you hear about us?"

"Uh, my mom? I told her I needed some music for the Pal—uh, my radio show and she told me I needed to come check this place out. Said you w-would have everything I was looking for?"

"Eh, we might." She shrugged. "You look a little young for a DJ. And don't you guys just play Top 40 garbage? I guess we've got some Bieber and Taylor Swift in the back. That new album of hers is blowing up like crazy right now."

I wrinkled my nose. "Uhh, no, please no. I get enough of Taylor Swift from my sister. I'm a s-student at Allora University. I've got my own show on WHPX on Friday nights." I blinked at myself. *Well... I guess it's true, for now anyway. Unless I screw up again.*

"Oh, so, what, EDM for the Molly poppers hitting the clubs? You can get 'Sandstorm' off Spotify. Though I think we've got a couple The Prodigy CDs I can let you have for a bargain if you want." She grinned, showing quite a bit of teeth.

"Uh, yeah, well… I mean I might need some of that stuff, I've got a gig coming up because I was invited to play a club, but that's just a one-time thing." *I hope.* "So I'm looking for some *good* EDM and I don't know where to start. My show, well, I mainly play what I like, 'cuz I'm on from 2 to 4 AM? I even have a few listeners?" *Why do I sound like I don't believe what I'm saying?*

Morrigan shrugged. "Oh yeah? Like what?"

"Well, punk and post-punk, mostly. Some New Wave, a little bit of early 90s alt rock, indie stuff, even throw in some Motown if I'm feeling it –"

"Hmm, okay. Well, maybe you are in the right place, kid." Her expression softened almost imperceptibly. Not enough for a human to notice, maybe, but I picked up on it clearly when the tightness eased around her eyes just the tiniest bit. "I won't give you the tour, it's not that big a store. I'll be up front if you need anything."

I nodded, murmuring my thanks as Morrigan slipped behind the counter and bent down behind it, mumbling under her breath. I took a walk down the aisle closest to the wall, which was lined with all sorts of music ephemera. Open, waist-high bins filled with neatly filed record sleeves, cassettes, and CD jewel cases were separated by tabs with handwritten labels.

Eventually I reached the Punk section, and I began thumbing through the LPs. *Let's see here. 4-Skins, 59 Times the Pain, Abrasive Wheels… oh shit, the Adverts?* I pulled the record out of the bin. It was in a large, opaque plastic bag that had been heat-sealed along one edge. Only the album title, *Crossing the Red Sea with the Adverts*, was visible.

I took the record up to the counter. "Hey, uh, Morrigan?"

There was a muffled thump from under the counter. The record store owner stood up, rubbing the back of her head. "Fucking... yeah, kid, you need something?"

I laid the LP carefully down on the counter. "Could I... could I look at this one? It's sealed, so I didn't want to just open it."

She looked down at the record. "Uhh, I dunno kid, this one's a little obscure—"

"Yeah, I know. The Adverts, active from, what, '76 to '79? First real instance of a female punk musician? Played at the original Roxy in London like nine times during its first 100 days? Those guys?"

Morrigan blinked at me for a second. Then she laughed, hard. "You little shit! Yeah, that's them. How the fuck did you even – you know what? Never mind." She shook her head and pulled a butterfly knife from her back pocket, flicking it open with ease. "Let me cut this open for you so you can take a look. Just be careful, okay?"

She slid the knife blade along the edge of the bag and pulled the album out, revealing the rest of the cover. It was hard to tell from my angle, but it looked as if there had been some writing in black Sharpie that had been added to the cover. "Oh, shit," Morrigan breathed.

She ran her fingers over the cover and set it down. "Listen, kid... I can't sell you this one. It's got, uh, sentimental value." She looked up at me. "I'm pretty sure this was reissued in '02, I probably have a copy of that somewhere. Let me check." She bustled away from the counter and set off briskly down the aisle, wiping at her eyes.

What was that about? Knowing it was completely none of my business, I stole a glance at the album cover. It took me a second to understand the writing since it was upside-down to me, but after a second it clicked, and my eyes grew wide.

To Morri – with all my love. Next year, in London with Lance! – Thorli

"What the fuck," I whispered. I spun it around and took a closer look. *That's... that's Mom's handwriting.*

Morrigan came back, holding a brighter, less beaten-up copy of the album. "Here, I knew we had another one, I can't believe this one ended up in the bins-" she stopped. "What's the matter, kid? Looks like you saw a ghost."

I picked up the LP on the counter. "This... who gave you this? Was it... was it Thorliekirin—Thorli Kriniacz?"

Morrigan jerked at the name. "Y-yeah. Wait, what? How the fuck did you know that? Do you... do you know Thorli, kid?"

I set the album down gently. "Kinda. She's my mom."

CHAPTER TWENTY

Morrigan just sort of stared at me for a second. "You," she said. "You're Thorli's kid? What the fuck – how did you – wait." She furrowed her brows. "Didn't you say your mom told you about this place?

I winced. "Y-yeah. She, uh, she didn't tell me anything else, though, I swear! I didn't know she knew you or anything. I mean I don't know why she—"

"She never mentioned me." Her voice was flat. "Wow, okay. Well... yeah. Your mom and I knew each other. Haven't seen her since the band broke up and she married that fucking pencil neck—uh, your dad, I guess."

"Uh... yeah, that's... that's him." I shifted awkwardly before realization hit me. "Wait, did you say 'the band'? You don't mean *the* band?" My heart leapt into my throat. "The... the Damsels?"

Her smile didn't reach her eyes. "Damsels of Distress, yup. I played bass. She really never mentioned me?"

"Uh, well she mentioned a Morri once or twice, but I had no idea it was short for Morrigan." My head was swimming. "Wait, Mom sent me here *knowing* you worked here. And she didn't tell me, either. I'm just as... shit. I'm pretty pissed, honestly."

"Yeah, imagine how I feel, kid." She sighed, running a

hand through her hair. "Listen, I'm sorry about giving you a hard time before. I thought you were just some trust-fund baby or something. If I'd known..." she trailed off, shrugging helplessly.

"Yeah, uh, I don't know what to say, either. I mean this is really fucking weird. Mom hardly *ever* talks about the Damsels. She won't even show us any pictures."

"Us? You got brothers and sisters, kid?"

"Yeah, believe it or not I'm one of triplets. Uh, fraternal, I guess. Surprised the hell out of Mom and Dad. I've got a sister and a brother, Mack and Dagmar." I paused uncomfortably. "Um, I'm Ricky, by the way."

This time the smile seemed a little more genuine, though it was tinged with sadness. "Well... I guess it's nice to officially meet you, Ricky. Still, this is a fucking trip, isn't it?" She reached over and tapped the album on the counter. "Looks like you've got her taste in music, at least?"

I smiled despite the situation. "Yeah, well, kinda. I'm the only one out of my sibs that's really into the kind of stuff she listens to. Mack takes after Dad - you'd never know it from looking at him, but he's a huge thrash metal fan. Dags, well, she's been groomed to take over the family business since she was a kid."

"That fucking fish cannery or whatever? Is that what's she's been doing all these years?" She snorted. "She said 'having to take over' was one of the big reasons she called it quits. Now she's dragging one of you guys into it, huh? Well, good for you living up to your old lady's ideals. At least somebody did." She gingerly picked up the signed Adverts album and slipped it back into the plastic. "Hey, how's Lance been? Your, uh, uncle, I guess? I haven't heard from *him* in years either, but he was always showing up and disappearing."

"Oh, uh... yeah. Lance? He's, uh..." I trailed off, not wanting to tell her. "He passed away about ten years ago." I paused. "I'm sorry."

Morrigan visibly deflated. "*Shit.*" She leaned back against one of the shelves. "Fuck. What happened?"

"No one really knows for sure." I rubbed the back of my neck, looking down at my feet. "We think he got mixed up with something he probably shouldn't have." I looked back up, meeting Morrigan's gaze. "But, well, if you knew him..."

"Yeah... yeah, I did." She sighed and forced a smile. "It sounds like Lance, at least." She cocked her head. "You know you look a little like him? He wasn't quite as tall, hair was different... but yeah, I see it."

"Thanks, that... that actually means a lot. We all miss him. You know he bought me my first guitar?"

She laughed gently. "Did he? I'm not surprised. You any good?"

"Nope, I'm fucking terrible." I grinned. "I've got a great ear, but I can't sing or play to save my life. So... yeah. Spinning records at 2 AM on Allora University Radio." I paused. "And, uh, I kinda, sorta scored an invitation to DJ a live set... at the Palace...?"

Morrigan's eyes grew wide. "You *what*? How the fuck did you manage that?"

I shrugged, my ears turning red. "I, uh, kinda went viral? Dags has like a million and a half social media followers, and she blew me up on her Insta. I guess that got somebody's attention. Thing is I don't know *shit* about dancehall music and Mom won't let me decline the offer and I'm pretty much ready to fake my death and move back up to Portland and—"

"Whoa, okay, okay!" Morrigan put her hands up, trying not to laugh. "Shit, kid, you're a mess. We better set you up, then, huh? Come on, I'll break out the reserves." She brandished the Adverts LP at me. "Not this one, though. You can have the reissue."

What followed next was surreal to say the least. Morrigan pulled out a few dusty boxes of LPs and cassettes from her back room and we went through them together. It was awkward at first, considering everything we had just been through, but after a while we settled into an easy rhythm – her pulling out music, me considering it, and then, more often than not, going off on a tangent about its merits.

Eventually there was a large stack of LPs and a smaller one of cassettes piled up on the counter, an amazing mix of stuff that had me truly excited about the prospect of digging through them and building some playlists. It was a crash course in adapting New Wave and prog punk for a live set, and I walked off with some real interesting stuff. The Cramps, Subhumans, Flipper, Wire, Television – there was even a Bad Brains cassette in the pile. Suddenly the idea of spinning records on the floor of the Palace of Wisdom didn't seem nearly as daunting, at least in the light cast by the overhead fluorescents.

Morrigan slid the last box back under the counter and dusted off her hands. She began ringing me up. "Fucking hell, kid, looks like I'll be able to pay rent this month after all."

"Yeah, well, let's just say it's on Mom." I pulled out a debit card. "That'll teach her to pull the wool over both our eyes for years, I guess?" I shook my head. "I still can't believe... I mean, why? Why shut you out like that? Why didn't she tell *us* about you? I'm sorry, Morrigan."

She shrugged. "Yeah, well, I don't think we're gonna get the answer to either question any time soon, you know? I mean unless you invite me to your next family reunion." She snorted, grinning. "Imagine *that* conversation over dinner! She still crazy about that nasty shit? The fucking... fish meatballs or whatever?"

I handed her the card. "Eh, it's an acquired taste, I guess. The sibs and I can't get enough of it, honestly."

She shook her head, handing my card back. "Yeah, I'm not

surprised it runs in the family." The ancient point-of-sale printer rattled and hummed, and she pulled the receipt free. She slipped it, and the music, into a pair of paper bags, then slid those into two plastic ones. "So, 2 to 4 AM Friday nights? 96.7?"

"Yeah, and the station rebroadcasts me the following night at 8 PM." I blinked. "Oh, don't tell me you're gonna tune in?" My ears grew hot. "I, uh… really?"

"Only if you agree to plug the place. I'm not exactly drowning in customers here." She gestured to the empty record store. "Things have been shit since The Roxy closed down a few years back. Fucking shame, too. You know the Damsels played there back in the day?"

"Huh. No, no I did not. Turns out there's a *lot* I don't know." I frowned. "What happened with that, anyway? I glanced inside the place through the window. It looks like it must have been one hell of a venue back in the day."

"Kid, you have no idea." She slid the bags over to me and I picked them up, one in each hand. I tested their weight. "Things are only gonna get worse, too. Old owners fucked off to God knows where one day. Vanished like a fart in the wind. Left behind a mountain of debt. Bank repossessed the place and now it's up on the auction block." She scowled. "I swear, whatever limp-dicked fuck of a development company that ends up owning that place better not turn it into goddamn luxury apartments. Fuckin' gentrifying shitbags."

"Jeez, Morrigan, you sound like Mom." I instantly regretted it as soon as I said it. Seeing her face just made it worse. "Shit, I'm sorry. I didn't-"

"No, it's all right. Not your fault, right? You didn't know." She closed her eyes for a second. "Listen, you come back, okay?" She opened her eyes again and looked directly at me. "I know I talk tough, but this place is really hanging on by a thread. Between The Roxy closing down and fucking Amazon, well…." She shrugged. "And maybe, uh, bring Thorli if you can? You know, for old times' sake? Besides, she kinda owes us both an explanation."

"Yeah, well, as long as you don't hit her with a baseball bat."

"No promises, kid." She grinned at me, the façade back up. "Now get out of here, I'm gonna close up early, pick up a fifth of Jack, and pass out on the couch in the back while watching Joan Jett music videos on YouTube all night."

I wasn't sure exactly what I was feeling when I stepped outside. My mind was racing, to be sure, trying to figure out what my mother had been thinking, both in cutting ties with Morrigan and sending me here. My eyebrows drew together as confusion, anger, and betrayal all went to war in my head. I think sadness was serving as referee.

I set one of the bags down and fished out my phone, checking the time. "Shit," I said, putting it back and picking the bag back up. It had gotten later than I thought. Luckily the bus stop wasn't far – I should be able to get back to Allora before it got too dark.

I rounded the corner and watched the UTA bus pull out into traffic. I groaned. *Well, the next one should be by soon.* About 20 minutes later, as promised, the next bus pulled up, a much older model that looked like it had seen better days. I wrinkled my nose at the strong smell of diesel fumes as I boarded, flashing my student ID at the driver. She nodded noncommittally and I moved towards the back, passing a handful of other passengers.

I sank into an empty bench seat, arranging my bags carefully on the floor between my knees. I had about a 45-minute ride ahead of me because of all the stops, but the good news was that it would drop me off right down the block from the school's south entrance. Then, just a short walk to Coindre Hall to stash the goods, get something to eat at the dining hall, and start planning some playlists.

CHAPTER TWENTY-ONE

T he bus shuddered to a halt. "Last stop!" the driver said.
I looked up from my phone, glanced out the window, and blinked. *This isn't Allora*, I thought. I checked the time, too – it had only been about 20 minutes since I had gotten on.

I picked up my bags, waiting for the moderate crowd to clear out before shuffling forward. "Hey," I said, "what's going on? I though this line goes all the way to the university."

The driver looked up at me from her seat. "Usually does," she said, "but the route's closed ahead and there's no detour." She pointed ahead. "Street fair. You can go a few blocks and pick up the next UTA station. Might have to make a couple transfers, but it'll get you pretty close."

I looked through the front windshield. Sure enough, the block ahead had been cordoned off with big blue sawhorses that had the words "UCPD" stenciled on them in white spray paint. Above it, a massive banner had been stretched across the street. It read "LA FESTA DI TUTTI I SANTI – CELEBRATING 75 YEARS!"

Shit. I thanked the driver and stepped out of the bus, taking a better look. The road ahead was packed with people, tourists and locals alike, all of them milling about and weaving their way through a maze of food stalls and carnival games. Live music boomed from speakers somewhere farther ahead.

I glanced down at my two bags filled with LPs and cassettes. *This is gonna take a while*, I thought. Taking a deep breath, I stepped past the barricades and into the crowd.

It was loud, and there were people everywhere. The scents of dozens of different types of street food mixed together wasn't helping either, especially when I walked past the stage where a cannoli-eating contest was being held. A Goblin wearing a backwards white baseball cap and a pastry-stained bib was shouting and pumping a fist in the air as the judges tried to hand him an ornate plastic trophy. "Second year in a row!" he bellowed. He turned to the runner-up, another Goblin, that was staring daggers at him. The winner shook his fist at him and slapped his upper arm in the classic Sicilian salute. "That's right, Joey, you goddamn ugly fuck, try again next year!"

Joey glowered. "I know where you sleep, you fuckin' *mamaluke*."

I shuffled past quickly, turning down the closest side street and away from the pressing crowd. Once I had gotten some breathing room, I leaned up against the wall of a nearby building, setting my bags down between my legs. I then fished my phone out and brought up the UTA app, checking the bus and subway maps.

Okay let's see here... Brentwood Avenue subway station. It was about three blocks west and four north, but it looked like just three stops down the line had a stand for the but to Allora across the street. *Back in time for some peace and quiet before Niko gets back.* I stuffed my phone back in my pocket, picked my bags back up, and set off.

The sun had begun to dip past the canyons of buildings by the time I got to the Brentwood Avenue station. It, too, was cordoned off, this time by dozens of UTA workers brandishing homemade signs and chanting slogans. One worker was shouting a call-and-response into a bullhorn, with the rest of the workers picking it up:

"What do we want?"

"A CONTRACT!"

"When do we want it?"

"NOW!"

I sighed. *Mom would kill me if I crossed a picket line*, I thought, calling up the UTA app again. I revised my path, walking another dozen blocks until I got to the next subway entrance, which was free of any picketing.

By this time the sun had fully set, and I was grateful that I just needed to take it for two stops before picking up my bus line. I waited a few minutes for the next subway and shuffled on, sinking gratefully into an empty seat for a quick break. I took my phone out and went back to work on my setlist.

The first stop came and went, humans and mythics coming on and getting off. The second was more of the same. Once the doors closed again, I stuffed my phone back into my pocket and gathered my things.

The subway's intercom chimed, and I looked up at the digital sign at the front of the car. The words "NEXT STOP CLOSED FOR RENOVATIONS" was scrolling slowly across from right to left.

I put my head in my hands. *I'm never getting back at this rate.* It was several minutes before the train came to the next stop after that one. I stepped out onto the platform, coming face-to-face with a large paper map of the UTA system set in a frame on the wall behind a sheet of scratched Plexiglass. *Now how far out of the way am I...?*

This subway line was out. It kept on going east, well past Allora University and then juked north along Destry Bay and out to the suburbs. As I traced my route on the map, I started counting blocks. *Ten, twelve, fourteen…*

My finger landed on the UTA stop I needed. There was an asterisk next to it, so I checked the map legend: LIMITED BUS SERVICE AT THIS STOP AFTER 8 PM. NEXT BUS SCHEDULED FOR 10:30 PM. I glanced over at the digital clock on the wall of the platform. It read 8:12.

My shoulders slumped. I rested my head on the clear Plexi and closed my eyes for a moment. "Fuuuuuuck," I breathed.

Opening my eyes, I looked at the map again. *What if I just walk right back to the dorms? How far could it be? We're almost in Allora now anyway…* I slid my finger back to the station and started tracing up. *Four blocks, five… shit.*

Allora University's south entrance was only about 12 blocks north of me. The problem was Tolon Park was in the way. I did some quick measurements and sighed. The park was wider than it was long, and going around would take forever.

Well, I'm not going through Tolon Park at night. That's a good way to get taken off the census, if Mom can be believed. Though… I took a closer look at the map. The park wasn't a perfect rectangle; the western edge was angled, and the path through was much shorter than going through the center. *Cutting through the Park there would shave a half hour off my walk. And I'd only be in there for a few minutes.*

My mother's words rang in my ears again. She'd been telling me to "stay the fuck out of Tolon Park at night" pretty much every day since I started classes.

I looked down at the two bags of music I had carried with me all the way from South Beckettsville. My stomach turned to ice at the memory of the pain and sadness in Morrigan's face when she saw Mom's handwriting on that Advents LP.

The hell with that, I thought. *Mom says a lot of things. I'm cutting through. What's the worst that could happen?*

CHAPTER TWENTY-TWO

I paused at the entrance to the park. It was black as pitch inside – or it would have been, if I had been human. The trees grew close along both sides of the little paved jogging path that led off through it, only illuminated by a handful of streetlamps at wide intervals.

I took a deep breath. *Come on, in and out, twenty minutes. Then back home. There's probably nobody this close to the edge anyway.*

I crossed the threshold of the park. Nothing terrible happened. I took another tentative step. The world still didn't end. I shrugged. *Guess Mom's just paranoid.*

It was a nice night. A slight wind curled through the trees, setting the turning leaves hissing gently in a way that reminded me of an incoming tide. I could see clearly that there was no one on the path in either direction. *Not even a Satyr or three looking for a good time*, I thought.

I hefted the bags in my hands and continued, passing an overflowing garbage bin. "Fucking hell," I muttered, glaring at it. "Humans." It smelled worse than it looked, half-eaten chicken wings and empty beer cans and... *oh god, is that...* I sniffed, and then gagged. *Ugh, yup. That's poop. And not baby poop either.*

That's full-grown human poop.

I shook my head, snorting to get the scent from my nostrils. I sneezed suddenly, the sound splitting the darkness. The entire path went silent.

Oh... shit? I froze in my tracks. *I probably just startled some raccoons or something. Or opossums. There's opossums in Tolon Park, right?*

I didn't wait around to find out. Wiping my nose on my sleeve, I set off down the path, my ears pricked and eyes peeled.

After a few moments the sounds of the forest seemed to return. I passed under a streetlamp and the wind picked up again. I filled my lungs, trying to calm my pulse rate, and stopped.

That smell. That's not a fucking opossum.

I heard the faintest of noises behind me and to my left, like a subtle click. I spun around in fright and yelped as something buzzed past me, followed by a high-pitched squeal, cut short by a dull, wet thump.

"Jesus fuck!" I hissed, backpedaling and looking around wildly. I almost tripped over my own feet. Glancing over my shoulder, I saw something sticking out of a tree trunk behind me and far to the left, the bark splintered from the impact.

A voice rang out from across the road. "This way, father! I do believe you struck the little beast!" The bottom dropped out of my stomach – I recognized that voice. It was the same one that had been tormenting me all semester in my Management Accounting class - the same one that had so "graciously" sent me that invitation to go hunting. Panicked, I dove into the underbrush, burrowing deep into a thicket of boxwood shrubs growing along the footpath and making myself as flat as possible.

The foliage on the other side of the path parted, and there he was in all his snide glory – Wyndham Summers, dressed in expensive-looking hunting gear, all hand-tooled leather. He had an ornate crossbow, all gleaming wood and faesteel filigree, slung on his shoulder. He swept his eyes across the road, raking past my hiding place. *Oh God, don't see me, don't see me....*

His gaze slipped from the boxwoods and alighted on the spot where the crossbow bolt had slammed into the tree. His face split into a terrifying grin and looked back through the opening in the underbrush behind him. "Bullseye, father! Pinned the little bastard right in place!"

A deeper, older voice answered. "Excellent, my boy. I knew our evening hunt would be fruitful." Another Sidhe emerged, tall and impossibly handsome like Summers. The family resemblance was uncanny, like looking at one of those social media filters that makes you look a few decades older. The comparison was even more pronounced, seeing as he was dressed almost identically to his son, down to the ornate crossbow in his hands.

Summers pointed, and the older Sidhe – his dad, apparently – turned to look. A cruel, triumphant smile creased his impeccable features. "Well, will you look at that. As I live and breathe! Looks like your old *pater familias* still has what it takes, eh?"

He strode across the footpath towards the tree and knelt down, plucking at the thighs of his hunting pants and hiking them up as he did so. "Look at you," he whispered, reaching out and grasping the still-quivering crossbow bolt with one deftly manicured hand.

From my angle I couldn't see what it was that he had hit, but I could hear what sounded like labored wheezing. It intensified as the Sidhe began turning the bolt. "Oh, no, none of that," he crooned softly, almost tenderly, before he pulled the bolt free with a vicious jerk, revealing a wickedly barbed tip dripping with silver blood. I winced.

There was a wet, rattling breath, like someone struggling

to speak. A guttural cough, and then, "Why?" The voice was weak, soft and gravelly. "*Iah tewake'nikonhraién:ta's.* We've... we've done nothing.... to you..."

The Sidhe's eyes went wide, his expression softening in mock compassion. "Oh, my poor little friend! I assure you, it's nothing personal. Just a bit of sport on a lazy autumn evening."

Summers walked over and pulled a long, glimmering hunting knife with an inlaid wooden hilt from a belt sheath. He handed it to the older Sidhe. "Here, father," he said. "Far be it for me to deny the honorable Earl Rethas the glory of his kill."

Summers's father took the knife wordlessly, turning the blade over in the orange sodium light of the streetlamp. His other hand kept its grip on whoever he had wounded in place against the tree and out of my sight. "Thank you, son," he murmured, before whipping his knife hand in one fluid motion.

There was a terrible squelching sound, followed by the soft thump of something hitting the ground and coming to rest at Rethas's feet.

"Hmm. A clean cut indeed." Rethas stood, knife hand covered in dripping silver. He held his other hand out to Summers, who deposited an embroidered silk handkerchief into his father's open palm. Rethas used it to clean the blade dispassionately before handing it back to his son. "Here, my boy, wrap up our little trophy and place it with the others. We've had a truly bountiful night. Almost wipes the taste of that vile bit of minstrelsy out of my mouth."

Summers bent down, wrapping something up about the size of a grapefruit in the handkerchief. He stuffed it into a large leather sack, already bulging with what looked like similar items. "I'm telling you, father, I had no idea that... that *worm* would have the audacity to select such a song—"

"Ah, but he did, did he not? Even after you ridiculed him to his face, not less than a fortnight prior?" Rethas turned to leave, passing Summers without sparing him a glance, not even slowing down as he pressed the curved, inlaid hilt of the hunting knife to his son's chest. "And then he chose to respond to our most gracious of invitations with such disrespect. Astonishing how it chose a song entitled 'Goodbye, Earl' if it didn't think that would be considered a direct threat."

Summers blanched in the glow of the streetlight, making his skin look ghoulish and wan. He struggled to re-sheath the hunting knife, hurrying after Rethas. "Father, please, allow me to avenge this slight! I already know where he sleeps. We could have his hide tanned and transformed into a lavish cloak, one that matches the Dragon-hide cape worn by the Crown Prince. Even the colors would match!"

Rethas scoffed. "Oh, and should I arrive at court with the head of a white Dragon on my shoulder without Prince Hadryn taking it as a slight? Though it might be an excellent way to orchestrate a family reunion of sorts. I'm sure your little college friend would appreciate that, wouldn't he?"

Silvery blood was oozing across the ground, down the slight incline and seeping into the earth beneath the boxwood I was sheltering in. The rivulet touched my outstretched hand. I screwed my eyes shut, bit my tongue, and tried not to scream.

Please leave, please leave, please just leave!

"Come, boy, we must away home. The night is still young, and we should—hm. What's this?"

I opened my eyes to see both Rethas and Summers looking down at the footpath where I had left my music. The older Sidhe was toeing one bag with a sumptuously tooled leather riding boot. "Is this... mortal trash?"

Summers knelt down, examining the outside of the bag. "'Morrigan's Music,'" he read aloud before opening it and peering inside. He pulled out the Adverts LP, turning it over in his hands for a moment. "This is... queer," he said. "Father, this wasn't here when we came by this way earlier."

"Truly? Hmm." Rethas reached into a quiver slung low across his hip, pulling out another crossbow bolt. He casually loaded his weapon. *Oh God. Ricky, do something.* "How quite droll. Perhaps you'll have a chance to avenge that slight before you know it, boy." His eyes scanned the underbrush, roving over the bushes where I had been hiding. I held my breath, not daring to move.

The tip of the Sidhe noble's crossbow dipped, almost imperceptibly. I cast my eyes to the left and right, looking wildly for a way out, seeing nothing but the two Fae, silhouetted in the light of the nearby streetlamp.

I cast my eyes to the side, looking for an exit – any exit – and yelped as something buzzed past my cheek, showering me with splintered tree bark. I scrambled out of the bushes and to my feet, right into the light of the streetlamp.

A cruel laugh split the silence. "Ah, there you are. I could practically smell you. A bit late for a stroll, isn't it? Don't you know that these are the hunting grounds of the Summer Court, worm?"

I froze dead in my tracks and turned, then fell back to the ground and scrabbled backwards off the jogging path. The streetlamp cast funhouse shadows along the ground as I did so. Another tree arrested my retreat, and I winced at the sudden impact. Rethas stepped into the circle of light, clearly revealing his haughty features, upswept ears, and cruel smile. He had nestled his massive crossbow in the crook of his arm. He loaded another wickedly sharp bolt, never taking his eyes off me. The ratchet mechanism clicked slowly.

I held one hand up to shield my eyes from the glare of the streetlamp. "I, uh... I mean... I'm n-n-not much sport, am I? Come on, haven't you ever heard of c-c-catch and release? You know, let a f-few seasons go by s-s-so they'll grow a b-b-bit bigger?"

The Sidhe's eyebrows shot heavenward. "Catch... and release? Oh, my stars and garters, my son! You were right when you said he was a water wyrm!" He flicked his eyes over to his left for a moment. Summers stepped forward, holding his own ornate crossbow. "This *is* the prey you've been hunting at university, isn't it?"

A predatory grin spread across the face of Summers. He hunkered down in front of me, cradling his crossbow in a casual threat. "Oh, yes, Father. This is Ruh-ruh-Ricky. Ricky, meet the honorable Earl Rethas, my esteemed sire." He smirked, looking back up at his father. "Of course, a White would look at things in terms of fishing."

"Ricky, eh? How *common.*" Rethas' eyes glittered dangerously, belying his courtly smile. "Tell me, Ricky – did you truly think your slight would go unanswered? That my progeny would simply stand aside when you played that ridiculous song on the radio? That *I* would allow such a slight to stand?"

I gaped at the Sidhe, stricken with disbelief. *It was just a song,* I wanted to shout. *It wasn't even about you!* Words failed me. I only watched, frozen to the spot, as Rethas slowly raised the crossbow to his shoulder, his fingers curling around the trigger.

My mother's voice echoed in my head: *Now or never, kid. Time to take that shot.* If there was ever a time for scales as hard as steel, it would be now. I closed my eyes.

A blinding flash of light illuminated the forest, making the Earl and his son both flinch, shouting and hiding their eyes. As the flash faded, I reared up in my full natural form, shaking the dirt and leaves off me from my former hiding place. Sometimes it's convenient being able to transform into a Dragon the size of a pickup truck towing a U-Haul.

Knowing I had mere moments before Rethas and Summers recovered, I whipped my tail, nearly half the length of my entire body in this form, hard. It further flattened the tree behind me and knocked the streetlamp from its moorings. The lamp rained a shower of sparks as it fell, striking the jogging path and plunging the area into darkness.

I drew as deep a breath as I could. *No more hiding now*, I thought, as I opened my jaws wide and unleashed a massive gout of white-hot flame. The asphalt of the jogging path grew shiny, steamed, and began to bubble; the bushes beyond combusted instantly.

I had bought myself just a moment in the chaos, and I needed to use it. Gathering all four of my legs under me, I flexed my front claws, digging them deep into the charred earth. In a single motion I tossed two great globs of steaming dirt and molten asphalt at the earl and his son, pushed off the ground with my back legs, and took to the sky.

I heard cursing and yelling below me, but I didn't spare a glance. Instead, I flapped my wings frantically, trying to gain enough altitude that I would be out of range of those damned Sidhe and their crossbows. I wheeled to my left and jerked as a crossbow bolt whizzed by, missing my muzzle by just inches. If I had been even a moment too slow—

A dizzying pain ripped through me as a crossbow bolt punched through my left wing membrane and lodged in my side. I roared in pain, corkscrewing in the air and nearly losing control. Every moment I was still aloft was agony, but I knew what would happen if I crashed inside Tolon Park. Despite feeling like I was ripping my wing to shreds, I flapped once, again, three times, and cleared the edge of the park.

I pulled my wings in as much as I could, shortening my span and pressing my injured membrane against my flank. Wherever the bolt was, I couldn't reach it – and I don't know if I could have pulled it free even if I had been able to grab it. The pain was extraordinary, like someone had cut open my head and poured acid directly into my brain. I was having trouble flying straight, and my vision was getting blurry.

There was only one place I could go that would be safe. I

just hoped I would get there before it was too late.

CHAPTER TWENTY-THREE

The adrenaline was rapidly draining from my body. My vision tunneled even further; every movement of my wings, my tail, even the simple act of breathing seemed excruciating. Still on I flew, slewing drunkenly across the sky and nearly colliding with a billboard.

I needed to gain altitude, but every time I spread my wings wider the cruel rip in my membrane would cause my flight path to hitch. At one point I could swear I felt it tearing even worse than it already had been. The pain nearly caused me to tumble from the sky.

After what seemed like an eternity of agony, I spotted my destination - the apartment block where my parents lived. If I could get to the third-floor fire escape....

My back left claw clipped a power line and nearly sent me into a flat spin. I was too low - I'd barely clear the second floor if I was lucky. Clenching my jaw, I bared my fangs and flared both my wings to their fullest, arresting my forward flight. I hovered for a split second, the taste of my own tears at the sides of my muzzle, and flapped as hard as I could.

I'd like to say I didn't cry out in pain. That I had dug deep within myself, gritted my teeth, and toughed my way through it.

But if I said that, I'd be lying.

My screech rattled windows and set off car alarms up and down the block. Flames leaked from my nostrils and seeped out from between my fangs as I rose in the sky, past the second floor, up to the third...

My forward momentum began to falter. I didn't have enough in me to try again. Instead I reached forward with all four of my legs, desperately straining to grab on to something, anything, that would stop me from falling to the pavement below.

A jolt ran through my front right leg as my claws made contact with the building. I clenched, claws digging into the stone and leaving long, deep marks in the façade. My legs scrabbled against the outer wall, eventually sinking both back feet into it as well and halting my slow slide downward. Then, my front left joined the other three.

I folded my wings tight against my body and craned my neck, looking up. The fire escape for the third floor was close. Pulling my left front claws free, I flexed my back legs, propelling me up the wall. Plaster and stone rained down as I laboriously climbed closer.

I transformed as I reached the fire escape, replacing my true form with my human one. I curled up into a ball, naked, shivering, and bloody, too weak to cry out, only faintly hearing the shouts of people far below in the aftermath of my mad flight to safety.

I heard the window open. "What the fuck is going on ou— oh my gods, Ricky!" Opening my eyes, I saw my mother silhouetted in the open frame. "Chad, it's Ricky, he's on the fire escape – he looks hurt!" She clambered out and knelt down next to me. "Fucking hell, Ricky, what's wrong? Let me see—" She touched my side. I cried out, and she pulled her hand back. "Ricky, you're cold as ice. Chad, where the fuck *are* you?"

"I'm here, I'm here, what the hell are you – oh *shit*." My father stared down at me and Mom, eyes wide. He clambered through the window as well. "Thorli, go get some blankets and the first aid kit. I'll get him inside."

Mom nodded silently, her face a mask of grief, and disappeared from sight. Dad took her place and laid his hand on my shoulder gently. I whimpered.

"Come on, Ricky, up we go." His voice was soft and soothing as he gathered me up in his arms. I hissed as pain blossomed in my left side, and I cried out again. Silvery blood spattered on the fire escape, hissing as it touched the metal.

"Shit, Chad, *come on*, get him in the apartment!" Mom was back, tucking my head into my father's chest as he navigated the open window. Tall as I was, it wasn't an easy task.

I don't remember much after that, only that I was laid down on something soft and warm. I was rolled onto my right side gently, only half-hearing my parents' panicked voices.

"Jesus, Chad, look at his side!"

"I see it, honey, hold on. Hand me the sponge. Let's clean him up – oh hell."

I sucked air through gritted teeth as the sponge touched my skin. My form fluxed, skin turning scaly, fingernails extending into claws, and then back to human.

"Ricky, breathe! You've got to calm down." My mother was cradling my head in her hands, her voice in my ear. "You fully transform inside and you'll blow what's left of the wall down into the street. You're all right, you're safe. We got you. We got you."

It took real effort to stop. My involuntary transformations slowed and then ceased. I unclenched my jaw, fully in human form, and drew a ragged breath. "Mom," I croaked, "I'm sorry, I'm so sorry… it's my fault, I didn't listen to you—" I gasped as the sponge touched my side again, feeling like flaming sandpaper against my skin.

"Shh, shh, it's okay. Try not to speak." My mother brushed the top of my head. "Dad's just cleaning your side to see how bad it is."

"Okay," I said, wincing as my father continued to clean the wound. "It… it was a c-c-crossbow bolt. Caught my l-left… *fuuuuck*… my left wing membrane. I was… I was trying to get away—" The pain in my side flared, and the rest of the sentence was lost in a muffled scream.

"Okay, I got it! I got it." My father's voice was tight. "Godsdamned… look at this, Thorli."

Mom gasped. "Are you fucking *kidding* me? Chad, that's—"

"Yup. Dragonsbane-tipped faesteel." Something dropped with a metal-on-metal clink. "Wicked, too. Designed to maim and weaken, even if it didn't hit a vital part." Dad put his hand on my forehead. It felt incredibly warm. "Ricky, my poor boy…."

"I'm sorry," I whimpered. "I… I missed my bus, and then there was a s-subway strike, and the n-next stop was c-c-closed for renovations." My mind seemed to be clearing slightly. "I thought I could get back to my dorm by just, just c-cutting through the corner of… Tolon…."

My voice cracked as a painful lump formed in my throat. "Stupid," I croaked, crying. "So stupid, I was so stupid—" The rest was just sobs.

"It's okay, Ricky. You're safe." Mom was stroking my head gently. I could feel my father poking around at the wound on my side. I hissed at the touch, but now that the broadhead had been pulled out of me, the pain was starting to subside slightly. "Tell me what happened. Was it… was it Sidhe?"

I nodded. "I heard them coming… so I hid in the underbrush. They… they were hunting something. Killed it, took a trophy. They were leaving when they s-saw something I had left in the path before I hid. They spotted me, so I t-transformed and used my breath, then tried to run." I winced. "Oh gods, they were looking for me. For *me*, Mom!"

"'Them?'" Dad asked as he continued cleaning my wound. "Was it a full hunting party?"

"N-no, it was just two of them. One of them was an earl. The other... oh god, it was his son. He's the same one who... my accounting class.... They thought I had bad-mouthed them on the air. Thought 'Goodbye, Earl' was me p-picking a fight..."

My father growled. "Did you get a name, Ricky?"

"Rethas," I breathed. "It was Earl Rethas."

My parents grew silent, both freezing. After a long moment, they went back to what they were doing. "Okay, Ricky - you just rest. We'll have this cleaned up in no time. It wasn't deep, you're lucky. Might take a little longer to heal than usual thanks to the Dragonsbane, but you'll be all right." My father bandaged my side and stood up, gathering the first aid supplies.

I was suddenly exhausted. "Okay," I mumbled. "I'm just gonna..."

Things got hazy after that. I dozed fitfully on the couch under a fuzzy gray blanket, half-listening to my parents' hushed conversation. It sounded like they had moved to the kitchen, but I was finding it hard to concentrate on what they were saying.

"... fucking Summer Court bullshit..."

".. the Queen..."

"... going to do? No way to prove it was them..."

"... Dragonsbane, Chad? It doesn't grow on fucking trees!"

"... word against theirs. They could claim Ricky attacked them–"

"... already lost a brother. Not losing my son too..."

Mom, I thought, my mind racing, *Mom I'm right here... I'm not going anywhere...*

CHAPTER TWENTY-FOUR

It was dark when I woke up. Completely disoriented, I tried to sit up with a start, but a sharp pain stopped me in my tracks. I clutched at my side, feeling at a gauze bandage in confusion until I remembered what I had just gone through. "Oh, gods," I croaked, sinking back down into the couch cushions.

A light snapped on to my right. My mother was sitting in an easy chair, a closed book across her lap. "Hey," she said. "How you feeling?"

I groaned. "Remember when Dad let us stay up late to watch WrestleMania 13 and Mack power-bombed me through that old glass coffee table?"

She chuckled. "I remember I was ready to ship you all off to Grandma Jutte for the whole summer after that."

I gave her a weak smile. "Yeah, well, this is almost as bad."

"Well, it can't be that awful if you're cracking jokes." She put her book down on the side table and got up. "You look thirsty. Want some water?"

I nodded, suddenly realizing how dry my throat was. "What time is it? And where's Dad?"

"Uhh…. almost 4:30 in the morning?" She was rummaging in the kitchen. "And I sent Dad to bed. He had the first shift." She came back with a full glass, ice tinkling in it as she walked. "Here, try to sit up a little."

I braced myself against the side of the couch and shifted my weight slowly. My side was throbbing. I leaned my back up against the arm rest and took the glass from my mother. "Thank you," I said.

"You got it, kid." She smiled, then sat back down in the armchair. "Just sip, don't go too hard or we'll be cleaning blood *and* puke from the couch cushions."

The cold water burned my throat like fire. I sputtered, eyes bulging, but managed to keep it down. "Shit," I coughed, "I'm so sorry, I didn't know where else to go-"

"Ricky, it's okay, you did the right thing. We're both just glad you're all right." She leaned forward, elbows on knees. "You're lucky you're alive, you know that? If that bolt had struck you head-on or gone even a half an inch deeper…."

"I know. And oh gods, Mom, I'm so sorry. I was just trying to get back to the dorms, I was on my way back from that record store you told me to visi— oh shit. *Shit.*" I sagged against the couch. "The music! *Fuck!* I had two big bags of LPs and cassettes with me, that's why I wanted to get home—"

"Hey, hey, it's okay. I'd rather have *you* than two bags of music." She paused. "Was it anything good, though?"

"Mom, it was a *treasure trove.*" I looked at her blearily. "But you already knew that it would be, didn't you? Just like you knew I would meet Morrigan."

My mother sighed. "Yeah. Yeah, I did." She paused. "So… how has she been?"

"Um. Angry. Sad. Hurt? A lot of different things. Especially after she learned who I was." I stared at her hard for a moment. Or at least as hard as I could, though it probably looked more like I was constipated than anything else. "I kind of felt the same way."

Her shoulders slumped. "I'm sorry, Ricky. I should have never sent you there. It's just... it was the only place that I *knew* you'd find what you're looking for–"

"Mom. What the fuck. Why didn't you *tell* us about Morrigan? Why didn't you tell us you and her were in the Damsels together? That she knew Uncle Lance?" That cold, tight feeling in the pit of my stomach was back. "You know she still has that Advents LP you gave her?" I said quietly.

Mom winced, shutting her eyes. She sighed. "It was... listen, Ricky. I wanted to tell you kids, I did, but it was just... it hurt too much." She looked out the window. "Morri and I were closer than sisters once, but, well, she didn't understand why I had to quit the band." She looked back. "How the hell was I supposed to explain it to her? *Sorry, love, I need to take over my clan's territory? Oh, and by the way, I can hold my breath for half an hour and survive in sub-arctic waters?*"

I opened my mouth, but words failed me. "You could have come up with *some*thing, couldn't you? Anything? I mean I know she's human, but she was...."

"Special to me." My mother nodded. "Outside of you, your siblings, and your father, she was the most important person in my life. Right up there with my brother." She sighed, swiping at her face. "But I had my clan duty. I tried to keep in touch, but, well... first you three came, and then Lance left, and... it all became too painful. Every time I thought of her, I just remembered everything that I had lost. That I couldn't ever have again." She sniffled, her hands falling heavily to her lap. "So, yeah. I ghosted her."

I let out a breath I didn't even know I had been holding. "I... I don't know what to say."

Mom shrugged, lifting her hands from her lap. "You didn't

know." She smiled a little, though it didn't really reach her eyes. "I'm sorry, Ricky. I'm sorry about not telling you about Morri, sorry about that Earl going after you, sorry you got hurt... and I'm really sorry about the music."

I nodded. "Thank you," I said. "And I'm sorry I didn't listen to you about Tolon Park, Mom."

"Oh honey," she said, getting up and hugging me. "I'm just so relieved you're safe." She pulled back from me, her arms on her shoulders. "You should probably drop that class you're in with that inbred bastard's son." She wrinkled her nose. "And you should *definitely* take a shower. You stink like a highway underpass mosh pit."

I laughed, then winced as my side complained. "Okay," I said. I handed her the water glass and stood up gingerly, wrapping the blanket around me. "Do you think you could get me something to wear? I, uh, well I kind of shredded everything when I took flight."

She nodded. "I'll find something. There's fresh towels in the hall closet. Go get yourself cleaned up."

I walked down the hallway, stopping to grab a towel. I flicked the light on in the bathroom and winced, both at the light and my reflection.

I looked like shit. More than usual, that was. Covered in dirt and grime, massive bags under my eyes, hair disheveled, dried silvery blood flaking off my side, bruises up and down my body. I turned off the main overhead light and flipped on the bulbs surrounding the vanity instead to cut the glare.

It was an adventure getting into the shower. I found it hard to stand for very long, so I pulled the shower head off the wall and sat on the tile bench inside the stall. I let the water heat up and then slowly began washing the muck and blood off me, the spray stinging against my skin.

I was about halfway through cleaning up, thankful my

parents' apartment building had unlimited hot water, when there was a knock on the door. "Hey," called my mother. "I found some extra clothes for you." The door cracked open and she snaked her arm through, leaving them on the counter.

"Thanks, Mom," I croaked. "I'll be out soon."

"Take your time, kid. Not goin' anywhere." She shut the door.

I took my mother's advice. I didn't have much choice, considering how long it took me to finish without opening that gash in my side back up. When I was done, I shut the water off and sat on the bench, catching my breath. Finally, I got out of the shower and dried off.

All right, let's see what we've got here. With the towel draped around my shoulders, I picked up the clothes my mother had left me. There was a pair of underwear, likely taken from Dad's drawers, ripped black jeans that looked like they had seen better days, a pair of socks, and a pair of scuffed and beaten-up New Balance shoes – also likely from my father. There was also a t-shirt that might have been white at one time but had long since faded to that nondescript non-color you get from washing it a thousand times.

"Huh." I turned the shirt over. There was a faded band logo across the front. "Tantric... Petting Zoo?" I shrugged and got dressed.

The sun was just beginning to stream through the windows when I came back out to the living room. Mom was cleaning up, pulling the slipcovers off the cushions and piling them on the coffee table. They were all stained silver and pocked with holes, my blood having eaten away at them like acid.

"Shit, I'm sorry," I said, leaning against the doorway.

My mother looked up. "Oh please, Ricky. You think I care about the couch? We're just glad you're okay." She grabbed a pile of clean, folded covers and began putting them back on the cushions. "How's your side?"

"Uh, better, I guess?" I touched the spot where the crossbow bolt had lodged in me and winced. "Still really tender."

"Yeah, that'll be the Dragonsbane." Dad came out of the kitchen doorway, holding three steaming mugs. "You're lucky it was just a graze, Ricky." The smell of hot cocoa filled my nostrils. He held out one of the mugs, and I took it carefully. There were mini marshmallows floating on top.

I chuckled, then winced. "That shit was no joke." I sat down carefully in an easy chair, cradling my hot cocoa. My father set another mug down on the coffee table.

Mom grimaced. "For fuck's sake, Chad, would it kill you to use a coaster?" She placed a clean cushion back on the couch, grabbed the mug, and sat down. "Your father's right, though. Dragonsbane can drop one of us like a sack of potatoes. So much for no fucking Dragon hunting."

I shivered despite the warm mug in my hands. *Had I really come so close to death?* "I... I... I'm sorry." My eyes welled up. "I'm so fucking sorry, I... I didn't listen to you, you *told* me to stay out of Tolon Park at night b-b-b-but-"

"Hey, none of that." My father sat down on the armrest of my chair. "I think you've paid more than enough for your mistake, right Thorli?"

"Hmph." She took a long sip from her mug, and then set it back down on the coffee table. On a coaster. "Someone's gonna pay," she growled. Her eyes flashed, her pupils tightening to cat-like slits.

"Hey, don't you go provoking the Sidhe. We can't jeopardize the *détente* with Queen Alana—"

"Damn it, Chad! What good is a *détente* if there are fucking *kúkalabbi* like this Earl Rethas doing whatever they want whenever her back is turned?"

"So what? Should we just go back to open warfare? Is that what you want?" My father's voice began to raise. "We can't lose anyone else! Your brother—"

"*Don't.*" My blood ran ice cold. I had only heard that tone of voice once from my mother before, and it was as scary now as it was when I was a fledgling. That wasn't the only reason, though. I remembered how Rethas and Summers had discussed having "another" white Dragonhide cloak. Because there already was one being worn by a Sidhe.

Mom was building up a head of steam. "Don't you *fucking* dare—"

"Guys, stop, stop!" I was standing up, though I don't even remember doing it. My pulse was hammering in my ears. "Listen... Mom, Dad, please. Rethas... said something. Something you need to hear."

I sat back down slowly, my parents both watching me. "He said..." I swallowed, trying to get the lump out of my throat. It didn't work. "He said that... that the Crown Prince has..."

"Has what, Ricky?" Mom's voice was calm, quiet. Soft. Dangerous.

I breathed a ragged sigh. "He's got a... a cloak." I paused. "A Dragon hide cloak." My father's brows came together hard. Mom blinked rapidly. "That's not all, though. Oh, gods... listen, he said it was..." I squeezed my eyes shut and took another deep breath. "He said it was a white Dragon hide."

My mother stared at me, her eyes wide. She sat down abruptly. "He... what?"

I winced. "Maybe it wasn't... I mean... Mom, we don't know-"

"Ricky." Dad laid a hand on my shoulder. "Give me and your mother a minute, okay?" His voice was soft, gentle.

I nodded dumbly and wandered into the kitchen, still

clutching my mug of cocoa. I could hear my father murmuring to Mom in that same tone of voice. Unable to bear what would be coming next, I set my mug down on the counter and pulled a pen and Post-It note out of a drawer.

"Going back to campus," I wrote. "I'm sorry." I left the note on the kitchen island.

I walked to the foyer. opened the door as quietly as I could and slipped through, closing it behind me. I paused there, my palm on the door, breathing, trying to fight off a deep feeling of dread.

"Okay," I whispered. "Okay, okay."

I stood up, pushing off the door. A terrible keening wail came from my parents' apartment. *There it is*, I thought. My own eyes stinging, I turned away and walked down the corridor to the elevator, the sound of my mother's mourning song following me.

CHAPTER
TWENTY-FIVE

The sun was well over the horizon when I stepped out onto the sidewalk. The street was a mess, fallen masonry and debris strewn along the gutters where emergency crews had likely pushed it aside as a temporary measure. There was even a line of orange traffic cones around one large chunk, obviously too heavy to move right then, that had fallen into the street.

I winced. *I really hope nobody saw me crash*, I thought.

The walk back to campus was blessedly short. With the sun up and shining the day was warming up nicely for early November and there wasn't a cloud in the sky – the kind of morning perfect for a nice walk. Not that I had a choice, considering I had lost my wallet and my student ID card somewhere in the middle of Tolon Park last night before crashing into the side of my parents' apartment building. It wasn't safe for me to go back to look for my things, even in the middle of the day.

That's fine, I'll just get Niko to let me in, I thought, reaching into my pocket. I cursed. My phone was gone, too, of course. Probably totaled, along with the clothes I had been wearing when I made my escape. No ID to get into my dorm, no phone to call my roommate to come let me in. *Well, I guess I'll just do this the hard way*.

It was still pretty early when I made it back to campus, though I was winded from the long walk; my side was throbbing after the first few blocks. Still, the quad was gorgeous this time of morning. The leaves had all finished turning around a week ago, and in the early morning sunlight the trees still had enough to have them awash in multicolored halos. Other than that, though, it was deserted – like any typical early weekend morning on a college campus.

I came up the footpath to the front façade of Coindre Hall, stepping into the long shadow cast by the brick residence hall. I took a seat on the stone steps. With nothing else to do, I waited and tried not to think about last night too much. I wasn't very successful.

I don't know how long I was out there, as I kept losing track of time. The building's shadow retreated as the sun rose higher; every once and a while, a student dressed in sweats went jogging by, but nobody came in or out of the dorm behind me. I just sat there, trying to tamp down the feeling that someone was about to sneak up behind me.

I jumped at the sound of hooves striking asphalt, shaken from my catastrophic daydreaming. My roommate was clomping up the footpath on his furry digitigrade legs. He was, to put it mildly, a mess. His hair was even more askew as usual and even his spiraling ram horns looked crooked, even though I knew that wasn't possible. Yet despite his markedly disheveled look, he was wearing a satisfied smile as he came up the path carrying a huge earthenware jug by a leather strap he had draped over his shoulder.

I cleared my throat. "Hey."

Niko blinked. "Ricky?" His face split into a huge grin. "The fuck are you doing out here?"

"I, uh, lost my ID." I paused. "And my phone."

"Are you kidding? Shit, man, that sucks. C'mon, I'll let you in. You're lucky I'm just getting home. Man, did you sleep in a bush? You look like hot garbage. Here, hold my amphora."

He pushed the giant jug into my hands. Whatever was inside sloshed heavily, smelling strongly of wine. It took him a while to dig out his ID and even longer for him to thread it through the card reader, as he missed it a few times. Finally, the lock beeped; he pulled the door open and stepped through, holding it for me.

I came inside and handed him the amphora back. The door shut behind us and I felt my anxiety subside just a little. "Thanks," he said, slinging it back over his shoulder. "So how the fuck did you lose your phone *and* your ID?" He glanced back over his shoulder as we walked down the hallway. "And what the fuck is a Tantric Petting Zoo?" He pointed at my chest.

"Huh?" I looked down, realizing he was talking about the name on my t-shirt. "Uhh... long story, man. Can we just... can we get back to the room? Please?"

Niko gave me a quizzical look. "Uh, yeah, sure." My roommate cocked his head. "Are you... you're not okay, are you?"

I shook my head silently. "I would... I'd feel better up in the room."

We went up the staircase to the third floor and came out onto the landing. "Man, seeing you on the steps this morning I was hoping you had gone out last night and gotten laid for once, but I'm wrong, aren't I?"

Niko let us into our room. I closed and locked the door behind us, then I went over to the window and closed the blinds. Only then did I sit down heavily on my bed.

My roommate set down his amphora on the floor next to his desk. It made a loud thunk as he did so and I jumped at the sound, eyes wide. My heart racing suddenly in my chest, I clawed myself backwards across my bed, not stopping until my back was pressed up against the wall. I think I might have even whimpered.

"Whoa, whoa, sorry!" Niko put his hands up, palms out, his eyes wide. "Fucking hell, dude, you are *tweaking*. Are you on something?"

I shook my head, closing my eyes. It took me a second to respond. "No, I'm not... I'm not on anything." I swallowed. "Except maybe adrenaline?" I opened my eyes back up; Niko had cocked his head at me like a confused German Shepherd. "I, uh... last night I...."

"Last night? Last night you what?" Niko's brow furrowed. "What the fuck happened last night, Ricky?"

I didn't have the words. Instead, I turned so that my left side was facing Niko and lifted the hem of my t-shirt.

He hissed. "Oh my gods! What... what *is* that? Did you get stabbed?"

I shook my head, dropping my shirt back down. "No, not stabbed. Well... kind of. I was... I was shot."

"Shot." Niko sat down on his own bed across from me. "With what? By *who*? Ricky, anyone with any sense wouldn't pick a fight with you unless they had a death wish. What the *fuck* is going on?"

I let out a ragged breath I didn't even know I had been holding. "Okay," I said. "Um. How much do you know about my people's history?"

"What, the draconics? You guys are literally Dragons. Shapeshifting, fire breathing engines of destruction. You're basically apex predators, or you would be if you ate other mythics. You're also, like, supposed to be impossibly hard to kill —"

"Yeah, well, not if we're shot with a Dragonsbane-tipped crossbow bolt."

"Oh no. Was it the Dragonhunters? The, uh, what are they called? The Knights of Saint George?"

I shook my head. "The Georgies don't use Dragonsbane." I paused. "It was the Sidhe."

"The *Sidhe*?" Niko blinked rapidly. "But don't the draconics and the Summer Court have a peace treaty?"

I pulled my knees up to my chest and wrapped my arms around my legs. "Yeah, it turns out when you're Fae nobility, you can do what you like as long as the City Guard don't catch you doing it." I just kind of stared at a spot across at the far wall. "I, uh... I ran, man. Transformed. Tried to fly away." It felt like there was a white-hot coal of electric ice in my throat. "That's when they shot me."

"Fuck, Ricky, I don't know what to say." Niko got up and sat down next to me, putting his hand on my shoulder. "How did you even get away?"

I sighed. "Pure chance," I said. "One of them... oh gods. You know that Sidhe I told you about from my Business Management class? Wyndham Summers?"

"The one who's been giving you shit since the first week of classes?"

I nodded. "It was him. He's... he's the son of an Earl of the Summer Court. They think I insulted them in one of my radio shows because I played 'Goodbye, Earl' that one time. The two of them were out looking for trouble last night, hunting. They found me."

"Wait, where in the City did this happen?"

I closed my eyes again. "It's my fault," I said after a moment. "It was late, and I had gotten off at the wrong stop. It would have taken me an hour to get back to campus if I had gone the regular way... so I cut through Tolon Park."

"Oh, Ricky." My roommate squeezed my shoulder. "That...

that wasn't smart."

"I know that now, dammit!"

Nicky pulled back, visibly shocked at my sudden anger. "Whoa, hey, sorry man!"

I swallowed. "No, I'm sorry. I didn't mean to... fuck." I took a ragged breath. "It's still really raw, you know? I'm only still here because of sheer dumb luck. I hid in the bushes when I heard them coming, but Summers and his dad were about to find my hiding spot. So I tried to escape." I swallowed. "I almost didn't."

"Well, fuck, dude." Niko looked aghast. "I'm so sorry. Are you... are you okay?"

I shook my head. "No, I'm not." I rubbed at the back of my neck. "You know when we transform, anything we're wearing gets destroyed usually? Lost everything. Shredded my clothes, totaled my ID and my phone. Left everything behind, just to get away." My heart sank. "My music, too."

"Your music?"

"Yeah, I had... fuck." I took a second as I found myself suddenly fighting back tears. "I went shopping yesterday, picked up a whole bunch of records and tapes."

"What, for the radio show?"

"Well, kinda. Hold on." I reached over to my desk and picked up the invitation I had received yesterday. I handed it to Niko.

My roommate took it in and grinned. "Aw, shit, Ricky. I heard you had made a splash on Halloween. This is great, congrats!"

"Yeah." I looked away, wiping my face with my good arm. "Except now I don't have the music I needed for that set. It's all gone, probably wrecked when I took off. All I've got to show for it is just a big goddamn hole in my side." I leaned forward, putting my head in my hands and cried.

"Whoa, okay, easy man. You're alive, that counts for something, right?" Niko started rubbing my back as I continued to be racked by sobs. "Come on, I mean I'm sure you could find some of this stuff online if it meant that much to you, right? Like, Spotify, or whatever?" He leaned in; I felt his breath in my ear. "Hey, I know what will cheer you up. Want a blowjob?"

My temper flared. "For *fuck's* sake—" I pushed Niko away from me, probably harder than I should have. "You asshole, this is serious! I almost *died*!"

"Okay, okay, sorry!" Niko backed away, his hands up, palms out. "Shit, I'm sorry Ricky. It was a joke. Well... kinda? I really thought it might help."

I glared at him, wiping my eyes. "Uh... no?"

He shrugged at me. "It was worth a try."

I stared at him in disbelief as an uncomfortable silence unfurled between us.

"You- you..." I choked on my words. "You... *fucking* Satyr." And then, without even realizing what I was doing, I started to laugh.

Niko grinned at me. "See? You're feeling better already."

I scoffed, shaking my head, and then winced as fresh spikes of pain shot up my side. "Yeah, uh, not so much." I paused, considering. "Okay, maybe a little. You can be a real asshole, though."

He shrugged. "You are what you eat, right?"

I laughed again, this time with more bitterness. "Shit, I'm gonna miss you, Niko."

My roommate quirked an eyebrow. "What? What are you talking about?"

"I have to go. I... I guess I came back to start packing up my stuff."

"Wait, what? You're moving out?"

"Moving out, dropping out, what's the difference? I can't be around here if Summers and his dad are gonna hunt me down." I shuddered. "They're not gonna stop. You haven't heard the stories about the Sidhe that I have. They used to hunt us for *sport*, Niko. And they still do. They like to… to turn our hides into capes and cloaks." I swallowed again. "Am I supposed to just go back to class and let Summers gut me like a fish?"

"What? No, Ricky—" Niko sputtered, just staring at me. Then he started laughing himself.

I glared at him. "What the hell, dude? You think that's funny?"

He shook his head, waving me off while he continued to laugh. "Ricky, you're a dumbass. You don't have to drop out. I mean, yeah, I'd love having a single room for the rest of the semester, but you don't have to go anywhere."

"What… what are you talking about?"

"Allora University is *neutral ground*, man." I stared at him, uncomprehending. "You know, like in *Highlander*? No killing fellow mythics allowed on school property. It's been like that since the beginning! Not even a Sidhe noble would dare try to push their luck."

"Wait, what? How is that even… I mean what's to stop them?"

"Uh, Lord Hades Himself?" He stood up, walking over to the window. "The pact is with Him, and He's the one that enforces the rule." He pulled up the blinds. "You think the campus gargoyles are just for show?"

He waved out the window at a gargoyle perched on the roof of the dorm across from us on the quad. It raised a clawed hand and returned the gesture. "See?" He put his fist up to his ear, thumb and pinky extended, and mouthed "call me" to the gargoyle. I didn't know they could blush.

I blinked. "Wait, are you serious?"

"Yup. As long as you're standing on school property, the gargoyles make sure nothing hinky happens. If it does, they report it to the Lord of the Underworld. And you do *not* want to get on his bad side." He shuddered.

"Holy shit." I sank down into my desk chair. "I... I don't have to leave?" I breathed. "I don't have to leave."

I started shaking. A moment later I was crying hard. Big, ugly sobs, the kind I'd imagine you'd cry after learning your cancer was in remission or something.

I felt Niko wrap his arms around me in a hug. "Easy, buddy, it's okay. I know. But you can relax." He let go and stood back up, giving me some space. "Summers can bark at you all he likes – the moment he tries to bite, he's fucked. I wouldn't step inside the same bathroom as him, but in public and on campus? You're totally safe."

I nodded, getting control of myself. "Okay, okay." I sighed, wiping at my eyes again. "Shit, I'm such a wreck. I'm sorry. And... well, thanks."

"Don't worry about it. You've been through the shit." He grinned at me. "Besides, you can always make it up to me, right? About that blowjo—"

I laughed through the tears. "Don't push your luck."

CHAPTER
TWENTY-SIX

I t took a couple of days to get myself back on track. That night, I emailed my parents, telling them I was planning to drop that business management class that I was in with Summers. "Better safe than sorry," I typed out on my laptop, which had thankfully not been with me when I lost everything else. I also asked them to cancel the debit card that had been in my wallet, since I had yet to get a replacement phone. Then, first thing the next morning, after a long and sleepless night, I swallowed my fear and went to the Records office to get a new ID printed up. That way I could stop hanging around the front door of Coindre Hall, waiting for someone to hold it open for me like I was some stereotypical Goblin looking to case the joint.

The rest of the day was really difficult. It took a supreme effort to go to the rest of the classes still on my schedule. I couldn't shake the feeling like I was being watched everywhere I went; every little sound made me flinch, even in light of what Niko told me. When I finally got back to my dorm room, the day was mostly gone – my relief was palpable when I let myself in with my own ID and then closed and locked the door to my dorm room behind me.

Niko had taken off early that day, according to the Post-It he had left on my laptop screen that stated he wouldn't be back until tomorrow afternoon. He had also added a "funny" doodle to the note, depicting, in great detail, what I assumed he would be up to that evening. I sighed and plucked the note off my laptop, crumpling it up and tossing it into the wastepaper basked under my desk. Then, I sat down, woke up my laptop... and stared out the window.

Did I really almost die the other night? My pulse began to speed up. Even as I could see students walking across the quad, I felt like I was back in Tolon Park. Back where a Dragonsbane-tipped crossbow bolt was pointed right at me. Back where a psychotic Sidhe noble had his finger on the trigger.

My side began to ache. I must have pressed my hand against the still-healing wound because the pain intensified suddenly. I hissed, but I also found myself free of the vivid, almost too-real memory that I had found myself inexplicably trapped in.

"Shit." I leaned forward in my desk chair, putting my head between my knees. I took some slow, calming breaths; my pulse slowed, and I sat back up.

My laptop screen was still on, a window for my web browser open from when I last used it. The home page for the school radio station was loaded up.

I sighed and dragged my finger across the touchpad, moving the cursor to where I could close the window. I stopped, considering. *Nah,* I thought. *I should at least check in.*

Instead of closing the window, I scrolled. About a third of the way down the page, the embedded stream for the station began coming out of my laptop's tinny built-in speakers.

"—don't *care* what the administration says, I'm gonna keep calling it Indigenous People's Day and you can't tell me otherwise. For the love of – listen. This college, hell the whole city is built on stolen land. And it started with that d-bag Columbus when his dumb ass tripped over the Taíno in the

Caribbean."

Curious, I kept scrolling until I got to the streaming menu. Under "Now Playing" it listed "Power Hour with Salka Delgado". I let the live stream continue to play as I clicked the Contact link and scrolled until I found the email address for Byron.

I clicked the link, bringing up my email client. I started typing.

Hi Byron,

Could you please pass along my email address to Anagen? I have their cell number but I lost my phone the other night, and I don't have any other contact information for them. I'd like to talk to them about our next shift.

I thanked him and signed the email, clicking send. Then I pulled out one of my textbooks and started doing the reading for tomorrow's class. I was about halfway through the chapter, taking notes on a legal pad, when my computer dinged. I looked up; Byron had written me back.

Ricky:

Sorry to hear about your phone. Hope you didn't lose anything else important. I passed your email address along to Anagen and told them what happened. I'm sure they'll catch up with you soon so you can coordinate next Friday's overnight shift.

Listen, I know I gave you two a hard time the other day but I also went over that night's logs, including all the listener feedback we got from your set. As long as you continue showing up for your shift without being tweaked on Special K like Chauncey was, the spot is yours as long as you want it. Keep up the good work.

Byron

P.S. Stay off the goddamn roof!

I finished reading the email, smiling for the first time since Niko told me I didn't have to drop out of school. I shot off a quick email to my mother, updating her on how I was doing today, before going back to studying as Salka Delgado continued in the background.

"Really, there are so many better heroes for Italian-Americans to look up to. Leonardo, Michelangelo – hell, any of the Ninja Turtles would be a better role model. And that's off the top of my head-"

My computer dinged again. "That was quick," I muttered, looking up and expecting to see an email back from my mother.

It wasn't Mom. Instead, it was from an allora.edu email address. The subject line read "THE FUCK HAPPENED 2 U"

"Ah," I said. "Anagen." I opened the email.

Rick WTF

I txtd u like 3446567 times between yesterday and today and I gotta find out from BYRON that you lost yr phone? Like a dumbass? We better still be on 4 Friday night. U chicken out and I'll haunt yr nightmares

email me back ASAP, nerd

I cradled my face in my hands. "So much empathy," I grumbled.

Another email came in as I was doing so, also from Anagen. This one had a subject line that read *"fuck that, join the station Discord"*

The email body had a hyperlink.

"Ughhhh." *They're not gonna leave you alone until you talk to them, you know that.* I clicked the link with a sigh. My Discord app launched, bringing me to the welcome screen for the station's server. There were half a dozen people logged in now. One read ItsAllGreek2Me.

They messaged me. *Rick?*

I sighed. *Yup. U ok Anagen?*

The "someone is typing" dots showed up in the message window. Then: *how tf did u lose yr phone you malaka?*

OK I gotta know - WTF is a malaka?

UR a malaka, u malaka

I took a slow breath before tapping out my reply. *It's kind of a long story. Lost my wallet and my student ID at the same time if it's any consolation?*

...what. How the hell did u manage that? Were u fucken mugged?

I stared at the message, unsure of what to say. My side began to ache again.

Rick? U still there? Wait... DID u get mugged??

Uh... kinda? No? Yes? It's complicated

Ru fkn srs? Who TF tries to mug a draconic?

Uh well listen I really don't wanna get into it online

OK well

The knot in my chest that I hadn't even noticed form began to subside. *C'mon, just let it go*, I thought.

It's still early. Coffee shop in the SUB should still be open. Get yr scrawny ass over there in 15 mins. I gotta hear this

NO EXCUSES RICK, U left me on read for 4 days, you owe me

I sighed.

Okay, okay, c u in a few

I slumped backward in my desk chair, hands on forehead. It had already begun to get dark out, and I felt my panic begin to rise.

No, dammit. I took a deep breath. *Niko said I'm safe on campus. Not even the Sidhe would risk pissing off Hades.* I breathed out. *I can do this.*

The walk to the Student Union Building wasn't far. A

moderate crowd of students were coming and going as I walked through the halls and around the corner towards the back of the first floor where the café was. A couple more students were there, standing in line at the counter while more were clustered around a few round wooden tables.

I scanned the room for Anagen, catching a glimpse of their Satyr horns at a table in the back near the windows. They saw me and I waved tentatively. They beckoned me over.

Anagen was dressed similarly to how they had been when I met them last week – black midi skirt, combat boots with the soles cut out to accommodate their hooves, and a gray zip-up hoodie over an untucked men's dress shirt. There were two cups of steaming hot cups on the table in front of them. "About time," they said as I sat down. "You can pay me back for the drink."

I leaned forward, giving the cup a sniff. "Uh… I'm not really much of a coffee drinker? But thanks?"

They waved my statement away. "Whatever. You gonna fill me in or what?"

I did. Anagen's eyes keep getting wider and wider until I felt like they were about to pop from their sockets and roll off the table. Finally, at the end of my tale, they just kind of stared at me for a moment.

"Okay," they began slowly. "Let me get this straight. You got an invitation from the Palace to spin some records, so you panicked and bought a whole mess of music from a vintage record store? And then you literally almost died trying to get that music back to your dorm? Because you pissed off the one Sidhe in the City that has a son in one of your classes? And then you tried to cut through Tolon Park, *a place Sidhe love to hang out,* in the middle of the night?"

I winced. "Uh… yeah. Y-yeah, that's pretty much it."

"And then you had to leave everything behind to escape and *still* got shot?"

I nodded.

They shook their head. "You're a godsdamned idiot, you know that?"

I wrinkled my nose at them. "H-hey, I almost *died*, you know!"

"Yup, I know." They drained their coffee cup. "Listen, I'm glad you're okay, but your mom was right - stay the hell out of Tolon Park at night unless you want your head mounted on some Sidhe's wall. And whatever those two assholes were hunting, I'd better report in about it. Sounds like they were poaching." They swirled the dregs of their cup, looking down at it as they did so. "You know, if you want some help figuring out what to play for your set at the Palace, I could give you a hand. We can get together Thursday night if you want?" Their eyes flicked back up, over the rim of their cup.

I smiled, relief flooding into me. "Are you serious? I need all the help I can get!"

Anagen nodded. "All right, then. When and where?"

"Hm." I scratched the back of my head. "Maybe the library? Thursday is Netflix and Chill Night in the dorm. It gets crowded with his polycule in there."

"Yeah, that sounds like Niko. 7:30?"

"Yeah, let me put it in my-" I went to grab my phone before realizing it wasn't on me. "Uh... maybe I should write it down." I looked around for a scrap of paper.

"Oh, for fuck's sake, Rick." Anagen plunged a hand into their bag and came back out with a Sharpie. "You better get your phone shit sorted. Here, gimme your hand."

I blinked. "Huh?"

"Your hand, Dragon King. Give it." They waited. "Oh, the hell with it. Come here!" They reached over and grabbed my right hand, pulling the cap off the Sharpie with their teeth. "And don't move!" they added as I tried to pull my hand back away. They leaned over, scribbling away with the marker on the back of my hand. "There," they said, letting go and straightening up.

I pulled it back, looking down at it. There, in big block letters, was a single sentence: *Thursday 7:30 library. Also, I am a big fat idiot.* "Gee, thanks," I said, looking back up.

Anagen had re-capped their Sharpie and was stuffing it back in their bag "Well, I think we're done here," they said brightly. "Guess I'll see you then, Rick." They stood up, sweeping their empty cup off the table. "Keep your scaly ass outta trouble until Thursday."

CHAPTER TWENTY-SEVEN

I spent the walk back to Coindre Hall with my hands jammed deep into the pockets of my hoodie, ears burning. The damn Sharpie wouldn't come off, no matter how much I scrubbed, either - I finally gave up when the scales on the back of my hand started throbbing. Short of taking a deep breath and scorching them off, I couldn't think of a solution, and the last thing I wanted was to explain to my RA how the fire sprinklers in the boys' bathroom got set off while I was in there.

Instead, I decided to finish studying and get some sleep. The room was incredibly quiet to the point where I found it nearly impossible to relax. I hadn't realized how used I'd gotten to Niko's snoring. That, and I found my mind racing as I lay there in the dark, thoughts returning again and again to that night in Tolon Park.

The silence was so maddening that I finally opened YouTube up on my laptop and queued up one of those videos that was nothing but hours of nature sounds. It took what felt like forever, but it finally seemed to do the trick; I drifted off somewhere around 1 in the morning.

I began to dream. I found myself trapped in an endless labyrinth of yellow corridors, lit by buzzing fluorescent lights and carpeted in a dingy beige. Something, or someone, was chasing me, getting closer and closer with each moment. It wasn't until I felt hot breath on the back of my neck that I finally woke up, heart hammering against my ribcage like a prisoner chipping away at their cell.

I sat up in bed. The room was lit only by the dim glow of my laptop screen as the video continued playing, accompanied by the sound of a distant seashore.

"Fucking hell," I murmured, picking an errant t-shirt up off the floor and wiping the cold sweat off my face. *I'm never gonna get any rest if this keeps up.*

I stood up and walked over to the window, pulling the blinds up. Light from the streetlamps streamed through, bathing the campus below in an orange glow. I cracked the window open, letting a cool breeze into the room, and just stared out into the night, across the silhouettes of Allora's skyline.

Another breeze blew in, causing me to shiver. I closed the window and dropped the blinds, plunging the room back into darkness, my only companion the pre-recorded cries of seagulls and the steady thrum of the surf. *Enough with the nature sounds*, I thought, sitting down in my desk chair and stopping the playback. *Maybe something else...*

Not for the first time that day, I really missed having my phone. I could have just loaded up Spotify, plunked a couple of earbuds in, and found something to listen to. Instead, I had to load it up on my laptop and start scrolling through my playlists for something, anything, that would drown out the doomsaying voices in my head.

I wasn't having much luck. The clock in the corner of my laptop screen read 4:23 and my eyes were starting to feel bleary when I finally found something – *Argybargy* by Squeeze. "Well, it's worth a try," I murmured. I clicked play, stood up, and got back into bed as the first track began playing.

They do it down on Camber Sands

They do it at Waikiki

Lazing about the beach all day,

At night the crickets creepy

I let go of a deep breath I didn't even know I was holding, settling into my pillow and listening. I wasn't proud of it, but listening to this album always relaxed me, even if it sounded like a collection of 80s sitcom theme songs.

"Pulling mussels from a shell," I hummed, terribly off-tune, as the first track began to fade. By the time Glenn Tillbrook started singing "Another Nail in My Heart," I had finally passed out.

The next couple of days were routine, if you considered "watching over your shoulder like a harp seal looking out for a hungry orca" routine. I had decided to drop my managerial accounting class, but I still wasn't taking any chances. Being told that school was neutral ground and trusting that Summers wouldn't try to pull something anyway were two very different things. In practice, it meant a lot of sticking to public places with plenty of foot traffic. Sure, humans might not register what was really going on, but there were enough mythics on campus that if I wasn't in sight of one of the gargoyles at least I felt like there were plenty of potential witnesses.

By the time Thursday rolled around, I was thoroughly exhausted. Part of me wanted to cancel on Anagen but I didn't want to ghost them; I felt like I owed them at least an explanation. I didn't want to do it over email or Discord, either; I hadn't gotten around to replacing my phone yet, since that would have required venturing off campus. I figured I could do it early Saturday morning.

So, it was about a quarter past seven when I shuffled in out of the early November darkness and walked through the doors of the school library, feet dragging and eyes bleary. Ellen was at the front desk, half-heartedly retrieving books from a bin on the other side of the book return slot and handing them to Naveen, who was scanning them in one at a time.

Ellen saw me first, her face lighting up. She tapped Naveen on the arm with a copy of *One Hundred Years of Solitude* and pointed me out. He waved and took the book from Ellen.

I waved back. "Hey, guys. Slow night?"

"Yeah, pretty much." Naveen scanned in the Márquez book and set it down to his right. "Thursdays are always pretty boring."

"You okay, Ricky? You look about as bad as I feel." Ellen cocked her head at me, giving me an appraising look.

I shrugged. "It's been... uh... a pretty nuts few days."

"Well judging by the bags under your eyes, it sure looks th–"

"Ellen, for fuck's sake." Naveen took another book from his co-worker. "I know misery loves company but leave him alone. You're the one who decided to go out to that frat party last night."

"Oh my *God* you're so fucking boring." She rolled her eyes and leaned towards me, dropping her voice to a conspiratorial whisper. "Nav's idea of a fun time is making sure all the microfiche are rewound tightly." She turned back to him. "You know, just because you don't drink doesn't mean you can't at least *try* to be fun."

I laughed despite myself. "Yeah, uh, not really the partying type either." I paused, looking back towards the main doors. "Truth is I, uh... well, I got mugged a few nights ago. Lost my wallet, my phone, and a whole bunch of other stuff I had been carrying. Mostly stuff for the radio show."

Naveen winced, putting the book he was about to scan down on the desk. "Damn, are you serious?"

"Yeah, shit, Ricky, are you okay? That sounds fucking

awful." Ellen's eyes went wide, true concern creeping into her voice.

"Yeah, uh..." I rubbed the back of my neck and gave a little shrug. "It sucked. But I'm okay." It was true, more or less. My side had healed up pretty well over the last couple of days, only occasionally giving me a twinge when I bent or twisted too quickly. "I, uh, I don't r-recommend it."

"Yeah, I'll bet." Ellen reached out and put her hand on top of mine. "I'm here if you wanna talk about it." She patted it a couple of times and then left it there.

"Uh.... thanks?" I gave Ellen what I hoped was my least awkward smile. I went to pull my hand away but she exerted a surprising amount of downward pressure, pinning me to the desk.

"Seriously, anything you need. Over a coffee, couple beers, a bowl or two - you name it." She ran her fingertips down the back of my hand, looking down at it. "Uh... why does your hand say 'I'm a big fat idiot?'"

"Because he is one. Right, Rick?"

I jumped at the sound of Anagen's voice behind me. Pulling my hand free of Ellen's grasp, I turned to see them standing there, head cocked to the side, arms crossed. They were dressed in a pleated burgundy midi skirt and their usual men's dress shirt, though they had it in a French tuck this evening. A gray herringbone knit scarf worn over a black faux leather jacket finished the ensemble.

I swallowed, relieved to be free of Ellen's grasp. "Oh, uh, hey?" I looked past them. There was a large tote bag at their feet. "What's that stuff...?"

"In a sec. Aren't you gonna introduce me?" They smiled at Naveen and Ellen, showing more teeth than usual. "Hi, I'm Anagen. I work with Rick at the radio station." They patted my shoulder. "He's a good boy, if a little green. Halfway decent taste in music, at least, anyway."

"Oh, uh, yeah sorry, this is Naveen and Ellen." I was slightly shocked at the sound of my own voice. *Why do I sound so nervous?*

"Nice to meet you," Naveen said. He nudged Ellen.

"Oh, uh, hi," she said gamely. "I love your makeup," she added.

"Thank you!" Anagen grinned wider, then turned back to me. "I like them. You can keep them."

I snorted. "Didn't realize I needed your permission, but okay?" I looked around, spying a nearby empty table. "Want to set up over there?"

"Yeah, that looks good. I'll meet you there." They turned, skirt swishing, and picked up the bag behind them.

"We're gonna work on some stuff for the radio station," I said in response to Naveen's questioning gaze. Ellen, for some reason, seemed more interested in watching Anagen walk to the table.

"Right, well, have fun," Naveen said. He picked up the book on the desk and scanned it in. "Back to work for us too I guess."

I nodded and turned, walking over to the table. Anagen had sat down and had crossed their legs, arranging their skirt tastefully. They brushed some dirt off one of their hooves. "She's cute," they said, as I sat down.

"Huh? Who, Ellen? Yeah, I guess so?" I was puzzled. The vibe was definitely off, but I couldn't exactly put my finger on it. "I'm really, uh..."

I looked back over my shoulder, catching Ellen looking at the two of us surreptitiously. She turned red and immediately buried herself in pulling books out of the return bin.

I turned back, dropping my voice a little. "I like Ellen," I said, shrugging, "but pretty sure not the way she wants me to?" I gave Anagen an awkward look.

"Oh yeah?" Anagen tugged on one of their horns absently.

"Uh-huh." *Yeah, no, the vibe is definitely off today.* I cleared my throat. "So, uh, you gonna tell me what's in the bag?"

"Ah, I guess I should, yeah." They reached down and hoisted it up, laying it down on the tabletop with a heavy thunk. "Got you a little something."

I cocked my head at them. "What do you mean?"

They began opening the bag, angling it away from me so I couldn't see what was inside. "Well, after you told me what happened the other night out at Tolon Park, I was so fucking annoyed with you that I just couldn't sleep. So, I went for a walk."

I felt my ears begin to burn. "Oh. Uh, s-sorry?" I felt that all-too familiar lump of ice in my chest beginning to form. "I duh-didn't mean to...?"

"Yeah, well, thinking of you getting almost made into a hashtag by Sidhe and Son really made me mad, you know?" They started rooting around in their back. "Plus, it turns out half a dozen Haudenosaunee nature spirits were murked the same night. I mean, come on, how are we supposed to *share* the park with the Sidhe if they're gonna treat it like their own personal Fleshlight? Blood doesn't make for very good lube, I'll have you know."

"Ugh, seriously?" I grimaced. "Thanks, now that's an image that'll be living in my head rent-free tonight."

"No problem." They pulled something out of the bag and laid it on the table. "And you're welcome for that, too."

I looked down. It was a muddy, beaten-up phone. The case was chipped in half a dozen places and the front screen had a spiderweb of cracks across it.

It was also mine.

"Holy shit," I said, picking it up. "Anagen, did you find my phone!?" I turned it over in my hands, incredulous.

"Yeah, I did. You really fucked up a whole section of the jogging path, you know. It looked like a tornado touched down in the middle of the park." I tried to turn on the phone, but nothing happened. "Oh, yeah, your battery's probably dead. I figure that if it's wrecked you could probably yank the SIM card out of it when you get a replacement. That way I won't have to update your phone number."

I laughed, almost wildly. "I can't believe – Anagen, thank you. You didn't have to do this." I looked up at them. "I mean, it's just a phone—"

"Yeah, I know, but I told you, I was pissed off and I couldn't sleep. Besides, that's not all I found." They reached into the bag again and pulled out a fat stack of LPs, setting them down on the table. They then held up the bag and jiggled it, the sound of plastic against plastic coming from inside. "Found a buncha CDs and tapes, too."

"Oh, my gods." I set my phone down and picked up the first record from the stack. It was a little dusty but otherwise seemed intact. "I can't believe you found them." I looked back up at them. "I... shit. Thank you. I really mean it."

They grinned at me. "You're welcome. Call it payback for making you climb that radio mast."

I sat back in my chair, looking back down at the stack of LPs. I laughed, shaking my head. "You... you really just saved my ass, man."

"Oh my god, Rick. How many times do I have to tell you? Not. A. Man." They sounded exasperated, but I could see they were grinning at me while they said it. "Besides I can't exactly let you make yourself a laughingstock at the Palace, can I? Have you gone down there and talked to Amelia yet?"

"What? Uh, no, I... well that kinda ended up on the back

burner after, uh... you know. Almost getting killed."

"Yeah, well now you've got your shit back, so no excuses. You should go down there Saturday, after sunset. Normally the bouncers would take one look at you and make you go to the end of the line, but if you still have that invitation, they'll let you in."

I winced. "Yeah, I, uh... I'm really worried about that. I don't know if I'm cut out for a live dance set."

Anagen blinked at me. "Wait, what? What makes you think you're gonna be spinning dance records?"

"Uh, because it's the Palace of Wisdom?" I gestured with my hands palm-up. "It's the biggest dance club in the City?"

Anagen closed their eyes and pinched the bridge of their nose. "Oh, for fuck's sake – Rick. You *maláka*. They're not gonna want you playing dance tracks."

"What? I don't understand."

"It's the *Palace*, Rick. They make their own rules. Yeah, they play plenty of dance music but most nights they cultivate a *vibe*. I haven't talked to Neira about it, she's busy as hell, but—"

"Neira?"

"The club's number-one DJ. She's a Nymph, older than shit. Was probably Orpheus' Music Theory professor. Rumor has it that she was actually an attendant to Euterpe and Terpsichore. She'll be the one signing off on your set. And I know for a *fact* that she's got a soft spot for New Wave." Anagen looked at me. "Rick, you okay? You look, uh, a little green."

"Uh, yeah... y-yeah, I'm okay." I stood up shakily. "Could you, uh, give me a second? I think I need to go throw up."

CHAPTER TWENTY-NINE

I didn't actually throw up. Getting weaned on fish heads kind of gives you an iron stomach, after all. Still, I did need a second to breathe in the bathroom stall. Elbows on thighs, head between knees, hands interlaced on the back of the neck. It's supposed to increase blood flow to the brain or something.

Whatever the reason, it seemed to work. After a few minutes, the thought of having to impress a millennia-old Nymph with my musical taste subsided from abject terror to just moderate anxiety, tolerable enough to stand up. I splashed some cool water on my face and scrubbed at it with a paper towel, then looked at myself in the mirror.

I'd seen better. Ellen had been right about the bags under my eyes. My hair was wild, and even my scales seemed dull. I blinked, wondering when it had been since I'd taken my last shower. *Not since that morning at Mom and Dad's...?*

I shook my head, balling up the paper towel and tossing it in the trash. "I gotta get my shit together," I murmured. With one last deep breath, I pushed the door to the bathroom open and walked back into the library.

Anagen was leaning back in their chair, scrolling on their phone. They looked up as I sat back down, a silent question on their face.

"Hey," I said gamely. "Sorry about that. I'm, uh... I feel better now?"

Anagen nodded, their face inscrutable. "Cool. You wanna work on some stuff, then?" They set their phone down.

"Uh, yeah, that'd be great." I pulled over the stack of LPs and spread them out along the table, checking each one's dust jacket for damage. "I think you saved just about all of them."

They shrugged. "Well, I found what I could."

"I can't believe you found *any* of them, honestly. I was, uh, literally in f-flight mode at that point."

"Honestly, Rick, it really wasn't difficult. I just asked the forest where your stuff was and the trees just... *led* me there. Forest spirit, remember? *I fýsi den kánei típota áchrista.*"

I cocked my head. "That wasn't Sigil, was it?"

"Nope. It's Greek. Aristotle. 'Nature does nothing uselessly.' The forest has answers for everything, if you just know how to ask."

"Wait, are you actually from Greece? You don't have even a trace of an accent."

"That's because I'm not. I'm from Toledo. I did do 'a year' in Greece, though." They made quotations marks with their fingers. "That was when I transitioned."

"Transitioned?" I felt like I was increasingly getting in over my head. "I don't get what you mean."

Anagen sighed. "Look, I was born human, okay? I, uh, 'joined the band' in sophomore year while I was in Thessaloniki. To let the process take its course. Horns, hooves, other, uh, things. Rushing that type of transformation can be painful or even dangerous."

Realization dawned. "Oh. Oh!" I could feel heat rushing up

the sides of my neck. "I'm sorry, I didn't know – I mean I knew that humans can Awaken into their mythic heritage sometimes but, uh..." I trailed off. "I guess I don't know much about Satyrs, huh?"

Anagen smirked. "Well, I'm sure I don't know shit about fuck when it comes to Dragon society so I guess we're even. Anyway, let's go over your playlist ideas, okay?"

Over the next half hour, Anagen definitely took the training wheels off. We got into more than one argument about music selection, with them really pushing me to justify my choices at a couple of places. In retrospect, it felt like they were prepping me for my conversation with Neira. Finally, though, we had not just hashed out another 2-hour set for the next night but a whole three pages of notes on creating a "curated experience" at the Palace.

Anagen's phone beeped. They looked down at it. "Welp, that's me," they said. "I better get my shit together if I want to catch the UTA out to the Palace without having to wait another hour."

I looked up at the clock on the wall. "Oh, yeah, it is getting late, huh? You, uh, you live at the Palace?"

"Nah, I live in Arcadia. Gotta go through the Palace to get there. Still cheaper than the dorms." They smirked. "Not everyone around here is Dragon royalty, Rick."

"Hey, that's n-not—" I stopped and thought about it. "Yeah, I guess you're right, huh?"

"'Course I am." They stood, picking up their jacket and shrugging into it. "So, I'll see you tomorrow night, then?"

I nodded, standing up as well. "Yeah. And, uh, thanks. Really. You didn't have to."

Anagen laughed. "Of course I did! I can't have you freaking out at the Palace. Besides, I want to borrow that Adverts album later." They paused, smiled, and then said, "But you're welcome.

See you later, Rick." They turned and walked off, skirt swishing.

It was high time I got back to Coindre Hall, so I started putting all the music Anagen had rescued for me back into the bag. After I had done, I stuffed my chewed-up looking phone into my pants, determined to see if it would still turn on once I plugged it into its charger in my dorm room.

I stopped by the front desk on my way out to say good night to Naveen and Ellen. They shared a glance between each other. Ellen's face slit in a shit-eating grin. "So, uh, what was all *that* about?"

I shook my head. "All what?"

Ellen laughed, putting her head in her hands. Naveen rolled his eyes. "Ricky. They're totally into you."

"What? Who, Anagen?" I blinked. "No, that's... that's fucking dumb."

Naveen arched an eyebrow at me. "Yeah, okay Ricky." Ellen was doubled over, wheezing. I couldn't tell if she was laughing or crying. "Anyway, see you around."

I shook my head again. "You guys are nuts," I said. I walked out into the night, the dry, fallen leaves crunching under my borrowed New Balances.

The moon was low on the horizon, partially obscured by the now mostly barren trees surrounding the school. Thankfully, there were still some students milling about, so I wasn't too worried about running into You-Know-Who this evening.

As I walked, I grew increasingly perplexed about what Naveen had just told me. *He's way off*, I thought. *There's no way. Besides, I'm not interested anyway.*

I wasn't lying to myself, either. I'd never really felt anything I could ever call "attraction" when it came to someone else. Not physical, anyway. That hadn't changed. And considering that Anagen was a Satyr, that kind of seemed like a deal-breaker if my roommate was any indication.

Oh, shit. I ground to a halt in the middle of the path. *My roommate.* I'd forgotten that it was movie night for Niko's polycule. I sighed, not looking forward to camping out in the hallway to my dorm room because there was a sock on the door again.

I scratched my forehead, thinking. The dining hall was nearby, and there was a computer lab on the first floor that I was pretty sure stayed open late. I could chill there for a while. Maybe borrow a charger and see if I could bring my phone back from the dead. *It's worth a try*, I thought, hefting my bag and setting back off.

I was in luck; the dining hall was closed at this time of night, but the computer lab was still open and mostly abandoned. I slipped inside and made a beeline for a study table, sitting myself down and pulling out my battered phone.

The table had a power bank inset in its top with a couple of different charging cords hard-wired into it. I picked through them and found the one that matched my phone, plugged it in, and crossed my fingers.

Nothing happened.

I sighed. *Figures*, I thought. *Well, maybe I can get the SIM card out.* I flipped it over, preparing to peel the cover off my phone when it buzzed suddenly. Startled, I turned it screen-side up and was greeted by a charging icon, though it was a little hard to see through the half a dozen cracks running through the glass.

I grinned. *Lucky break*, I thought, setting the phone down gingerly. I let it charge for about half a minute before picking it up again and holding down the power button.

The screen flashed. It began going through its startup sequence, and before long I was staring at my lock screen. "Well, shit," I murmured, pressing my thumb to the fingerprint reader.

It kicked back an error message. I tried again to no avail. Brow furrowed, I took a corner of the hem of my hoodie, rubbed the bezel of my phone, and tried one more time. Finally, it unlocked, the screen flooding with missed message notifications.

I tapped at the phone, running the pad of my finger along the touchscreen. The response was sluggish, but it did seem to work well enough. Still, I would likely need a replacement sometime soon. For now, though...

I began writing out a text to my mother but thought better of it. We really hadn't talked much since she found out about what had probably happened to Uncle Lance. I figured I'd give her a little more space. Instead, I texted Dad:

Anagen found my phone in Tolon Park! They gave it back to me tonight. And it even still works! Kinda. They found a bunch of the music I left behind, too. Talk about good luck!

A few moments later and my phone buzzed as my father's reply came in.

That's great! You're lucky you have them watching your back like that. Maybe you should ask them to go with you when you go to the Palace? You're still going, right?

I thought about it for a second, wondering if it was a good idea or not after what Naveen and Ellen said. *Is that something I'm comfortable asking them?*

I started tapping again. *Maybe? I was gonna maybe ask Dags but that might be a better idea*

I sent the message, then decided to bite the bullet.

How's Mom?

It took a minute or so for the reply to come back.

About as well as you'd expect. Old wounds reopening. She'll be okay though, don't worry about her. You need to take care of yourself, too. She told me about how you met Morri. I'm sorry we didn't tell you about her, Ricky. It wasn't my place, you know?

I sighed, not even knowing where to start with that.

Well, I guess the cat's out of the bag, now. I'll talk to Mom about that some other time, she's got enough on her mind. Anyway it's getting late, I just wanted to let you know what's up. I'll TTYL. Love you both

I checked the time on my phone, squinting through the cracked screen. It was probably late enough that movie night had broken up for the evening, so I unplugged the phone and stuffed it into my pocket. Reassured by the familiar weight there, I left the computer lab.

It turned out my hunch was right - I wasn't greeted by a sock on the door. Relieved, I keyed my way into the room and found Niko perched on the windowsill, having removed the screen. He was dangling his feet over the edge, dressed in an open silk robe and nothing else, taking a drag from a cigarette.

"Heya, Ricky," Niko said languidly. He grinned at me and took a deep drag, blowing a plume of blue smoke out the open window.

I wrinkled my nose. "Niko, the room smells like musk ox and bleach. And you know we're not supposed to be smoking inside."

"Why do you think I took the screen out?" He inhaled, pinching the smoke between his thumb and forefinger. It sparked as he did so. "Want a drag? It's a clove. You might like it." He turned to me to offer it, his robe displaying his pride and joy. Again.

I waved him off, turning my head away. "Uh, nah, I'm good. I don't need any help breathing smoke. You wanna put that away? It's like baby's arm holding an apple."

"Prude." He wrapped the robe around him and belted it. "There, feel better?"

"Slightly, thank you." I sat down on my bed, setting the bag gingerly to the floor. "Have a good time with the squad tonight?"

"As always." He flicked some ash out of the window. "What's in the bag?"

"Oh, you're not gonna believe this." I pulled my banged-up phone from my pocket and brandished it. "Anagen met me at the library and dropped off as much of my stuff that they could find at Tolon Park. My phone even still works!" I set it down on my desk.

Niko nodded. "Yup, that's Anagen all over. They're the Herald, after all. Not surprised."

I cocked my head at him, pausing as I bent to take off my shoes. "Herald?"

"Yeah, you know how every Satyr has a specific role in our culture?"

"Uh, no? Was I supposed to?"

Niko rolled his eyes. "Well, I guess not. I mean it's not a secret but we don't really go around talking about it too much with other mythics I guess. But yeah, satyr society is stratified by role. Healer, warrior, so on." He took another drag and then flicked it out the window. "Anagen's role is Herald. They go everywhere, talk to everyone. Wading into Tolon Park to find your stuff is par for the course."

I wrinkled my nose. "Dude, that was still lit."

Niko slid off the windowsill, bending down to pick up the screen. "It's fine, it's a wet night. Gimme a hand with this?"

"Yeah, gimme a sec." I pulled off my other shoe and stood up, helping Niko guide the screen back into the window. "But what does being Herald have to do with going and getting my stuff?"

"Well, you talked to them about what happened the other

day, didn't you?"

"Yeah. They called me a big fat idiot for cutting through Tolon Park in the middle of the night."

"Well, if the shoe fits..." Niko pushed on the screen experimentally and then nodded. "Yeah, that's in, thanks. No, the thing is that they listened to what you said. And, well, they decided to do something about it. That's not really a Herald thing, though, that's more of an Anagen thing."

I sat back down on the bed. "Oh, so they weren't just kind of doing what they're expected to do?"

"What?" Niko snorted, flopping down on his own bed, draping his robe across him in what I can only assume he thought was in an alluring way. "No, of course not. You're not a Satyr. They didn't have any obligation to go out of their way. Like I said, if Anagen did that, it's because they wanted to."

I rubbed at my forehead, taking in this new information. "Huh, okay."

"But that's Anagen to a tee. You know they're not like some other Satyrs, right?"

"Well, I know they're nonbinary and that they were born human, but—"

Niko shook his head. "No, well yes, but not just that. They're different because they're not..." He paused. "Uh, how do I put this.... You know how we've got a rep for being walking erections?"

I glared at him. "Noooo. Really?"

Niko rolled his eyes. "Honestly, you don't know what you're missing."

"Nah, I'm good, dude."

"Suit yourself." He shrugged. "But to the point, not all Satyrs are polyamorous pansexuals. Sure, plenty of us are, considering 'pan' is right in the name. But there's all kinds of sexualities and gender expressions in Satyr culture. Room for everyone, no matter what floats their boat. And it's never a guessing game, either. We've literally got it written on our skin." He waved his hand. The air prickled as he did so; his arms and chest shimmered, and an intricate display of tattoos, many of which were written in Sigil, appeared over his body.

Niko grinned. "Nice, right? We usually keep 'em hidden when we're in mixed company, since humans can read Sigil and we don't always want to advertise. You ever get a glimpse of Anagen's tats, you'll know what I'm talking about – they keep them glamoured so that only the designs are visible, not the words."

"Huh." I could see, quite clearly, that many of Niko's tattoos described his likes and dislikes in the bedroom. I squinted, translating aloud. *"Fetishization of pocket-sized monstrous creatures...* what the hell does that mean?"

Niko winked at me. "Can't figure it out?"

I scratched my head for a moment before it dawned on me. "Bahamut's balls. Is that a *Pokémon* fetish?"

"Gotta catch 'em all, baby." Laughing, he waved his hand again. His tattoos faded.

I put my head in his hands. "Information I didn't need." I picked my head up, looking at Niko in puzzlement. "But what does this have to do with Anagen?"

"Well, they're actually *not* a walking hard-on. Have you ever heard of the term demisexual?"

I shook my head. "I don't think so?"

"Being demi means that there has to be a romantic bond with someone before you feel sexual attraction towards them. One of Anagen's tats makes that clear. Like I said, it's rare but not unheard of."

"Huh. Well, that explains a few things, I guess. Like why

they didn't flash me the moment they were alone in a room with me. Unlike *some* Satyrs I won't mention." I gave Niko a mock glare. That had been an interesting first day on campus, to be sure.

Niko laughed, getting up off the bed. "Hey, I just call 'em like I see 'em. I like that nervous twink energy you've got." He picked his towel up off the hook behind the door. "Anyway, I gotta grab a shower and then head out for the night. If I don't see you tomorrow, good luck with the radio show. And, you know, everything else."

"All right, thanks Niko. I appreciate it. Hey, before you go, you never said what your role was?"

"Who, me? Healer. I'm pre-med, you know. I've always liked exploring other people's anatomy, after all." He winked at me, grabbed his shower caddy, and clomped out the door.

CHAPTER THIRTY

The talk I'd had with Niko certainly gave me plenty to think about, but it sure didn't clear up any of my confusion about whether Anagen was interested in me or not. The whole thing was mostly academic considering I didn't feel that way about them, but then again that wasn't really different considering how I didn't feel "that way" about anyone. Still, Anagen had become more than just the person I worked with at the radio station, especially after the stunt we pulled on Halloween night, all to keep the broadcast on the air. Combine that with how they went hunting for my phone and the music I left behind, and, well, they had become a friend. And a pretty good one. Even if they seemed to enjoy torturing me.

I guess the one thing I was worried about was that if Anagen *did* have feelings for me, and I didn't return them, whether that meant bad news for this friendship. It wasn't like the situation with Ellen. I knew she had a crush on me – even *I* noticed some things, after all – but my strict policy of "don't engage" seemed to be keeping me out of trouble so far. Naveen did his best to keep her in line whenever I visited the library, which helped as well. On top of that, well, Ellen was human. I couldn't exactly be myself around her.

I kept thinking about it as I got ready for bed that evening. Having people in my life that I could be honest with – fellow mythics, people who I could look at as friends – was kinda new for me.

I plugged my newly-resurrected phone into its charger and crawled into bed, still feeling unsure of what to do. Or even if there was anything that I *should* do. What I did know for sure, though, is that I was grateful that mythics like Niko and Anagen were in my life.

The next day was cold and overcast, with blustery wind gusts pulling the last few leaves that had been clinging to the trees off from their branches. They danced through the sky and skittered dryly along Allora University's footpaths. Campus was mostly deserted, considering that only clueless freshmen like myself had signed up for classes that met on Fridays. For the rest of the collegiate world, the weekend had started the night before.

The wind was like a baptism against my scales that morning, bringing the slightest hint of sea air mingled with the crisp, sharp scent of the slowly decomposing leaves and grass, mixed with the smoky flavor of the shawarma stand two blocks from campus. Tying everything together was the ever-present buzz of car exhaust from nearby streets. Oh, and wet garbage. Gotta love the City.

It wasn't that undercurrent of rotting trash that was bothering me today, though. It wasn't tonight's broadcast, either - despite everything that Naveen, Ellen, and Niko had brought up last night, that was far from my mind. Not even the prospect of having to go down to the Palace and meet with a Nymph older than most human civilizations was bothering me at that moment. What was on my mind right then was that I was currently walking to my Managerial Accounting class that morning. I had to get paperwork signed by Professor Trevanche to finalize my withdrawal.

I had already missed my chance earlier that week, as I had chickened out when it came to seeing Summers in class again. All the ironclad security in the world provided by gargoyles and overseen by Hades himself hadn't been enough to make me want to rub elbows with someone who had literally tried to kill me just a few days ago. The withdrawal period for the semester was almost over, though, so unless I wanted it to tank my GPA, I had to tough it out.

Easier said than done, I thought to myself, walking up the steps to Old Main and slinking down the corridor towards my classroom. I slowed down as I drew closer to the open door, craning my neck to get a better look inside; it seemed to be about two-thirds full, typical for a Friday morning. So far, the desk where Summers habitually sat was empty.

I let out a breath I hadn't realized I'd been holding and walked inside, making my way to my own seat near the window. I figured I would talk to Trevanche after class was over out of respect for him. Seemed like I owed him that much. Wasn't his fault that humans went gaga whenever Sidhe turned on the charm around them.

The hawthorn tree outside was mostly bare of leaves at this point, its windswept branches little more than thorns and clusters of small, dark red berries. I didn't spare it more than a glance, though, as I sank down into the desk chair and pulled out my textbook, trying my hardest to not act as terrified as I felt. I had to stop myself from turning to look at the open doorway every time I heard another student come in.

Finally, Professor Trevanche came in and started class. I was tense throughout, but by the end Summers had still not shown up; the knot in my stomach began to undo itself. By the end of the class period, I wasn't quite enjoying myself considering the subject matter, but at least I felt somewhat less like there was a target on my back.

The class ended and I packed up, eager to get back to my dorm room and begin preparing for my show this evening. I asked Trevanche to sign my paperwork, slipped out the door, and walked down the hallway, losing myself in the hum of the crowd of students as we all shuffled towards the front door.

I had decided to ask Anagen if they would come with me to the Palace this weekend to help me navigate whatever strange social waters might be behind those velvet ropes. I figured I'd treat her to dinner at Uncle Dave's diner beforehand, maybe stop by Morrigan's if there was enough time—

Distracted as I was, I never saw it coming. Someone grabbed the back of my hoodie, yanking me off balance and backwards into the first-floor men's bathroom. I let out a panicked squawk as I was pushed roughly to the ground and surrounded by a half-dozen figures. They were all tall, lithe, and with upswept, pointed ears.

I tried to scramble to my feet. "Hey, what the fu—" My world exploded in pain as someone struck me, hard, across the face. Literal stars sparked across my vision. I could taste something acidic at the back of my throat. I looked down; drops of silvery blood were dripping on the bathroom tiles in front of me, landing on a single pointed tooth. It had transformed to full size after being knocked from my jaw.

"You're not going anywhere, wyrm." I looked up blearily, still barely comprehending what was going on. "You might have gotten away last time, you slippery little shit, but now I've got you."

"S-Summers?" I squinted up at him, then winced. I put a hand up to my throbbing jaw. My tongue found the raw socket where my tooth had been. "Y-you can't... campus is supposed to be n-nuh—"

"Neutral ground?" He smirked, dropping down on his haunches. "Oh, we would never, *ever* seek to violate the terms of that agreement, would we, boys?" A malevolent titter from the Sidhe's cronies washed over me like a riptide. "It's not *our* fault if clumsy Ruh-ruh-Ricky tripped on his way into the *bathroom*, now is it?"

Summers reached down, plucking my tooth from the tile. "You can't hide forever, you sneaky little shit. Nice trick, making me think you were a full White, by the way. Imagine my surprise when you breathed *fire* at us. I forgot you lizards can cross-breed." He tucked the tooth into a pants pocket and stood up, dusting his hands off. "You should really be more careful, Ricky. You don't want to get into any more... accidents." He jerked a head at his coterie and they all filed out, laughing.

The door banged loudly as the last one left, making me jerk and bite my tongue. I moaned as the pain in my jaw redoubled. "Fuuuuck," I mumbled.

It took me a minute to get back to my feet. I dragged myself over to the sink and looked at myself in the mirror. *Yup, big fat lip and blood all over my clothes. Great.* Gingerly, I washed my face and got as much blood as I could off my shirt, pausing when I smelled something burning. Turning around, I saw the spot where my blood had landed had turned black and begun smoking.

"Shit," I said, panicking. By the time I had cleaned up most of it by scrubbing at it with soggy paper towels, the blackened stain had grown to about the circumference of a grapefruit. Still, it looked like my blood had stopped actively eating away at the tile. *Hope my tooth burns a hole in that asshole's designer pants,* I thought as I pushed open the door to the bathroom and out into the now-deserted hallway.

By the time I had got back to Coindre Hall, the throbbing in my jaw had subsided to a dull but annoying ache. I had the room to myself again this evening - a blessing, as I didn't really want to explain to Niko how I had been sucker-punched because I hadn't been paying attention. Instead, I pulled a bottle of water that had been chilling in our communal mini-fridge and held it up against my face, hissing as the cold plastic touched my scales.

I groaned, flopping back on my bed. "All over a stupid fucking song," I grumbled. "It's not even *about* you two dickheads!" I sighed, closing my eyes and trying to will my heart to slow its frantic hammering in my chest.

I don't need this, I thought. *Can I really not go anywhere without watching my back?*

My phone buzzed. I pulled it out of my pocket with a sigh and thumbed it on, bringing it up to my face to squint at it. It was a message from Anagen.

Hope ur ready for tonight, nerd. Better show me it was worth it rescuing all that vinyl for you

I sat up, setting the bottle down on my desk and gripping my phone with both hands. *I'll be there*, I typed back. I paused, thinking. *Also, you feel like doing me another favor? Talk to you about it in a few hours.*

Anagen sent me back an animated .gif in reply, a clip of David from *Schitt's Creek* rolling his eyes and saying "'kay." I laughed, weakly, then winced as my jaw twinged.

That's not a no, I typed back.

A few moments later, another message came through. *Fine but u'll owe me. Even more than before. Talk later. Don't be late, malaka*

I sighed, slumping back down on the bed, a feeling of relief washing over me. Looking over at my desk, I saw the rescued LPs and cassettes that I had left piled there last night. "Well," I said aloud, "better get to work."

CHAPTER THIRTY-ONE

Several hours later, I was skittering across campus like a nervous rock crab running for cover from one end of Kettle Cove to the other. I had thrown a spare hoodie over the large plastic crate of vinyl and cassettes I was carrying with me while I made my way towards the Student Union Building, giving anyone who so much as glanced my way the ol' hairy eyeball to see if it was Summers and his goons out for more of my blood.

I made it through the SUB's main entrance and into the elevator, not daring to breathe until the doors closed shut. My pulse, which had been thundering in my ears from fear and exertion, finally began to slacken. *Can Dragons have heart attacks?* I wondered idly as I checked the bin I held in my arms.

The elevator dinged, and I stepped out into a blissfully empty hallway. There was no one waiting for me this time when I rounded the corner to the station, just light spilling out from the open door. I walked through into the office, fighting the urge to kick it closed and lock it behind me.

"Hey, it's me," I called out, setting the bin down on the desk. I didn't get a reply. After a short pause where I had to force myself to keep from being concerned, I called out again. "Anagen?"

This time the response came almost immediately. "In the back!"

"Okay," I called out, relief flooding me. I went to pick up the bin of music, but before I did, I walked back over to the open doorway and stuck my head through. The hallway was still empty.

I stood there for a moment, just listening. Nothing but the typical sounds of a large, empty campus building at almost 1 in the morning. Most nights I found it comforting. Tonight, though....

"Rick? You coming or what?"

"Huh?" I pulled my head back in. "Uh, y-yeah, be right there!" I stepped out of the doorway and turned to grab my music. But not before closing the door to the radio station. I then locked it, for good measure. Picking up the bin, I looked back at the now-closed door and immediately felt better.

I stepped deeper into the station, passing by Soundra in Studio A. The Vampire casually flipped me off when I waved to her. I found Anagen in Studio C, hunched over the ancient computer. They looked up at me as they entered. "I got everything I'll need for tonight," I said. "Didn't have the time to copy stuff over to digital though, so I'll have to spin some of these the old-fashioned way. These turntables and tape decks in here still work, right?" Anagen was looking at me, brows furrowed. "What?"

They pointed at my face. "The fuck happened to you, Rick? You look like you came in second in a chainsaw fight."

I sighed, putting the bin down on the threadbare carpet. "Uh, I had a little accident?" I gave them what I hoped was a sheepish grin. It turned into a wince.

Anagen muttered something in Greek before jumping to their feet. "Fucking hell, Rick, did you get a... a *tooth* knocked out?"

"Huh?" I tongued the tender socket where my lower incisor had been just a few hours ago. "Oh, y-yeah. It's okay, it'll grow back in just a couple days. Draconic, remember?"

"That's not what I meant." Anagen crossed their arms and glowered. "What the fuck happened to you?"

I bit my lip, instantly regretting it as it sent another twinge of pain across my jaw. "I, uh, well... you know that Sidhe fuckboy? The one with the psychotic dad that tried to kill me in Tolon Park?" They nodded. "Well, he, uh... he sucker-punched me. In the men's bathroom."

Anagen's eyebrows shot up into their hairline. "He *what*?"

I bent down and began rummaging through my bin. "Yeah, you know, typical bully, right? He knows he coulda gotten caught if he tried anything out in the open, so he has me dragged out of sight and tries to split my jaw open. Just a friendly little warning." I grimaced, keeping my eyes on what I was doing. "Guess he was pissed he d-didn't get a kill shot the other night."

Hands shaking, I pulled an LP from the bin and stood back up. Anagen was looking straight at me, an inscrutable expression on their face. "Rick. Are you up for this tonight? We can always just pull a rebroadcast from a couple weeks ago if you're not up to it."

I shook my head. "N-no," I said. "I want to do this. This is, like, one of the only places left on campus where I feel like I don't have to watch my back, you know?"

Anagen chewed their lip, still looking at me. "Okay," they said finally. "But this is some fucked up shit, Rick."

"Thank you," I said, letting out a breath I hadn't even known I was holding. "And yeah, it is." I slumped down in the creaky office chair, holding the LP in my hands. "I never wanted any of this."

"No shit, Sherlock." Anagen grabbed one of the folding chairs from the wall and set it up across from me. "Here," they said, motioning for the vinyl in my hands. "Pull 'em out and hand 'em over. Let's see what you got here, okay?"

They took the LP from me. I bent down to grab the next one in my playlist. "So, this turntable works, right?"

"Yeah, it'll get the job done. Not the most reliable, but it'll do. Definitely gonna recommend you back these up and bring digital track copies in the future, though. Some of this shit looks old as hell."

I nodded. "Yeah, it's almost all vintage. Couple reissues here and there, but most of them are original pressings." I came back up with a handful of cassettes. "These I'm less worried about, they're a little more durable."

I held out the tapes to Anagen. They took the cassettes and set them both on the table, on top of the LPs. "So, changing the subject. What's this favor you need so badly?"

I bent back down to fish another vinyl from my bin. "Well, you know how the Palace wants me to do a set sometime soon?"

They nodded. "Yeah, we talked about it last night, remember?"

"Well, I've never been there myself. I don't know anything about the place. Would you... would you mind going with me? Maybe sometime this weekend? So I don't feel completely clueless walking in there?"

They cocked their head at me, giving me an appraising look. "Yeah, I guess we could do that. It'll have to be after nightfall though, Amelia won't show up until after sundown." Anagen tugged on one of their horns for a moment. "I know. You can treat me to dinner before that. There, that's my price."

I chuckled. "Yeah, that's fine. I'd be happy to. You ever been to the K Street Diner?"

"What, that greasy spoon out in South Beckett? Never been. Is the food any good?"

"Better than you expect. So, it's a deal?"

Anagen pursed their lips for a moment, visibly mulling it over. "All right," they said, "but you're paying." They stood up, clapping me on the shoulder. "You got this? I got some shit to do in the other booth."

I nodded. "Yeah, I'm good. And, uh, Anagen? Thanks."

They grinned at me. "Don't thank me yet," they said, walking out.

It felt like a huge weight had been lifted from my shoulders. I bent back down, pulling the rest of the music from my bin, and began arranging it in the order I'd be playing it that night. Before long, I had decided on a play order.

My anxiety slowly returned as it grew closer to my slot time. I had begun to get used to this feeling, though; it was a strange combination of both nervousness and excitement that seemed to get just slightly more bearable every time I went on the air. I tried not to think about everyone who would be tuning in the day after when the station rebroadcasted it for a wider audience.

Before I knew it, Anagen let me know it was just about time to begin. I clumsily slipped the headphones over my pointed ears and looked at the top of my pile.

My jaw was still throbbing, now more an annoyance than anything else. The dull ache was driving me crazy, as was the empty socket where one of my teeth should have been. Somewhere, somehow, the fear I had felt in the moment was giving over to another emotion altogether.

I reached back down to the bin and pulled another LP, a pristine copy of NoFX's *The War on Errorism*. The record came out of the sleeve with a satisfying swish of vinyl against paper. I placed it on the turntable, the seconds ticking down as I set the needle down on it carefully.

The ON AIR sign lit up, and I thumbed the mic button.

"Hey everyone, welcome to The Night Nest. Thanks for joining me tonight. I'm Ruh-Ricky Gold, and I've got another two hours of music for you." I could hear my voice repeating back to me faintly. As always, it helped me relax. "I'm prepped for you folks tonight, thanks to Morrigan's Music and Vinyl down in South Beckettsville. Got some, uh, deep cuts for you this evening. In fact, I, uh, I thought we'd start with something special." I paused for a heartbeat, not really sure if I should be doing this. "I ran into someone at Tolon Park the other night on the way back from Morrigan's. Had to leave in a real hurry, so, sorry I had to fly." I smirked a little at that.

I hadn't quite spontaneously combusted at that point, so I found myself getting bolder I started the turntable. The record began to spin. "Seriously, though, nice guy. Real c-class act. I hear he'd been trying to get into Allora for a while, too."

I started fading in the audio on the turntable as the lyrics kicked in.

He's not smart, a C student

And that's after buying his way into school

Beady eyes, and he's kinda dyslexic

Can he read? No one's really quite sure

I adjusted the balance again, breaking in over the first verse. "So, uh, it's amazing what money can buy when you don't have talent. Or smarts. I'm sure the university's new wing will begin construction soon. You know, the one named after his dad. Anyway, this one's for you, buddy."

And with that, I muted my mic, just in time for the chorus to kick in.

Idiot son of an asshole

He's the idiot son of an asshole

Idiot son of an asshole

He's the idiot son of an asshole

I leaned back in my chair and grinned. Yeah, it was petty, and probably a bad idea, but let's face it – it made me feel better. Plus, with both him and his crazy father already trying to kill me, it's not like things could get any worse, could they?

CHAPTER THIRTY-TWO

"Y ou're kidding, right? This place?"

It was the day after, and Anagen and I had made plans to meet up at the UTA stop just a couple blocks from the diner. I had gotten there first, killing time on my phone and keeping an eye on the crowd until they stepped off the bus for the short walk to 69th and K.

"Hey, looks can be deceiving." I could understand what they meant, though. Uncle Dave might own all three floors, but the brick building that housed the diner and his duplex apartment above it didn't really look like much from the outside. "This place has been here for decades for a reason."

Anagen wrinkled their nose but followed me up the short flight of steps to the diner entrance. "Is it because the owner's been bribing the Health Department?"

I opened the door and stopped dead in the vestibule. "What the hell?" There were people waiting to be seated. More than a few people. Another quick glance and I saw that most of the booths were full, too. "Okay, this is weird."

"What's weird?" Anagen brushed up against me from behind, putting one of their hands on my shoulder and pulling me down. "Dammit Rick, quit being taller than me." I shimmied over to give them a better line of sight. "Huh, a little early for the dinner rush, isn't it?"

"Yeah, I mean, I haven't seen it this busy since, uh..." I scratched my head. "Actually, I can't remember ever seeing it this busy." I peered through the crowd, catching sight of someone in a waitress uniform as they rang someone up at the hostess stand. "I think that's Sharon," I said, waving to get her attention.

She ran a customer's card and handed it back to them, then looked up. I caught her eye and she smiled, waving back, then held up a finger and mouthed the words "one sec." I nodded in return.

Sharon finished settling the customer's bill and stepped out from around the hostess stand. "Hannah," she called out, "can you seat the next table? I'll be right back!" Down the aisle to her left, Hannah mutely raised a hand in acknowledgement without turning around.

Sharon beckoned us over, and we slipped through the small crowd at the door. I murmured apologies as I brushed past them, Anagen trailing in my wake.

"Hey kiddo," she said wearily. "What brings you out here today?"

"Hey," I said, looking around. "My friend Anagen and I wanted to grab something to eat." They waved, giving Sharon a friendly smile. "You guys look, uh... really busy, though." In addition to the crowd, there was something else new - a beaten-up jukebox had been set up near the entrance to the restrooms. "Is that the Wurlitzer?"

Sharon nodded. "Yup, your uncle had it moved downstairs right after Halloween. Right around when this new crowd started showing up. He said something about an ad he ran on the radio?"

"An ad? He doesn't have a marketing budget, how did he

—" I swallowed, realization dawning. "Ohh. Oh God. I, uh, I guess I better check in with him."

Sharon shrugged, grinning slightly. "He's back there, working his little rear end off. Never seen him so irritated. Or so happy. Go on, you know the way back!" She stepped aside, letting us pass. "Nice to meet you, sweetie," she said as Anagen stepped by. "Ricky so rarely brings by his friends."

Anagen beamed at Sharon. My ears grew hot as I mumbled a goodbye and led the way through to the kitchen door. "Come on," I said, "I'll introduce you."

I pushed the swinging door open and stepped through, holding it for Anagen as they followed. The kitchen was nearly as hectic as the dining area. Multiple burners were lit, the fryer was bubbling away, and my uncle was there in the thick of it like a conductor in an orchestra pit. He had one spatula in his right hand and another gripped firmly by his tail as he worked the grill.

"Uncle Dave? What the hell is going on out there?"

He craned his neck around, taking in my presence. "Sorry, kid," he said. "You picked a bad day to come by for a visit! I'm busier than a three-legged centaur in an ass-kicking contest right now." He turned back to the grill, going back to conducting his symphony. "Though I guess you could see that, huh?"

"Yeah, uh... wow." I looked back at Anagen. They were surveying the kitchen with a practiced eye. "Uh, is this because of the plug I slipped in on Halloween night?"

Uncle Dave laughed, shaking his head. "You played it," he said, grinning. He shot me an appreciative look. "What was all that about never playing any AC/DC, huh?" He fished two finished burger patties from the grill and placed them expertly down on a pair of plates on the counter, slapped the buns on top of them, and then moved them to the pass-through. "Order up!" he shouted, hitting the desk bell with the spatula he held in his tail.

I shared a glance with Anagen. "Yeah, uh, sorry? It was kind of a spur-of-the moment thing, I guess I shoulda checked with you first—"

"You kidding, kid?" He turned to us completely, having earned himself a moment of respite. "I had to move the Wurlitzer down here because so many new customers wanted to hear some music while they ate. This keeps up and I'll have to hire another cook!" He grinned toothily. "Who's your friend?"

"Oh, this is—"

"Hi, I'm Anagen." They stepped forward, smiling. "I'm Rick's board operator at the radio station."

"No shit. So it looks like I owe the both of you, then. Come here!" Before I could even back up, my uncle swept us both into a hug. All I could smell was fry grease and his "special" cigarettes.

"Oof, okay, okay!" I said, struggling as he squashed the two of us together. He let us go with a laugh and turned back to the grill. I looked at him appraisingly. "Hey, did you... did you get a little taller or something?"

"Did I?" He shrugged, pulling some onion rings out of the deep fryer and shaking the basket, letting it rest for a moment. "I dunno, maybe? It's been a while since I felt this alive, I'll tell ya that much. You guys want something to eat?"

I shared a glance with Anagen. They nodded. "Well, I mean you're really slammed out there, I don't want to—"

"Sure do," Anagen said. "We'll wait for a booth to open up." They gestured out the pass-through to a pair of open stools at the bar. "Nice to meet you," they said, pushing open the kitchen door. Dave nodded to them amicably.

I stood there for a second, dumbfounded. "Uh, I guess we'll... we'll wait?"

My uncle looked over at me again, a questioning look on

his face. With his free hand, he pantomimed a curving ram's horn on his head.

"It's, uh, a long story," I said, backing through the kitchen door. "I'll fill you in, I promise." He waved me off, grinning, and dumped the basket of onion rings out onto a plate.

I slid onto the barstool next to Anagen. They were paging through the diner's menu with interest. "So that's your uncle, huh?"

"Yup," I said. "My dad's brother, they're both Clan Argent." I shrugged, then smiled up at Hannah as she walked by on her way to a booth. She patted my head, ruffling my hair.

Anagen looked up from the menu. "Jeez, she's taller than you," they said, squinting at her. "A mythic, too?"

I nodded. "Werelioness. She's the diner's unofficial bouncer."

Anagen laughed. "This place is, uh, certainly interesting." They then looked back at the menu. "So, what's good here?"

I shrugged. "Depends what you like, really. Some people swear by the Reubens. Get here early enough and the French toast is really good, but Uncle Dave stops serving breakfast at around 10:30."

"Huh." They flipped through the pages, scanning each one. "Kinda weird that a diner doesn't do all-day breakfast."

"Small-scale operation," I said. "It's always been just Dave on the grill back there, though one of the waitresses can pitch in if necessary. He never had enough business for more." The chime over the front door went off, and I craned my neck around to see a pair of college-aged humans join the line to be seated. "Well, not before today, at least."

"Hmm." Anagen closed the menu and set it down. "I think I'll try the veggie panini. What are you getting?"

Hannah sidled up. "Let me guess. The fried haddock,

substitute fries for your favorite brand of potato chips?" She looked down at the both of us, her expression all business but for a familiar glint in her eyes.

"And a hot cocoa," I added, grinning.

She grinned back, her sharp canines prominent, as she set down two napkin-wrapped sets of silverware. "And anything to drink for you, Ricky's Friend Who He Hasn't Introduced Yet?"

My ears grew hot as I tried to stammer a reply. "I, uh, th- this is—"

"Anagen," they said, looking up at Hannah brightly. "I work with Rick at the radio station." They smirked. "And a water is fine, please!"

Hannah barked a short, terse chuckle – which, for her, was like a belly laugh. "Nice to meet you, Anagen. I'll get your orders in. Think fast, Ricky!" She turned, bumping into me with her hip and nearly knocking me off the stool on her way back to the passthrough.

Anagen tittered as I righted myself, perching back on the stool. "Seems you're pretty well-liked here," they said.

"Yeah, something like that. Hannah has liked manhandling me like a werecub ever since she started working here. I think it's her way of expressing affection." I reached up to rub the scales at the back of my neck and winced as my upper arm lifted, a twinge of pain traveling down my side. "Shit," I hissed, pressing my palm into my side.

Anagen's eyebrows shot up. "Yikes, what's that about?"

I poked tenderly at my side. "It's this fucking arrow wound," I said. "Taking forever to heal up. The Dragonsbane is really kicking my ass." The pain subsided enough for me to drop my arm. "S-sorry," I said.

They shook their head. "Nothing to apologize for," they said. "You're not the one that pulled the trigger, remember?"

"Yeah, I mean... I guess?" I didn't meet Anagen's gaze. Instead. I reached out and started fiddling with a ketchup bottle on the lunch counter. "I am the idiot that chose to walk through Tolon Park after dark, though."

I looked back over at Anagen in time to see them rolling their eyes. "We're not our mistakes, Rick. They're how we learn. I mean, you think I was born the perfect specimen that I am today?" They smirked and mimed buffing their fingernails on their shirt.

I laughed, shaking my head, then looked up as Hannah set down our drinks across from us on the lunch counter - a clear glass of ice water with a straw and a steaming mug of hot cocoa, topped with whipped cream and a sprinkle of cinnamon. She left with a wink. "Thank you!" I called out after her. She raised a hand in recognition without turning around.

Anagen picked up the straw, ripping the wrapper from the top of it and fiddling with it for a moment. "So," they said, "how does a silver draconic, one that's uncle to the Dragon king, end up working as a short order cook?"

I grimaced. "Well, you know how Dragons' identities are tied to their hoards, right?"

They nodded. "Yeah, that's common knowledge."

"Well, if one of us suddenly loses our hoard, like if it ends up getting, say, tanked due to an investment scam run by a Coyote..." I shrugged, a pained expression on my face. "Let's just say my uncle used to be a lot taller. Right now, his 'hoard' consists of the building and whatever the diner makes him."

"Well, it does seem like it's pretty busy now. I guess that plug on Halloween helped." They pinched far end of their straw wrapper and put the other end up to their lips.

"Yeah, I hope it stays that—" I sputtered, suddenly hit in the face with a paper wrapper. Anagen laughed as I glared at them. I balled up the wrapper and tossed it back at them; they deflected it with a palm. It skittered across the lunch counter. I rolled my eyes.

They shrugged, grinning. "Come on, you can't tell me you never shot a drink straw across the table at dinner as a kid?" They stuck their now-bare straw into their water and took a sip.

I shook my head, smirking at them. "No, I was usually the target. Usually of my brother."

"Ah, yes, the elusive Other Sibling. What's his deal?"

I shrugged. "Eh, I mean we don't have the strongest relationship. My brother's a bit of a dudebro, but when he stops trying to be someone he isn't he can be a pretty chill guy. Totally different than my sister, she's… well I'll be honest, she's snarky as hell. Constantly messing with me, but it's never really from a mean-spirited place. I know that she would have my back if I ever needed her to. My brother? Well, I hope so. We were closer when we were younger. Family stuff kind of saw us grow apart a little."

"Yeah, that can happen. Sibling relationships are hard. Are you the youngest?"

I shook my head. "Technically we're triplets, but we're fraternal so we look nothing alike. My brother takes after my dad as a silver, my sister is definitely more like my mom even down to the white scales, and I'm stuck in the middle. Best-slash-worst of both worlds, depending on how you look at it. We've got a pretty big extended family on both sides, but they're spread pretty thin, so we don't see each other much. My Uncle Dave is maybe the exception to that." As if on cue, a silvery Dragon head on a long, slender neck threaded out the passthrough for a moment, scanning the diner. I waved; my uncle winked at me and pulled his head back in.

I looked back at Anagen. They were regarding me thoughtfully. "Uh," I said, blinking a few times. "What about you? Any family?"

They gave me an inscrutable smile. "Just about all of Arcadia," they said. Then they shrugged. "Well, at least now. My, uh, human family? From before I transitioned? I don't really talk to them." They wrinkled their nose at me. "They had a whole-ass problem with the 'not a man, not a woman' thing."

I winced. "Shit, I'm sorry. Didn't mean to open old wounds."

They waved me off. "Don't worry about it. I'm much happier this way, living my truth. Do I miss my folks sometimes? Of course I do. But they weren't interested in who I was, only who they wanted me to be. So, yeah. It sucked. And it hurt. Still does, but less now, you know?"

I gave them what I hoped was a sympathetic smile. "Uhh, I guess? I mean, not really? Like I never wanted to be the Ra'saar, but I don't have a choice. That's coming for me one way or the other." The order bell dinged; I looked up in time to see Hannah grab two platters from the pass-through and head our way. "Ah, looks like our food's here," I said.

Anagen laughed, unwrapping their silverware. "Saved by the bell. C'mon, let's eat – I'm starving. "

CHAPTER THIRTY-THREE

The food was a welcome reprieve. It's hard to put your foot in your mouth when you're eating, after all, though obviously not for lack of trying on my part. Plus, it had been a while since I'd had the time to properly enjoy my uncle's cooking.

Anagen let me off the hook as well. They dug into their panini, making sounds of approval as they ate. They did stop to peer curiously at the small bag of potato chips that arrived on my plate with my food, though. "What brand is that?" they mumbled, mouth full of grilled veggies, motioning at my plate.

"Huh, these?" I picked up the bag and turned it towards them. In the front of the packaging was a caricature of a deer skull with a bib tucked around its neck, a crossed knife and fork under it. The words "Hungry Wendy's All-Dressed Potato Chips" were emblazoned in a ring around the image.

Anagen set down their panini and took the bag from me. "Hmm," they said, turning it over in their hands. "'Product of Canada.' What the hell is All-Dressed?"

I laughed, taking the bag back from them and pulling it open from the top. "It's a combination of ketchup, barbecue, sour cream and onion, and salt and vinegar. We used to eat these all the time back up in Portland." I pulled out a chip and took a deep, appreciative sniff. "Can't get them this far south of the border. My uncle imports them for me." I popped the chip into my mouth, crunching happily as the flavors exploded across my palate. "Want one?" I offered them the open bag.

Anagen smirked, shaking their head at me. "I'll, uh, stick to my fries, thanks." They picked one up off their plate and dipped it in some ketchup for emphasis. "So, by Portland, you mean...?"

"Maine," I said, popping another chip into my mouth. "Right on the coast. The US branch of the family business is headquartered there." I picked up my fork and speared a piece of my haddock. "North Atlantic deep-sea fishing thing," I said before popping it in my mouth.

Anagen reached for their water. "Oh yeah? So you grew up there?" They took a sip. "How'd you avoid growing up sounding like the Gorton's Fisherman?"

I took another bite, chewing and swallowing before responding. "Speech therapy."

Anagen laughed, then looked at me. "Wait, seriously?"

I nodded. "But not for that. My stutter was absolutely *awful* as a kid. Real Porky Pig style. You know how you can hear it whenever I'm stressed out, like when I'm w-worried about talking on the air?" They nodded. "Well, it was like that, but constantly. All. The. Time. Say what you want about public schools, but Longfellow Elementary helped make me into the, uh, *incredibly* c-confident person I am today."

"Public school? It sounds like your family has more money than Hades. Plus, you're the fucking king of the Dragons. You didn't go to boarding school? I find that hard to believe."

I shook my head, taking a long sip of my own from my hot cocoa. "Nah, Mom insisted. All three of us went, even though Dad's side of the family was really against it. My Grandma

Jutte threw a fucking fit, let me tell you. All my cousins were doing the whole boarding/private/finishing school thing and we were holding bake sales so we could afford to go to the Boston Museum of Art on field trips in high school." I shrugged. "I was fine with it. Trust me, the last thing I wanted to do was end up in one of those adolescent viper pits with other draconics."

"Yeah, I'll bet." Anagen dug back in, and I took that as a cue to do the same; for a few minutes we just enjoyed our meals, letting the sounds of the diner wash over us – the unique mix of silverware clinking against plates and the hum of conversation.

Soon later, Anagen pushed their plate forward, wiping their mouth with their napkin. "Not bad," they said. Then, their phone chimed, and they pulled it out to look at it briefly. "Hmm. I know we planned to go to the Palace after this, but it's still gonna be a while before nightfall. Amy won't be around until then." They looked around. "And as much as your uncle's diner seems pretty cool, I really don't wanna spend the next two hours hanging around here."

I scratched at my cheek, thinking. "Well, I dunno what we could – oh, I know. You want to see the record store? It's a hole-in-the-wall but considering how you saved my ass I feel like I owe you a visit. Besides, I'd like to see Morrigan again."

"Hmm... yeah, that sounds like a nice way to kill a couple hours. And yeah, you do owe me."

I grinned, pulling out my wallet. "What, treating you to the diner isn't enough? I see how it is. C'mon, let's get outta here before Hannah pins me down to the counter and starts cleaning me behind my ears."

I grabbed the check from off the counter and went to pay for our meal, Anagen following behind. After paying, I turned to go and bumped into another patron as they were coming in.

"Sorry!" I said, looking down at them. "I didn't-" I blinked. "Professor Chen?"

My Music Theory professor was standing there, dressed in a battered windbreaker. A dark-skinned man stood next to him, pulling a scarf from around his neck. "Oh, hello, Ricky! Funny running into you here. Literally." He smiled amicably up at me before noticing the Satyr by my side. "Anagen, right? You were in my Music Production class last spring, weren't you?"

They nodded. "Good to see you again," they said. "And you too, Lawrence!" They waved at the man next to Chen. "How's the animal shelter?"

"Busy as always," Lawrence said, the skin around his eyes wrinkling as he smiled. "Believe it or not we're partnering with the hockey team soon for a corgi-themed adoption drive. Either of you looking for a new pet?"

"Don't you dare," Chen said playfully. "They've got finals soon! Though I feel like Ricky here won't have to worry about his Music Theory exam. I hear you've been tearing up the airwaves at the station."

I smiled, rubbing the back of my neck. "Y-yeah, I, uh... yeah I'm glad I took that flyer from you that day in class. Thanks."

"Yeah, well I had a feeling you would be a good fit. I'm glad to see you stuck with it, Ricky." He gave me a genuine smile.

I returned it. "Me too. Well, we're on our way out. See you in class!" I nodded politely to Lawrence. "N-nice meeting you," I said. Anagen waved as we slipped past them and left the diner.

A brisk wind blew down K Street, bringing with it the promise of a winter that wasn't so far off as it had been just a few weeks ago. It wasn't much of a bother for me, but Anagen seemed to be grateful when we slipped inside the bus stop and the wind stopped buffeting us.

"A little too chilly for you?"

They curled their lip. "I'm not Mr. Tumnus. I need more than a scarf to keep warm."

I gave them an incredulous look. "You've got furry legs! How are you even cold?"

They crossed their arms. "I spent a year in Thessaloniki, remember? It doesn't exactly snow in Greece very often unless you're up in the mountains. And it's perpetual summer in Arcadia. So, I don't wanna hear it."

I shrugged, grinning. "Suit yourself," I said. "Cold never bothers me. In fact, I kinda like it. We'd fly out to Halfway Rock Lighthouse of the coast and go swimming in the winter when we were hatchlings." The next UTA bus rounded the corner and began lumbering towards us. "I was never quite as strong a swimmer as Mom and Dags, but I was a hell of a lot better than Dad and my brother."

Anagen wrinkled their nose at me. "You're a freak of nature, Rick. I knew I liked you for a reason." The bus rumbled around the corner, and they stamped their feet. "About fucking time. I'd be freezing my tits off if I still had any."

The bus came to a stop, and we clambered on, both flashing our school IDs to the human driver. About half the seats were full, but we were able to find two empty ones across from each other near the rear set of doors.

"So, tell me about this place," Anagen said, hunkering down into their coat. The bus pulled out into traffic. "This is out near South Beckett, you said?"

I nodded. "The neighborhood is a little run-down, but it looks like it would've been nuts back in the day. Morrigan is three doors down from this old live music venue that's closed now, but about 20 or 30 years ago it was something else. I guess there's just no competing with the Palace of Wisdom, is there?"

Anagen shrugged, rocking gently back and forth with the movement of the bus. "It's not all it's cracked up to be, believe me. You know I live there, right?"

"Yeah, you mentioned that the other day. What, are there

apartments in there somewhere, or...?"

"Nah, it's a permanent portal to Arcadia. And it's the best place for brand-new Satyrs to learn the ropes of what it means to do what it is we do. Plus, newbies like me usually end up with the shit jobs."

I smirked, reaching out to a nearby grab rail to steady myself as the bus went around a curve. "They don't have you cleaning toilets in there, do they?"

"I wish. I swear, that would be preferable to having to run casks of Arcadian Reserve to the Fae. It's fine if it's to the Dwarves or even the Trolls most of the time, but I'd rather deliver to the Phouka if I could help it."

"Uh, what about, you know, the Sidhe?"

Anagen shrugged. "It depends. If I'm delivering to court, it's all formal and ritualized. I walk in with my cask, there's bowing and scraping, and I walk out with a barrel or two of honey harvested from dreams. The Arcadian Dryads make some bomb-ass mead out of it, let me tell you."

My eyebrows shot up. "Wait, dream honey? I thought that would fuck you up if a non-Fae ate it?"

"Settle down, Pooh Bear. Nobody's sticking their head in there and going to town. Whatever the Dryads do to it, it makes it safe to drink. Worth like a hundred fifty bucks a *glass*, but safe."

The bus turned another corner. I looked up at the digital readout for the next destination – it read SOUTH BECKETTSVILLE. "We're getting close," I said, standing up. "Just a short walk from the next stop."

"All right." Anagen stood as well, losing their footing as the bus lurched. They stumbled a bit, and I caught them. "Shit, thanks Rick." They clung to me for a second and then righted themself, dusting off their skirt with one hand while holding on to me with the other. "Fucking City traffic. Good thing I've got my own personal grab bar with you here. Seriously, are your siblings this tall, too?"

"Ehhh, not really?" I shrugged. "It's, uh... part of who I am, I guess?" I looked across the bus surreptitiously. Luckily, most draconics don't ride the UTA. "Goldens tend to grow to be among the largest. Our human form kind of mirrors that."

"Oh yeah?" Anagen poked at my chest and felt my upper arm. "I don't feel much muscle under there. No wonder Niko is all up in your business. He's got a thing for twinks." Smirking, they gave my bicep another appraising squeeze.

"Oh my gods, don't start," I moaned, brushing their hand off me. They let go. "I swear, he's a walking hard-on."

"He's a Satyr, Rick." The bus slowed to a halt, its air brakes hissing. We stepped down off the bus and back into the chilly November air. "Kinda in the job description."

"Yeah, I know, but, uh, I mean he did say that not all Satyrs are like that." I turned to begin walking towards the record store. Anagen fell in beside me. "I mean, he, uh, he s-said you weren't like that."

"Why, Rick! You askin' about me, were you?" Anagen gave me the side eye, a predatory look on their face. "You doin' some reconnaissance, eh?"

My ears grew hot. "What? N-no, I mean it just c-cuh-came up in conversation—"

Anagen laughed. "Relax, Rick, I'm just fucking with you. Yes, it's true, I'm demi. It's a little on the rare side but it's not unheard of. Just like it's not impossible to find other enbie Satyrs."

"I, uh, that means you're attracted to, uh..." I furrowed my brow. "How's that work again?"

Anagen shook their head as we strolled down the sidewalk. "It means that in order for me to feel sexual attraction to anyone, there needs to be an emotional connection of some sort first. Niko is different. His sexuality is more 'traditional,' if there is such a thing for Satyrs."

"You mean, if there's a hole, he needs to fill it?"

Anagen barked a laugh. "Something like that. Most people just sort of assume that a typical Satyr would stick it in mud if he thought it would wiggle, but that's just a stereotype. Still, stereotypes come from somewhere, don't they, Mister I-Sit-On-a-Pile-of-Gold-Coins-And-Eat-Anyone-Who-Takes-Any-From-Me?"

I snorted. "Point taken." We turned a corner and I pointed ahead. "Ah, here we are, down there on the right. C'mon."

"Wait, where? The abandoned storefront!?"

"It's not abandoned! It's just, uh..." I made a pained expression. "Look, the block has seen better days, all right?"

The wind gusted down the street. Anagen sidestepped a stray plastic bag as it tumbled down the sidewalk. "I can see that."

"C'mon, give it a chance." We arrived at the entrance. Light shone faintly from within between the gaps of the different yellowed music posters that had been plastered across the front display windows and the door. "Just wait until you meet Morrigan. She's pretty old school."

I pulled on the handle, holding the door open for Anagen as they slipped in behind me. The little bell over the doorframe tinkled. "Hey Morrigan," I called out, "you around? It's me, Rick-"

I stopped dead in my tracks. Anagen slammed into me from behind, bouncing off me. "Shit! Rick, you *maláka*, what the fuck's your problem?"

"Uh." I swallowed. I looked down the first narrow aisle of LPs and cassettes. Morrigan was standing at the far end of the store, deep in conversation with someone else. Someone I had last seen pointing a crossbow at my heart while their son stood beside them, sneering down at me. "Uh, Anagen... w-we got a problem."

CHAPTER THIRTY-FOUR

The door slammed shut behind us hard, the bell on its frame chiming again. Rethas looked over at the sound; as he broke his gaze, a shiver ran through Morrigan. She slumped slightly on her feet, a dazed expression spreading across her features.

The Sidhe raised his finely sculpted eyebrows at the interruption. Then, upon seeing us there – or seeing me, at least – his eyes narrowed imperceptibly. "Well," he said, his voice a mask of joviality, "would you look at what the Satyr dragged in. Quite literally, in this case." A hand strayed to his side, as if he was reaching for a weapon that wasn't there, dressed as he was in an impeccably tailored three-piece suit.

I worked my jaw, my mind in a haze. "W-what... why... how?"

Rethas pulled a scrap of charred paper from the breast pocket of his waistcoat. "Oh, it's quite simple, really." He unfolded it and, producing a pince-nez from another pocket, held it aloft, peering through it. "'Morrigan's Music and Vinyl,'" he intoned. "Left behind after our last little chat in Tolon Park, along with the rest of the merchandise you acquired from this humble mortal shopkeep."

He stuffed his pince-nez back into his waistcoat. With

his other hand, he crumpled the receipt and dropped it unceremoniously. It skittered across the worn linoleum, coming to a stop against the wall beneath an ancient-looking fire extinguisher. "All useless bits of ephemera, I'm sure. The true prize, of course, was to find this place here – a place you might return to sometime soon. Imagine my surprise when you serve yourself up to me on a silver platter." He began to take measured steps toward me, that same cruel grin playing across his impossibly handsome face. "Tell me, little lizard, how *did* you manage to get away? That Dragonsbane would have felled an elder white – or an adult silver, whichever you are."

I backpedaled, my heart slamming against my ribcage from within. "I don't... I-"

"Knock it off, Blue Blood." Anagen brushed past me, pushing me back behind them. "I don't know what sick game you're playing, but you just admitted to being in Tolon Park while attacking the Ra... uh, Rick, here, with a Dragonsbane weapon – a clear violation of the treaty between your people and his." They crossed their arms, staring down the Sidhe. "Was this, perhaps, on the night that more than half a dozen Jogah, the grandchildren of Hinun, were found beheaded, one not far from the site of the alleged attack?"

Rethas sneered, but he stopped his advance. "I can't speak to what you're referring, young Satyr. Unless you're alluding to the vicious, unprovoked attack that this young drake here launched against both me and my son while we were out hunting in Tolon Park? Which is, by decree and treaty, shared between both Arcadia and the Kingdom of Rainbows? The truth is I only fired after this beast of a worm attacked us first, attempting to scorch us with his fire."

"*What?*" I had finally found my voice. "Bullshit! I was running for my life-"

"Rick," Anagen growled at me, flicking their eyes at me for a moment. "Shut the fuck up." They shifted their attention back to the Sidhe. "Nevertheless, the 'beast of a worm' here has a wound in his side that I have personally seen. A wound that has still not fully healed – something that only a Dragonsbane-tipped arrow would cause. Tell me, why were you in Tolon Park with Dragonsbane weapons, if not without intent to hunt – and kill – a Dragon?"

Rethas' face contorted with rage, but only for a moment. In a flash, he had regained his composure. The smile that graced his features never reached his eyes. "I have no desire to bandy words with you at the moment, Satyr," he said, his voice low and dangerous. "I will, instead, take my leave – if you would so kindly permit me to do so."

Anagen stepped to the side, pulling me along with them. Rethas walked slowly toward the exit, head held high. He placed a well-manicured hand on the door. "Perhaps we shall meet once more, little Dragon. When there are fewer impediments to a longer... conversation." The bell above the door tinkled once more as he pulled it open.

"Wait!" I stepped forward, even as Anagen grabbed me around the arm to stop me. "I n-need to know. W-why are you doing this? Over a s-stupid radio show? What the fuck is your problem?"

"My 'problem?'" Rethas looked over his shoulder at me. "My 'problem' is that all the other mythics in this brave New World, the place my kin have chosen as their home, refuse to *know their place*. As if any of you *beasts* could dare be considered our equals."

"Are you kidding me? You... you're insane, you know that? N-none of us were here first. The d-Dragons, the Fae, the Satyrs, we all *came* here from the Old World. We're all immigrants, you don't deserve better treatment just because—"

"Immigrants?" Rethas' lip curled. His eyes flashed with malice. "Don't be absurd. Immigration is for *commoners*. Smallfolk. The tired, the poor, the... wretched masses thronging the slums and barrios of this cursed world. For brownie turnspits and the vile, gangrel, potato-eating offspring of the blasted Riordan."

Rethas spat on the floor, causing me to jump back. He grinned mirthlessly. "The Sidhe don't immigrate. We expand. We conquer. Establish kingdoms, empires that last for a thousand human lifetimes. We take what we wish, fool worm, regardless of if it is offered, just as the prince took the life of your kin. We. *Colonize*." He stepped through the open doorway. "And we let nothing stand in our way." The bell over the door rang once more as it closed behind him.

I slumped back against the counter, my pulse up around my ears. As I did so, Anagen rushed over to the door, peered through one of the gaps in the music posters, and then quickly locked it from the inside. "Pan on a pogo stick, that guy is an absolute fucking lunatic. What the hell was he trying to do here?"

"Ricky? Ricky, is that... is that you?" I looked up. Morrigan was standing in the middle of the aisle, rocking unsteadily on her feet. She shook her head groggily.

"Oh, shit, hold on. Um, Anagen, can you help me—"

"Right." The two of us stepped forward, supporting Morrigan on either side. We walked her to the back of the store and sat her down gently on a ratty couch. She slouched drunkenly into the cushions.

"Looks like he put the Sidhe whammy on her hard," Anagen said, leaning over Morrigan and looking into her eyes. "You think he was pumping her for information on you or something?"

"Who knows?" I kneeled down next to the couch, grabbing Morrigan's hands and giving them a squeeze. "Hey, yeah, it's me," I said gently. "You... uh, looks like you fainted, or had a seizure or something. Take it easy. What do you remember?"

Morrigan fought to focus her attention on me. "I... I dunno. It's all really hazy. Some really bougie guy came in, started asking me some questions..." She shook her head again, this time with a little more force. "Next thing I know you were there, and I felt like that one time Thorli and I split half a bag of —" She looked at me. "Uh, never mind."

Anagen frowned, looking around the record store. "You don't remember anything he said to you?"

Morrigan looked up blearily from the couch. "I... no, I really don't. That's pretty fuckin' weird, isn't it?" There was a pause, as she glanced between Anagen and me, a pointed look on her face.

"Oh, right!" I tried to give Morrigan my least awkward smile, failing miserably. "Morrigan, this is, uh, Anagen. They w-work at the radio station with me. I wanted to show your store off to them."

Morrigan gave Anagen an appraising look before nodding. "Nice to meet you," she said, "though I wish it was under better circumstances. I assure you I usually don't just pass out of nowhere like that."

Anagen gave her a warm smile. "We all have our moments," they said, offering her a hand up. "Don't worry about it."

Morrigan took it, standing back up uncertainly. "Seriously," she said, "I guess I should thank whoever's looking out for me that you two came along when you did. Was there anyone else here when you walked in? I hope I didn't say anything weird to that guy before."

I opened my mouth, but Anagen jammed me in the ribs. "I'm pretty sure it was just us," they said. "You good?"

"Yeah, I think so." Morrigan did seem like she had finally shaken off the worst of the effects of a human speaking directly to a Sidhe for a prolonged period of time. "So, uh, Ricky, I tuned into your show a couple of times so far. I gotta admit, you're not half bad."

I smiled at her. "R-really? That's, uh, that's great, thank you!" Anagen cleared their throat. "Uhh, I owe it all to them, though," I added, hooking a thumb at Anagen. "They taught me everything I know about radio. Uh, so far, anyway."

"Good thing I haven't taught him everything that *I* know, yet." They grinned, patting my shoulder.

Morrigan chuckled. "You guys make a cute couple. How long you been going out?"

My mind went blank. "I... what?"

Anagen laughed, hard. "Oh, we haven't gotten to that part... yet. The night is still young, though."

Suddenly, the sound of breaking glass rang through the store. I spun around in time to see shards of the front window come tumbling down, clattering onto the ancient drum set that had been on display there. Behind it was a large, shadowy figure dressed in dark clothes and clutching a tire iron. They were wearing a dark knit cap and had black bandanna tied across their mouth.

"Whoa, what the fuck!?" Morrigan lunged forward, losing her balance as she did so. Anagen caught her before she could fall to the ground, glaring at the broken window.

Another figure, dressed similarly to the first and just as hulking, came into view. "Our master sends his regards," they growled, their voice deep and gravelly. They lifted one hand, hefting a large glass bottle with a rag stuffed in it. In the other hand was a disposable lighter.

"Oh shit," I breathed as realization hit me. "No, no stop--"

Too late, they lit the fuse of the Molotov and tossed it in through the broken window. It shattered across the back of the front counter, engulfing it almost instantly in green, searing flame.

The two assailants turned to go. *"Død over våre fiender!"* the one carrying the crowbar bellowed before they disappeared into the night, obscured by already billowing smoke.

"Shit, shit!" Morrigan stumbled again as Anagen steadied her. "Fucking fire extinguisher! Ricky!" She pointed, and I looked over. There it was, hanging on the wall – right above where Rethas had tossed the store receipt I had left behind. I stared at it.

"Rick, *move!*" Anagen's shout shook me out of my reverie. I stumbled over to the wall and pulled the fire extinguisher from its hook, fumbling with the pin.

"Okay, I'm on it!" I shouted over the sound of growing flames. I looked up at the black, oily smoke that was rapidly filling the room. I spared a look over my shoulder. "Is there a back door?"

Morrigan was nodding, her hand over her mouth. Anagen was holding her up again. "It comes out on the alleyway," she shouted, then coughed. "Fuck! Ricky, hurry up and get out of there!" She led Anagen through a doorway into the recesses of the store.

This is nuts, I thought, finally pulling the pin from the extinguisher. I aimed the nozzle and squeezed the trigger like the RA had shown us the first week of classes, and a jet of white, powdery smoke shot from the nozzle.

The moment it met the flames, I knew something was wrong. The fire guttered for a moment, but then it looked like it burned stronger than ever before, the flames an even brighter shade of green. In a moment, the entire front third of the record store seemed to be ablaze.

I backed away, dropping the fire extinguisher on the floor and reflexively shifted my form, strengthening the scales across my body to keep safe from the heat. My nictitating membranes slid into place, protecting me from the acrid smoke. My clothes felt tight, straining against my new form, and I struggled to control my transformation to not shred them completely. I could taste the smoke clearly now, my body working overtime to filter the particles from my lungs.

This was clearly not a mortal fire. Whatever was in that bottle was likely mythic in origin, considering both the color of the flames as well as how it seemed to shrug off mundane attempts to put it out.

The smell of melting vinyl filled my nostrils. I could see clearly that the fire had spread to the first row of LPs, veridian flames dancing over their cardstock sleeves. "Oh, fuck that," I hissed, and took a deep breath.

Being born a gold Dragon didn't have many perks for me so far. What it did offer me, though, was the ability to breathe more than just fire. In fact, I could breathe anything that a member of any other Dragonflight could.

I breathed out. A blast of icy wind and snow left my mouth in a wide cone, rolling over the flames, causing them to gutter and spark before literally freezing them in place. The remnants of the plate glass display window erupted out into the street as my breath flash-froze the front of the store, sending smoke and shards of frozen green fire tumbling out the open frame.

I sagged against the closest shelf, catching my breath. Wisps of frost clung to the front of my clothes. I brushed them off and they crackled as they fell, landing on the floor and shattering.

I looked around the store. Most of the damage looked like it had been contained, but the front of the place was a total wreck. The counter had been slagged nearly completely, with a melted lump of plastic and metal being the only indication that there had ever been a point-of-sale computer there. The front display case was torched as well, and the paneling across the front of the store was burned away, revealing scorched and pitted brickwork underneath.

"Bahamut's balls," I muttered, stepping over the useless fire extinguisher. I held my hand out to the front door, feeling for any heat, but it seemed my breath had taken care of that problem. The door had had its glass blown out too, so I didn't bother unlocking it - instead, I stepped through the shattered door frame and out onto the debris-strewn sidewalk.

"Ricky!" Morrigan came staggering out of the closest alleyway, Anagen supporting her. "You got the fire out! Good job, kid!" She stopped, catching sight of the ruined front of her store. "Oh. Oh, shit." She slumped to the pavement.

"Morrigan? Shit!" I knelt down next to her. "Are you okay?" I looked up at Anagen. "You didn't call the fire department, did you?"

"I did better than that," they said grimly, pointing. I turned in the direction she indicated. A fire truck, an ambulance, and an unmarked police cruiser, all with their lights on, came careening around the corner. "I called the City Guard."

CHAPTER THIRTY-FIVE

"Right, so let's go over this again, this time for the record. Name?"

I looked at the City Guard as he clicked his pen and set it to paper. He was dressed in plainclothes, with his badge of office around his neck. The name on the badge read CANMORE. "Ricky— uh, Frederick Konacsz. 314 Coindre Hall, Allora University." I coughed. "Draconic," I added, lamely.

The constable nodded. "Student, then. And your Satyr friend here?"

"Anagen Nimenos. I live at the Palace, also a student at Allora University. Rick and I work together at the campus radio station."

Canmore scratched away at his pocket notebook. "So is that what brought you out to, uh..." he looked up at the still-smoldering awning. "Morrigan's Music?"

I nodded. "I had b-bought some records and tapes a few weeks ago." I paused, looking over at the ambulance where Morrigan was being treated. She was sitting up, holding an oxygen mask to her face as a paramedic was checking her vitals. "I, uh, the owner's a f-friend of my mother's, actually."

The constable nodded, taking more notes, then stopped. "A non-mythic?" He looked up at me, his eyes curious. Through the smell of ash and melted vinyl, I caught his scent clearly –

horses and hounds. *A Phouka*, I thought.

"They, uh, they were in a band together back in the '80s. Went their separate ways shortly before I was hatched." I looked up at the façade of the storefront. "How bad's the damage?"

"Well, it could have been worse." Canmore glanced up at the charred brick and melted glass. "That human's lucky you came by when you did. Breath of Loki isn't like mortal accelerants." He looked back at me. "You're a white Dragon?"

My stomach flip-flopped. "Uh, m-mixed lineage, actually," I said. "Dad's a silver, but Mom is Clan Snow. I, uh, take after her." I reached wildly for a way to change the subject. "What's Breath of Loki?"

"It's an alchemical fire concoction. That's why the fire was green and you had to use your breath to extinguish it." The constable pulled a handkerchief out of his pocket and kneeled down, picking a shard of glass from the sidewalk. He stood back up with it. "Smelled it a mile away. Literally. Here, take a whiff."

I leaned forward and inhaled, instantly gagging at the stench. "Ugh, it's awful. The hell is it made out of?"

"Trade secret, apparently." He dropped the remnants of the broken bottle to the pavement, brushing off his hands. "Seen it typically used by Troll anarchists. Which matches the snippet of Norwegian you heard from the assailants. You sure this human hadn't run afoul of any Fae that you know of?"

Anagen and I shared a look. "I mean, not directly, no. Uh... I mean... m-maybe I might be... kind of responsible?"

Cannmore eyed me appraisingly. "I don't mean to sound offensive, Mister Konacsz, but you don't seem the kind of Dragon that gets into fights with Trolls."

My ears grew hot. "I'm not! N-not really. I mean, there's this Sidhe in one of my college classes – he's been t-torturing me all semester...."

"Have you been physically assaulted?"

I pressed my lips together. "I d-don't want to cause any trouble—"

"He's put him through the wringer, Constable." Anagen scowled, crossing their arms. "Tormenting him on and off campus. Intimidating him, dragging him into bathrooms and giving him black eyes, him and his shithead father even went after him one night in Tolon Park. They had *Dragonsbane* crossbow bolts. Fucking blue bloods. Uh, no offense."

The Phouka shook his head. "None taken. Those are some serious allegations, though. Do you have a name or noble house?"

I cut Anagen off before they could continue. "N-no, sir, sorry." I caught Anagen's gaze, pleading silently with them not to push the issue.

"Hmm. All right. Well, nothing to be done then, is there?" He dug in his pocket, pulling out a business card. "If you, uh, find out more about them, contact me. We'll look into it. Otherwise, this just looks like jotun street violence. South Beckett isn't exactly Destry Bay."

I took the card from him, nodding. "I'll r-remember that."

Canmore nodded one more time, then turned away to talk to a Guardsman on the scene. Anagen grabbed me by the arm and dragged me a few feet down the sidewalk, pushing me into an alleyway.

"Ow, ow-hey, stop!" I tried to pull away.

"Shut up, you *maláka*," they hissed. "Phouka can hear a pin drop from 50 feet in a crowded orgy." They let go, looking back at the way we had come, before turning on me. "Why the hell didn't you tell them it was Rethas?"

"Because if my mother taught me anything it's to never trust a fucking cop! And I didn't want to make things worse!"

"Make things *worse?*" Anagen pointed back behind themselves towards the end of the alley, presumably at the record store's smoldering exterior. "They tried to burn down the place! *With us in it!* How much worse could it *get*, Rick?"

"I don't know! These shitheads are insane! This whole thing started because of a misunderstanding, remember? Some... some p-perceived insult. Over the *radio*. Like any of that actually fucking matters!" I leaned back against the brick wall of the alley and slumped down to sit on a trash-strewn stoop. "Fucking Sidhe."

Anagen sighed, then plopped down next to me. They dug in the folds of their skirt, pulling out a silver case. "Yeah," they said, opening the case. The smell of cloves filled the alley, mingling with the scent of soot and old garbage. "You really stepped in it, didn't you?"

"Story of my life," I grumbled, looking down the alley. I heard a soft click and turned back in time to see Anagen light a black cigarette with a disposable lighter. They took a long drag, the tip of their cig sparking and crackling. "I didn't know you smoked?"

"Emergencies only," they said, exhaling a plume of smoke. They slipped the lighter back into the case and snapped it shut. It disappeared into the folds of their skirt. They took another long drag, then leaned their head back against the wall and exhaled.

I took another experimental sniff. "That smells like the same brand Niko smokes. Cloves?"

They nodded, smirking. "Yup. I know it's cliché, but whatever." They shrugged, then looked over at me. "Want a drag?" They held their hand out.

I snorted halfheartedly, considering. I reached up and took it from them, eyeing it critically. "Fuck it," I said finally, and took an experimental puff.

I gagged, holding the lit cigarette away from me while I

waved the smoke away with my other hand. "Ugh," I choked out. "I think I'll stick to breathing smoke the natural way."

Anagen laughed, taking the cigarette back from me, their fingers brushing mine. "Suit yourself," they said, taking another drag and then expertly flicking ash off the tip.

I coughed again, then turned my head away from Anagen. Taking a deep breath, I concentrated and let loose with a short-lived gout of flame from deep in my throat, scouring the taste of cigarette smoke from my mouth. "That's better," I said, wiping at my mouth and turning back. "Sorry."

"I meant to ask you about that, by the way."

"What, the breathing fire thing? I'm a Dragon."

"No, you idiot, the fact that you breathed ice just before, and *now* you just breathed fire. Is this a Dragon King thing?"

I sighed. "Yeah. If they concentrate, a gold Dragon can use any kind of breath any of the other clans can. Fire, ice, acid, lightning, you name it."

"Hm." They arched an eyebrow at me. "You're just full of surprises, Rick. At least you know how to show a person a good time." They socked my shoulder playfully. "Have to admit, I haven't been on a date this interesting in a long while."

I looked at them blankly. "Uh, w-what—"

Before I knew what was happening, Anagen leaned in, grabbed a handful of my shirt, and pulled themself close, pressing their lips to mine. They then let me go, pushing back gently, a mischievous grin on their face.

The taste of cinnamon and cloves lingered on my lips. I blinked rapidly at them. "Uh, I... wh..."

Anagen cocked their head at me, then laughed. "Did I break something just now? Has Ricky.exe stopped responding?" They leaned forward again, this time putting an ear to my chest. "I think I can hear dial-up modem noises."

I laughed reflexively. "I mean, I d-didn't know we were on a da—" Anagen pulled their head back up, kissing me again, aggressively this time. Startled even further, I pulled back, trying to extricate myself from them. "Whoa, hey, wait, please, I don't—"

Anagen leaned back away from me, an uncertain look on their face. "What's wrong?" they said, sounding confused.

"Um," I said. "Anagen, I like you—"

They smiled a little, pulling on one of their horns. "I like you too, Ricky." They met my gaze and their smile faltered. "I sense a 'but' in there, though. What is it?"

I grimaced. "I think I, uh... I think I g-gave you the wrong impression."

"Oh." Their shoulders fell, but their expression remained neutral. Anagen's eyes grew guarded. "Wow, uh, okay. Is it...?" They gestured helplessly at themself. "Is it because I'm...?"

I looked at them in incomprehension. "Because you're... what?"

"Well, you know. I'm, uh, not a girl? Or a dude? Is it a nonbinary thing...?"

My eyes widened. "What? No, no, oh gods, no – that has nothing to do with it, I swear!"

"Well then what is it?" They furrowed their brows and dropped their hands into their lap. "I... well, I thought we had a connection just there."

I winced. "It's not that, Anagen, it's just..." I sighed, leaning my head back against the alley wall and closing my eyes. "Um... I d-don't know how to explain this. Not exactly." I opened my eyes, looking back at them. "Listen, it's not because I'm not attracted to you in particular - I'm not attracted to anybody. I never have been." I shrugged. "I know, it sounds like a cop-out, but I swear it's true. I've never even been in a relationship before."

Anagen cocked their head at me. "Because... you don't feel sexual attraction?"

"Yeah, I... I just don't. I never have." I sighed. "I know, there's probably something wrong with me, right?"

Anagen sighed, then started laughing. Hard.

I blinked. "Wh... what's so funny?"

Anagen waved me off, still wracked with laughter. They eventually caught their breath, wiping at their eyes. "Fucking figures."

"Okay, I'm really confused. Why the hell did you *laugh* at that?"

"Oh, Ricky. You complete dumbass." They wiped at their face, still smiling. "Or maybe I'm the dumbass. The first person I fall for after transitioning and they're ace." They laughed again, shaking their head.

I just sort of looked at them for a second. "Wh... what? Ace?"

"Ace! You know, *asexual*. As in not feeling sexual attraction toward any gender?"

I shook my head, still not comprehending. "Wait, what? You mean that's... that's a thing?"

Anagen slapped their forehead. "By the gods, Ricky. Take a gender studies class, fucking hell - yes, asexuality *is a thing*. And that thing is you. Er, your sexuality, anyway. Congratulations, you just joined the Queer community. Your toaster is in the mail."

My head felt like it was swimming. "Uh... what?"

"Oh, for gods' sake. Get in the fucking QUILTBAG, Shinji."

CHAPTER THIRTY-SIX

I just stared at them, my brain trying to catch up with what I had just been told. "I... I don't understand. I thought, uh, 'Queer' was for anything that wasn't considered the social norm, you know? Like—"

"Like someone who doesn't feel sexual attraction toward anyone, regardless of gender?" Anagen smirked at me. "That sounds pretty 'outside the social norm' to me in a world where the white cis het dudes are in charge by default. At least on the mundane side of things." They shrugged. "Mythics are different, of course, though you can still get plenty of weird looks from folks outside certain communities. Like with the Sidhe, they're all about bloodlines and genealogies, right? You're expected to marry a member of the opposite sex and produce offspring. At least on paper, anyway. What they do behind closed doors, away from the prying eyes of the court, is another thing altogether. You can't tell me it isn't different in draconic culture, can you?"

I thought about it for a minute. "Well," I began slowly, "with so many Dragons lost to open warfare with the Sidhe in the past, repopulation is the biggest goal. Most, uh, mating between Dragons is usually handled like a business transaction, I guess? We're usually raised communally by the clan's females to keep us safe, though there are close records kept of lineages and stuff like that." I rubbed the back of my neck. "My parents are definitely not the norm in that case. Word is my Grandma

Jutte nearly lost her mind when her son up and *married* a Snow Clan female. Of course, she changed her tune once me and my siblings hatched, but even then, she only went from openly disliking Mom to barely tolerating her." I looked over at Anagen. "Otherwise, who you, uh, have a relationship with really doesn't matter if it's not intended for mating purposes. Gay, straight, none of that's really important in our world. But still, I never heard of someone like me."

"Well, you're literally going to be king someday, aren't you? Doesn't that mean you'll be in demand for making little Rickys of your own one day?"

I sighed. "Yeah, and the thought of that makes me sick to my stomach. I mean, can I tell you? I don't even masturbate. Like, once or twice, maybe? But it was closer to scratching an itch than anything else. There's just... nothing there. It's why I feel like something's wrong with me."

Anagen put their hands on top of mine and met my gaze. "Ricky. You're not broken, it's just how you are. Listen, back before I became a Satyr, I was raised by my family as a girl, even though I never felt like one. And making matters worse, it wasn't just a feeling like I was really a boy, either – hell, that would have made things easier. Thing was I didn't feel like one or the other. It took a long time for me to figure out that 'non-binary' was where I felt like I was truly who I wanted to be. And even longer to figure out the whole 'non-human' thing on top of that." They squeezed my hand, and I squeezed back. "So I get it. Besides, being demi is often considered under the ace umbrella because, for some of us, it's so rare to find someone they have a truly deep connection with."

They dropped their head slightly, gazing down at the dirty pavement of the alley. "I gotta admit, though, there's just something about you." They looked up, locking eyes with me once more. "I just think you're pretty cool. And I genuinely like spending time with you. Plus, your taste in music isn't half bad."

They squeezed my hand again. "You know, just because you're asexual doesn't mean you're necessary aromantic. You can still be in a relationship without it being sexual."

I swallowed roughly. "Um, Anagen, I..."

Their eyes grew subtly wider. "Yes?" Their expression was inscrutable.

The words stuck in my throat as I looked back at them, really looked at them for what felt like the first time tonight. Their hair was in shambles, face covered with soot from the fire, makeup smeared, and clothes rumpled. Yet beneath all that was a person that I had come to really care about in ways that weren't familial, or even as a simple friend or acquaintance. Even if I didn't want to sleep with them, I liked being around them. And I wanted more of that.

I took a deep breath. "Okay, wow. Uh, I don't know what I'm doing. Like, I really don't. But... I like you. A lot. And, uh, I guess if you're interested in pursuing something, then I am... too...?"

Anagen grinned at me. "Good," they said, leaning in and putting their forehead against mine, careful not to butt me with their horns. "Hey, I know this might be more than a little scary, okay? A lot of this is new for me, too. But, well, why don't we figure this out together? As long as we're honest with each other, right?"

I nodded, my heart hammering in my chest. "Uh, okay." We sat there for a moment, pressed together, our foreheads touching, holding hands. "Um... what happens next?"

Anagen wrinkled their nose for a moment, as if deep in thought. "Well, first I'm gonna kiss you again. Then, we're gonna get up, dust ourselves off, and get our asses over to the Palace. I need a change of clothes, and you still have to meet Neira."

I nodded. "Okay." Anagen smiled, and leaned in. "Wait," I said.

They pulled back a little. "What is it?"

"What you said before. 'Get in the fucking QUILTBAG, Shinji.' Was that a goddamn *Evangelion* reference?"

Anagen laughed. "You're such a fucking dork." They kissed me.

It wasn't terrible. It didn't light some fire within me or anything, but it was... nice? It felt intimate, like something you would only do with someone you were closer to than anyone else. I liked that.

True to their word, Anagen broke the kiss after a moment and hauled themself to their feet. They then offered a hand down to me. I took it, standing up myself. "So," I said. "Uh, should we, like, hold hands, or something? How does this work?"

Anagen rolled their eyes. "Gods, you're like a little lost puppy. Come here." They took my arm and snaked it around their waist, doing the same thing back to me. "Come on, let's go grab the UTA for Allora."

We did just that, walking down the alley and out onto the sidewalk once more. The closest bus stop wasn't far, and we stood there, waiting for one to pull up. It wasn't long before the next one rolled to a stop.

It was packed at this time of night, so the two of us stood as the bus wound its way through the City. I don't remember much of the trip, to be honest, as my mind was buzzing with everything that had just happened in the span of what felt like no time at all - running into Rethas at the record store, scrambling to stop what had obviously been his goons trying to burn the place down, talking to the City Guard... and then the conversation in the alleyway. It was a lot.

I pulled out the business card that Constable Canmore had handed me before we left, looking down at it. Anagen peered over my shoulder. "Having second thoughts about coming clean?"

I bit my lip. "I dunno. I just want this whole thing to go away, you know? But... I feel like it's not going to. Like it's just gonna get worse and worse. I mean, this guy's got it out for me, and for Dragons in general. What if he goes after another draconic in the City?" My brows furrowed. "He already tried to burn down Morrigan's. What if he comes for my family?" I looked down at them. "What if he comes for you? It's not like there's too many enbie Satyrs in the City."

"Aww, that's very sweet, Ricky." They patted my cheek, taking the card from me and stashing it somewhere in their skirt. "Don't worry about me. I'm tougher than I look. Besides, even the craziest Fae knows not to fuck with an Arcadian. Not if they don't want the entire Summer Court cut off from the Palace, *and* the finest booze in the City." They frowned. "You're not wrong, though. You, uh, you might want to put a call into your folks, tell them to keep an eye out."

I nodded, pulling my phone from my pocket. "Yeah, I think that's a good idea." I unlocked it, pulling up my address book. "Besides, I need to tell them what happened at Morrigan's." I tapped a number and put the phone up to my ear.

It rang twice. *"Ricky?"* My mother sounded concerned. *"You're calling – what's up?"*

I winced. "Yeah, hi Mom. I dunno how to tell you this—"

"What's wrong? Are you okay?" Her voice muffled for a minute. *"Chad, it's Ricky. Something's up."* Her voice came back clearer again. *"We're coming back from dinner, like a block from home. What's happening?"*

I sighed. "Okay, um, listen, Anagen and I went to go see Morrigan today at the record store. Something happened while we were there." I paused. "When we walked in, Rethas was there. He had put the Sidhe whammy on Morrigan and was pumping her for information."

My mother swore, loudly, in Icelandic. *"That blue-blooded*

bastard. I swear, if he did anything to her—"

"Mom! Listen, this is important!" I sighed. "She's okay. Well, barely. Rethas left after we showed up. But... well..." I looked over at Anagen. They gestured me on. "The store was attacked right after by a couple of Trolls dressed all in black. They broke the front window and tossed some sort of mythic version of a Molotov through. We put the fire out, but the entire storefront was torched." The line was silent. "Mom? Mom are you there?"

"Was she hurt?" My mother's voice sounded strained.

"N-no, Anagen got her out while I used my breath to put out the fire. She was being treated by the paramedics when we left. She's okay."

"You're sure she was okay?" I could hear my father's voice in the background, and Mom replied to him. *"What? No, it's.... it's bad, Chad. Rethas. Again."* Her voice grew hard. *"He tried to burn Morri's record store to the ground. With our son still in it."* Dad's voice again, sounding angry and frightened - something I never thought I'd hear. Then, Mom was clear in my ear once more. *"Where are you now? Are you coming home? You're not by yourself, are you?"*

"I'm okay, we're both okay, me and Anagen. We're heading to the Palace of Wisdom on the UTA right now." The bus lurched as it came to a stop. Passengers filed off while new ones stepped on.

Anagen leaned in. "We'll be safe there, Ricky's Mom! We've got bouncers the size of Minotaurs out front!"

"Who was that? Was that Anagen?"

"Yeah, we're, uh, we're t-together." I met the Satyr's eyes. They grinned at me. "Been together all day, They're gonna introduce me to the people I need to talk to about, uh, that invitation to DJ a set, remember?"

"Okay, but for fuck's sake be careful. And when you're done,

you call us back and we'll come get you ourselves, okay? No taking the bus, or the train. Not by yourself, and not tonight. Hold on." I heard a door open. *"Hey, are you guys looking for anything?"*

"Apartment 4G," a gruff voice said. *"Got a bottled water delivery from Somerset Holdings for 'em."*

"Oh, yeah, I think they're out for the night. You can leave it by their door, we'll let you in." There was the jingling of keys, a buzz, and the sound of another door opening.

"Thanks, ma'am. Come on, let's get this done. Drinks at Under the Bridge after this."

"Sorry, Ricky, was letting some delivery folks in for the Pierces. Listen, we're about to take the elevator up. Promise me you'll call after you're done at the Palace, okay? And that you'll wait for us to pick you up?"

"Okay, Mom, I promise. But listen, please be careful, if Rethas went after Morrigan, he could send people after anyone. You, Dad, Dags, Mack—"

"Ricky, I'll warn them. It'll be okay. You did the right thing, now we're on the lookout." The elevator dinged. *"Please, please be careful."* She paused. *"Remember your uncle."*

I swallowed, hard. "I do, Mom. I love you."

"I know you do, kid. We'll see you soon." The line went dead.

I slipped my phone back into my pocket and looked over at Anagen. "Well, that's that," I said. "She was really rattled."

"Yeah, how could she not be?" They pointed out the window. "We're coming up on our stop. You ready?"

I swallowed the lump that began forming in my throat. "I guess? I mean how bad could it be?"

They leaned up and pecked me on the cheek. "You'll be fine," they said, squeezing my hand. The bus rolled to a stop again, about a block and a half away from the Palace. I could already hear the bass beat, even from here. "Come on, it's time to meet the family."

CHAPTER THIRTY-SEVEN

T he Palace of Wisdom wasn't your typical club. Well, to mortal eyes, it was pretty much exactly what you would imagine as the City's number-one spot for nightlife. Velvet rope at the entrance, long line of people waiting to get in, muffled dance music coming from behind a pair of brass-inlaid wooden doors. There was even a long red carpet lining the sidewalk outside, leading right to the entrance. The building itself began life as an opera house around a hundred years ago. Its all-brick exterior still bore marks of that history, like the large marquee out front. Tonight it read "NEW WAVE NIGHT WITH DJ NEIRA."

"You're in luck," Anagen said, pointing up at the sign. "She's spinning tonight. You can catch her before she goes on and have that chat."

"Great," I said, trying to sound like I wasn't frightened out of my wits.

"You'll be fine," they said. "Just don't make a complete ass of yourself." They tugged me forward, past the line of non-mythics waiting to be let in, to the front doors. A pair of truly massive, hulking Satyrs were stationed out front, wearing a pair of cloaks and nothing else.

"Oh, gods," I mumbled. "And I thought Niko was packing."

"Say hello to the twins," Anagen said, waving as we came close. "Evening, boys! Got some fresh meat for Neira. Little Ricky here wants to be a DJ." They reached up and ruffled my hair.

The leftmost Satyr laughed, his voice like a pair of boulders rubbing together slowly. "You look like shit, Anagen." Still, he unhooked the velvet rope and pulled it aside for us. "Did you sleep in a dumpster?"

"Tell you later. C'mon, Ricky." They grabbed my hand and pulled me after them. The Satyr clipped the rope back behind us while the other pulled the door open.

A titter of disapproval went through the crowded line. "Hey!" one of the twins bellowed. "They *work* here. Next one 'a' you bitches about it and you're outta here!" The grumbles ceased nearly immediately.

Anagen led me inside into a small, wood-paneled foyer. Another set of doors led deeper into the venue. The deep bass of dance music grew ever louder. "First things first, we go to check in with Amy. She'll get you into the back to wait for Neira while I go change. I'll meet up with you there, okay?" I nodded, seemingly robbed of my ability to speak.

After its brief stint as an opera house and then a movie theater, the Palace had been reconditioned as a dance hall. The foyer we were in now, where the ticket booths would have been originally, had three sets of doors leading to the interior of the venue. Anagen led me forward a few short steps to a small alcove with a counter. A sign above the alcove read "COAT CHECK." A woman stood behind the counter, head down, phone in hands.

"Amy!" Anagen called out. The woman looked up. She smiled at Anagen, revealing blood-red eyes and prominent incisors. "There you are," she said. "Where've you been? And who's this?" She gave me an appraising look.

Anagen pushed me forward. "Uh... Ruh-Ricky Konacsz," I

said, digging in my pocket. I pulled out the invitation that had been delivered to me the other day. "I was t-told to present this to you. Lady Amelia, I, uh, presume?"

She took the card from me and glanced over it. "*You're Ricky Gold?*" she said, her face expressionless.

My ears felt hot. "Uh... yeah?"

There was a long beat, then Amelia broke into a toothy grin. "You're a pretty good disk jockey, kid. You know Neira asked for you personally?"

"Wh... she did?"

"Yup. We're all late-nighters here, Ricky – there's nothing like listening to your set at 2 in the morning after a shift ends. Our doors never close but we all need breaks. Plus, my sister won't shut the fuck up about you."

I cocked my head at the Vampire. "Your, uh, your sister?"

Amelia nodded. "You've met her. She's got the Friday night slot right before you at the radio station."

My eyes grew wide. "Wait, are you talking about Soundra? I thought she hated my guts!"

Amelia laughed throatily. "Oh, she does. But she really, really likes your taste in music. Though it's more she's looking out for Anagen here. The thing with Chauncey, well—"

I winced. "Yeah, tell me about it."

She shook her head. "Well, you've got our thanks for ousting him. Plus, your Halloween show went over really well."

"Wow, really? Uh, I mean thanks." I rubbed the back of my neck. "Really, I wouldn't be here today unless Anagen pushed me into it. So, it's kinda their fault." I looked over at them – they were grinning, almost like a proud parent.

"Oh, I know, they wouldn't shut up about you either. Though, Anagen, the two of you have been holding out on me –

didn't tell me he was so handsome!" She handed the invitation back to me. I stuffed it into a pocket wordlessly as both Amelia and Anagen shared a laugh.

"We didn't want you getting any ideas." They matched Amelia's grin. "Is Neira in yet? I can take him back. I really need to get changed anyway."

Amelia nodded. "Yeah, you can leave him in the waiting room until she's ready for him." She smiled at me, much in the same way someone might when their waiter set a nice, juicy steak down in front of them. Her eyes gleamed. "Hope to see you again soon, Ricky."

Anagen began dragging me away. "S-same here," I managed to get out before nearly tripping over my own feet.

We pushed through the interior doors to the main part of the venue, emerging into a cavernous room. Across from us, against the far side of the room and down a whole level, was a large wooden stage flanked by a red curtained proscenium; an expansive dance floor was before it. Ringing the floor on three sides was a mezzanine; on the left and right were twin bars that ran along both walls with accompanying stools, tables, and booths, all with an eclectic mix of mythics and mortals drinking and talking. In the center and directly before us, leading down to the packed dance floor, was a wide, ornate set of stairs that led down to the lower level.

Anagen led me down that staircase, weaving expertly through the crowd. "Come on, you *malákas*, let's get you into the back."

"The back? Where—?" I looked ahead. There, along the side of the stage, was an unobtrusive door on the lower level. Anagen led me to it and pulled it open, pushing me inside. They followed after, closing the door behind me. The sounds of the dance floor dropped to nearly nothing.

"Welcome to The Back," they said, their voice ringing in

my ears. They pointed down the long, wood-paneled corridor. "Dressing rooms and rehearsal space for live acts, business offices, spaces for private parties, and a direct line to Arcadia, so don't go wandering off." I swallowed reflexively as they padded down the hallway, their hooves thudding dully against the thick carpet. "Here we go," they said, stopping at another door. "Right through here's the waiting room. I'll let Neira know you're here and then go get changed. I'm tired of smelling like soot and melted vinyl." They shooed me in, giving my hand a squeeze. "Go on. And good luck, Ricky." They clomped off down the hallway.

I took a deep breath and opened the door, revealing a tastefully appointed waiting room on the other side. A collection of nice, expensive-looking couches and easy chairs, a fully-equipped sidebar next to a freestanding water cooler, and a large tank filled with exotic fish completed the decor. The filter bubbled comfortingly.

There was also another person in the room, a willowy young woman sitting on one couch. She had long, sea-foam green hair and was listening to her phone over a set of expensive-looking headphones with her eyes closed.

I cocked my head at her. She looked familiar, but I couldn't quite place her. Those headphones were recognizable, too – GS 300Xs. Top of the line and not cheap. I knew I'd seen her before somewhere, but where?

I let go of the door to the waiting room and it swung shut behind me, closing with an audible thud. I jumped, and the woman opened her eyes, looking around the room. "Oh," she said, smiling. "I didn't hear you come in." She pulled her headphones down, then gave me a double-take. "You... do I know you?"

"You know, I get the same feeling?" I sat down across from her, getting a closer look. "Do you go to Allora University? I could swear I've seen you on campus before. Or..." I looked closer. There were gill slits on either side of her neck.

She grinned. "Or maybe on the bus, Shoal-Serpent?"

I blinked, then laughed. "Right! The bus, like, a month and a half ago! Hello, Sea-Sister. You... you said you DJ at the Palace on the weekends, didn't you?"

She nodded, smiling. "I did. I finished that project I was working on when we ran into each other, by the way."

I leaned back against the couch, feeling relieved at running into a friendly face. "Ooh, that's exciting. How did it turn out?"

"Oh, I'm pretty happy with it, though I don't know if I'll ever be fully satisfied. But you know how that goes, I'm sure. That's actually why I'm here tonight – I'm looking forward to giving it a test run with a live audience."

"Yikes. That sounds absolutely terrifying."

"Doesn't it, though?" She leaned forward, her eyes sparkling. "That moment before you drop the needle, and you're looking out over the crowd from the booth... there's nothing else like it in this world or the next." She smiled serenely. "Scoring the soundtrack to a perfect night is its own reward, especially when the whole Palace starts vibing in unison."

I nodded. "Yeah, I mean, for sure, but having the entire crowd rely on you like that? I'll be honest, it would scare the absolute crap out of me." I shifted uncomfortably. "That's actually part of why *I'm* here tonight."

"Oh?" One of her eyebrows shot up. "What do you mean?"

"Well, uh..." I pawed at my pockets, pulling the invitation out. "I'm kinda f-fighting off that fear right now, actually. I got this in the mail recently." I held it out to her.

She took it, scanning it carefully. "'Dear Mister Gold,'" she read aloud. "Wait, WPHX?" She looked up. "Are you *Ricky* Gold?"

I stared at her. "Uhh... come on, you can't say you've heard of me? I'm on at 2 in the morning!"

She shook her head, smiling. "Amelia puts you on every Friday night. Or, well, Saturday morning, I suppose. Normally she changes the station after Soundra's set is over, but after you had to fill in that night, she's been keeping you on." She grinned, flipping the invitation over to look at the Palace logo on the front. "At first, it was just to piss off her sister, but then once she realized you had decent taste in music it became a tradition. And to think, I shared a bus ride with the City's hottest up-and-coming radio DJ, even before he knew it."

I shook my head. "T-that's very kind of you," I said, "but I, uh, honestly I kinda fell into this."

"Yeah, but you love it, don't you?" She gave me an appraising look. "I've seen it before." I shrugged, unsure of how to answer that. "Well, do you think you're ready for spinning live records, *Mister Gold?*" Her eyes sparkled.

I grimaced. "Uhh, no?" I laughed. "Honestly, I have *no* idea what I'm doing. I'm scared out of my wits just sitting here. I'm supposed to meet with this Nymph tonight so she can, I dunno, see if I've got what it takes or something? She's supposed to be the best. I have no idea what I'm in for. Uh, Neira? Do you know her?"

"Hmm, Neira? What have you heard about her?"

"Just that she's practically legendary. Been around forever, she's the Palace's number-one DJ, has rubbed shoulders with actual Muses." I shivered. "And she'll be the one signing off on any set I come up with. Which is fucking terrifying. Other than that, I heard she's got a soft spot for New Wave... uh..." I looked at the woman across from me. She was smiling expectantly. My blood ran cold.

"Nice to meet you, Ricky," she said, handing back my invitation. "I'm Neira."

CHAPTER THIRTY-EIGHT

I blinked at the Nymph. "Yuh... what? I mean, uh, oh." I looked down at the invitation she had handed back to me, then up at her. She was smiling sweetly. "Uh, really? Oh, okay. Wow. Um... hi?"

She laughed. "Sorry," she said. "I couldn't help myself when I recognized you from the bus a couple of months ago. Seems like some things are just fated to happen, huh?"

"Uh, yeah, I guess so?" I gave her what most likely an incredibly awkward smile. "Sorry, kinda looking for a hole to crawl into right now." I grinned weakly.

She shook her head. "Don't worry about it. I swear it wasn't mean-spirited. I guess you can consider it your first lesson as a DJ – expect the unexpected, huh?"

"Wait, are you serious? I mean aren't we supposed to, uh, I dunno, talk about it first? I d-don't know the first thing about spinning records live."

"Everybody starts somewhere." She smiled again. "Relax, Ricky, I'm not gonna throw you to the wolves just yet. Trust me, I've been doing this for a *very* long time, and I'm a pretty good judge of character at this point. There will be a lot you're going to have to learn before I let you loose in the DJ booth, though. How do you feel about shadowing me tonight for a set? As long as you don't touch anything. Because if you even so much as breathe on my deck, you're out on your ass." She winked at me.

"Uh, y-yeah, that would be great! Thank you? I mean, this whole thing has got me shitting bricks worse than my first night on the air—"

The door to the waiting room opened. Anagen, now looking decidedly less rumpled in clean clothes and a freshly-washed face, stuck their head in. "Hey Ricky, I can't find Neira any— oh! There she is." They came inside, closing the door behind them. "She's not teasing you, is she? Because that's my job."

Neira smiled. "*Yasou*, Anagenimenos. Are you the one who brought this little lost lamb to us this evening?"

"I did, though it was an adventure getting his scaly ass here." They clomped over and sat down on the couch next to me, putting their hooves up on the coffee table. "Ricky and I spent the day dodging the crazy Sidhe noble that's obsessed with turning him into a throw rug."

Neira quirked a fashionable eyebrow. "Well, he's safe here. You know that, right Ricky? Only an absolute *malákas* would try to cause trouble within the Palace."

I smiled weakly. "I, uh, I feel like you're severely overestimating the common sense of this guy, but I hope you're right."

There was another knock on the door. It swung open to reveal a Troll in a blue work uniform carrying two massive water jugs with ease. "Delivery," he said gruffly.

Neira waved him in, pointing to the water cooler against the wall. "Right over here, please?" He nodded, stepping inside. Another worker holding a clipboard, similarly dressed and with a baseball cap emblazoned with "Somerset Holdings" across the front jammed low down on his face, followed him in. The second one walked across to Neira and handed her the clipboard silently, his back to me.

She took it from him, picking up the attached pen and signing off at the bottom. "Thank you," she said again, handing it back. She looked up at the worker. "Haven't seen you before," she said. "Is Hathor out today?"

"I'm filling in," the worker said. My blood ran cold. I knew that voice. "It's a special occasion today." He turned around, pulling his cap off and grinning at me malevolently. "Isn't it, Ruh-ruh-Ricky?"

I moved to stand but a heavy pair of hands clamped down on my shoulders from behind. I looked up to see the Troll leering down at me. I felt something sharp pressing into my neck. "Don't," he growled.

"What is this?" Neira, brows furrowed, went to rise from her seat, only to have Summers spin around and backhand her viciously. She fell back down with a cry.

"Nobody move," Summers said, "or little Ricky here gets to bleed out in front of both of you." I winced as the Troll dug harder into my neck scales.

Anagen's eyes were wide with rage. "Are you fucking insane? This is the Palace, you can't bring weapons in here! Amy would have stopped you!"

The Sidhe smirked. "You'd be amazed how much leeway a pair of humble delivery boys has when it comes to getting into places. Besides, we're not carrying weapons, are we?" Summers looked over at the Troll and chuckled. "It's not like that bloodsucker at the front desk would have asked us why we've got a razor-sharp sliver of a Dragon tooth in each of our pockets." He reached into his coveralls, pulling it out and brandishing it.

Anagen swore. "You fucker. You can't possibly think you'll walk out of here if you hurt him, do you?" They made a move to get up; as they did so, the Troll dug his own sliver into my neck, hard. I gasped in pain as a tiny rivulet of my own blood began to drip.

Just great, I thought. *I'm going to be killed by my own tooth.*

"Oh, we're not going to do *anything* to Ricky right here," Summers said. "He's late for a very important meeting with my father, though." He circled around the back of the couch, nudging the Troll out of the way. I felt the pressure against my neck lessen for a moment as the two switched positions. "He's coming with me. Quietly, and without causing a fuss. Or his little friend here, well... let's just say I know that Satyrs aren't nearly as resilient as draconics."

The Troll, now standing directly behind Anagen, glowered. A silvery bead of my blood gleamed on the improvised Dragon tooth shiv in his hand.

"You're going to regret this." Neira's voice was cold as ice. She was glaring daggers at both Summers and the Troll.

"What, are we going to be banned from this shithole? Big fucking deal. I'll cry into my new dragonhide cloak." Sommers grabbed me by the back of my hoodie and hauled me to my feet. He dug the tip of his own weapon painfully into my back. "Let's go, asshole." He turned his head to his henchman. "If the Nymph tries anything, slit the Satyr's throat," he said. The Troll nodded.

I was manhandled through the open door and out into the hallway. We paused in front of the door to the dance floor. "Here we go, nice and easy," he hissed, his breath hot against my ear. "You let on that anything's up and you won't make it out the front door. You understand?" I nodded, swallowing hard. "Good boy. Now open the door and walk to the exit. Slow," he added, poking me hard in the back for good measure. "Remember, you pull any shit and your little Satyr friend bleeds out all over the carpet in that waiting room. And keep your eyes straight ahead."

Heart slamming against my ribcage like a steam hammer, I pushed open the door to the dance floor and walked out, buffeted by the sound of the music. The walk to the front door felt like an eternity as we weaved through the crowd and up the stairway to the upper level. Summers marched me past Amelia's coat check, into the wood-paneled vestibule, and then out into the open air and past the two Satyr bouncers.

There, parked on the curb with its hazard lights on, was a Somerset Holdings delivery truck. Another Troll dressed in a delivery outfit was leaning up against the side. Summers walked me past the truck, jerking his head at the worker as he did so. The Troll fell in step behind us as we walked past the truck and kept going.

"Wh-where are you taking me?" I said.

"Shut up," Summers replied. "I told you, you're late for a meeting." We continued down the block. We made an abrupt left turn, ducking down into an alleyway that separated the Palace from the building next to it. We must have been near the dance floor because I could hear the muffled thrum of music as it beat against the wall.

Rethas was standing there, clearly waiting for me. He was dressed as he had been earlier that day, save for the addition of an ornate rapier slung low against his hip. He grinned as Summers pushed me roughly, sending me sprawling to the dirty pavement. "Good work, Wyndham my boy. I see our guest has arrived."

I looked up at him from the ground. "You're f-fucking insane, you know that!?"

"Am I? What strikes me as foolish is struggling against fate. Come now, don't make a fuss about this. Unless you *want* the rest of your family to meet the same end as that mortal merchandiser's quaint little shop?" He stroked the hilt of his sword. "I have a pair of my best there now, waiting for a call. Do you know what Breath of Loki can do to an entire city block, if you've got enough of it? Not even a whole nest of Dragons could put out all the flames before it consumed them. You don't want to die with their lives on your conscience, do you?" He smirked.

I gritted my teeth. "You're full of shit," I said.

"Am I? You know we Fae are famous for not being capable of lying. That means when we say something, you can trust it to be true."

I glared up at Rethas, thinking back to how my parents been letting some delivery workers into their apartment building when I was on the phone with them. "Fine. Just... just swear you won't hurt them. Please."

Rethas grinned, showing altogether too many teeth. "Why, you have my word – I'll not lift a hand against them." I sagged, breathing a sigh of relief. The Sidhe chuckled darkly. "Good little worm." He looked up at the Troll. "You, go watch the alley entrance. See that we're not disturbed. Son, stay here and keep our guest from reneging on our agreement. It's time for your father to go to work."

The Troll nodded, letting me go and skulking off the way we came. Summers stepped up behind me while I knelt in the dirty alleyway, his hand heavy on my shoulder. He looked disinterested, even bored – like he had done this dozens of times before and this was just another day for him.

I glared up at Rethas. "Is... is this really necessary? All over some stupid shit I said on... on the fucking radio?"

"What?" The Sidhe laughed. "Oh, my dear boy. You sweet summer child. Do you think I care about any of that? Don't be absurd." He crouched down on his haunches, meeting my gaze directly. "No, I knew from the first moment that my son told me there was... a draconic... attending Allora University that this day would come."

He reached out, grabbing me roughly by the chin in a viselike grip, turning my head this way and that like he was examining a prize horse. "No," he went on as he continued to examine me, "instead, I instructed Wyndham here to antagonize you at every opportunity he could to test your mettle. The droll, petty little insults you hurled into the wind from your cozy perch were just icing on the cake. They gave me all the excuses we needed to escalate."

As if on cue, Summers pulled his phone out of his pocket. "Father," he said a moment later, "they're in position at the Dragon's apartment building and awaiting your orders."

"Ah, excellent." Rethas let me go and stood, pulling a pocket square from his jacket. He fastidiously cleaned his hands, as if touching me had somehow dirtied him. He stared down at me. "Tell them to proceed."

"What?" I struggled to rise, but Summers behind me clamped down on my shoulder, keeping me on my knees. "But you – you gave me your word! You said you wouldn't hurt them!"

Rethas turned away from me. "Ah, yes, I did, did I not? That no harm would come to your family *by my hands*. And I told the truth – I won't touch them. My loyal retainers, however? That's a different story." He looked back over his shoulder at me. "You should really think more carefully when you strike a bargain with one of the Fae, you foolish worm. Just because we can't lie doesn't mean we won't stretch the truth." He turned back to Summers. "Do it."

"Yes, Father." Summers released me from his grip, grabbing his phone with both hands.

From Rethas' smirk, it was clear he felt I was soundly defeated. Tricked into putting myself in danger, manipulated into trusting him with the fate of my family in only the way a Sidhe could twist the truth – surely I would simply accept the fact that I was helpless, at his mercy, and would soon be joining my family in death, our tanned and preserved hides on display at some Fae estate somewhere.

I'll admit that for a moment I felt abject terror, just as he likely predicted. Here's the thing about fear, though - the typical response to it, physiologically, is fight or flight. Most times in my life, I chose to run.

Tonight, though? With the lives of my family at stake? This time things were different. This time, I wasn't going anywhere.

CHAPTER THIRTY-NINE

I knew I had hardly any time to spare. If Summers sent that text, the whole city block where my parents lived, and everyone living there, would be burned down to the ground, mythics and non-mythics alike.

At this point, I didn't care what happened to me – I knew I was probably fucked. I had maybe one chance to do something about it before I ended up draped over Rethas' shoulder like a mink coat on some rich white lady from Destry Bay.

In the split second I had left, I willed myself to partially transform. Once more, my scales grew and hardened; a long, spiked tail erupted from the small of my back, ripping through the fabric of my jeans, and whipped up behind me. It speared Summers' phone out of his hands and he shouted in shock, falling backwards against the alley wall. The back of his head collided with a sickening crunch. He slumped to the ground, motionless, leaving a smear of blue on the brickwork.

I stood up as my wings sprouted from my back, similarly shredding my hoodie, just as my shoes disintegrated as my feet transformed into digitigrade claws. The rest of my body followed suit; fingers lengthening into talons, face transitioning to a scaly, armored muzzle. I glowered down at Rethas from my new height, a good six inches taller than I had been before.

The Sidhe backpedaled a step, gripping the hilt of his rapier with a look of shock on his face that soon gave way to a perverse joy. "Looks like the worm has some fight in him after all," he said, pulling the weapon from its sheath. It gleamed dully in the dim light of the alleyway.

"Don't," I said, whipping my tail back and forth. I backpedaled, coming up against Summers' unconscious body, and placed a clawed foot on his chest. "Or do you not care what happens to your son?"

Rethas' eyebrows shot up. "Oh, how delightful. What do the mortals call it in their charming Western films? A 'Mexican standoff'? Charming." The Troll at the mouth of the alley had come running after hearing the commotion, but he stopped short as Rethas held a hand up. "Fine. Let my servant here collect my useless progeny and go in peace."

"For what in return?" I growled. "More half-truths and weasel words?"

Rethas sneered again. In the dim light, he reminded me of someone I'd seen before, though I couldn't quite place it. I only knew every time he did that, it filled me with revulsion. "Very well. Pick up my son's phone and send a message to recall my servants. They, and all who reside in their vicinity, will remain free from harm."

Unwilling to take my eyes off the Sidhe, I snaked my tail out and scooped up Summers' phone. I tossed it at Rethas, who caught it nimbly. "You do it, and then show me." I pressed my foot down on Summers' chest. He groaned weakly.

"You worms. So mistrustful." He deftly tapped out a reply and then tossed the phone back to me.

I flicked my eyes down, taking in the words on the screen. *Abort mission,* read the latest message. As I did so, an acknowledgement came in response.

"There," Rethas said. "Satisfied?"

"Not nearly," I said. I crushed the phone in my claw and tossed it to the side, the electronics raining down to the dirty alley pavement. "But a deal's a deal." I took my foot off Summers and stepped away; the Troll hooked his hands under the younger Sidhe's armpits and dragged him off.

"Well," Rethas said, smirking again, "now that you've played your only card, what will you do now?" He shifted his stance subtly, placing his weight on his back heel. "You seem to have run out of options. A wiser creature would have negotiated his own safety as well. 'Catch and release,' didn't you call it?"

I bared my teeth at him. "Get fucked, you inbred idiot."

He cocked his head at me. "A strange hill to die on, to be sure. But at least you'll be dead." He lunged, the tip of his rapier flashing in the dim light.

I was never much of a fighter when I was younger. Yeah, Mom and Dad made us all take some self-defense classes, but even when we were all hatchlings, I never liked getting physical. It always seemed smarter to me to avoid getting into a fight altogether if you could. Still, when your brother enjoys roughhousing with you whether you want to participate or not, you do learn a few things.

Rethas came in high, aiming to skewer me like a kebab. I scrambled to the side, pulling my wings in close to my body to prevent them from getting sliced, and tried to put a little distance between the two of us. The only problem was that the Sidhe was now between me and the mouth of the alley.

Rethas spared a glance behind him and smiled, obviously thinking the same. "Come now," he said, his voice dripping condescension. "You're not going to run, are you? You'll only die tired."

"Fucking hell, do you *ever* shut up?" I cast my eyes around the alley, looking for any options. I knew I couldn't win a fight against him - he'd probably been training with that stupid pigsticker of his for decades, if not centuries. It was too narrow to fully transform in here without blowing out building walls, and he was so close that by the time I took a deep breath, he'd be on me immediately.

Rethas advanced on me once more, his lip curled in derision. Again, something tickled the back of my brain at his expression, making me loathe him even more than I already did. He lunged again; this time I saw it coming, and I batted the flat of the blade away from me with the back of one scaly paw. The impact made my teeth rattle.

I backed up some more, suddenly finding myself flush against the outside wall of the Palace as the dance beat reverberated through the brick. I had just a moment to breathe before Rethas was on me again, stabbing and slashing at me. I wheeled away just in time; his rapier, no doubt made from faesteel and tipped with Dragonsbane, gouged deep channels in the wall, releasing a shower of masonry.

This is getting me nowhere, I thought, my mind racing. *I've got to get the hell out of this alley or he's gonna fucking kill me.* I flicked my eyes from the Sidhe to the damaged wall, now behind him.

Rethas snarled at me. "Come on, you stupid creature! Fight me or die like the craven beast you are. This whole thing has become a pantomime!"

At those words it clicked. The pale, angular features, the lithe frame, the naked arrogance, the scowling sneer – I knew who Rethas reminded me of, and why it turned my stomach. All he was missing was a heroin chic pallor and padlock on a chain around his neck. Oh, and Nancy Spungen clinging to his side.

I took one last step back. "You know what, you're right," I said. "I've had enough of this shit. And more than enough of you, you Gary Oldman-looking motherfucker." I sprang at him.

As far as mythics go, Sidhe are supernaturally fast and

strong. Lithe, athletic, agile, and incredibly tough – every inch the elven stereotype that mortal writers attributed to them over the centuries. Yet for all their graceful, dancer-like prowess, it still took an entire hunting party of them to take down a full-grown Dragon. And that was because it didn't matter how strong or tough an individual Sidhe was – even just one of us would always be stronger.

I slammed into Rethas, pinning his sword arm to his body. He let out a cry of surprise as the both of us collided with the weakened outer wall of the Palace, blasting through to the other side in a shower of broken bricks and mortar.

We tumbled into the open space together as screams erupted all around us, even as the dance music continued. I lost my grip on him and we pulled apart; I smashed through a pair of barstools before I could sink my claws into the floor to stop me from moving.

I scrambled to my feet, looking around wildly for Rethas. The crowd was roiling, mythics and mortals alike panicking and pushing in every direction, buffeting me as I fought against the tide of bodies.

It was too late when I spotted the Sidhe, his impeccable outfit ruined and his face bleeding from half a dozen cuts. Rethas had lost ahold of the rapier as we careened through the wall; instead, he had an ornate faesteel dagger clutched in his fist in a reverse grip. With a snarl, he slashed at me.

The crowd was too thick; I couldn't get away in time. The blade came up in a silver flash. I jerked my head to the side and a line of fire erupted across the side of my face, from below my left eye to above my brow ridge. I stumbled backwards, blinded my own blood, colliding with the stair rail that protected the bar area from the dance floor below. Flailing and howling from the pain, I went over it backwards.

The landing knocked the wind out of me. I gasped, desperately trying to fill my lungs, to get my limbs working again, but every breath sent lightning bolts of agony through me from the wound on my face. *Dragonsbane*, I thought wildly. The still-healing scar on my side from where Rethas' crossbow bolt had become lodged in me weeks ago throbbed, inflamed once again by the new wound.

"Ricky!" I turned my head, trying through the haze of pain to see who had called me. From up on the raised stage, I could see two people standing there. I blinked, my nictitating membranes clearing the dirt and blood from my eyes, and they sprang into focus: Neira and Anagen, both looking disheveled. Beside them was the unconscious body of a Troll dressed in a blue work uniform.

Anagen was shouting at me. "Ricky, get up! *Get up,* you idiot! He's coming!" They pointed.

I turned my head to see Rethas clambering over the railing. He had taken the time to retrieve his rapier and he slashed the air around him, sending the crowd fleeing from him.

He landed heavily on the dance floor, his former grace largely forgotten. The Sidhe's eyes were wild, burning with hate as he approached me. The blade of his sword wavered in his grip. "Finally," he panted, coming to a halt over me, "it's time to end this farce, worm." He raised his weapon high over his head.

I coughed, spitting a wad of bloody phlegm onto the floor. There was no one around us – it was just me and him. "You're right," I croaked, "it is." I closed my eyes. With the last of my strength, I willed myself to fully transform.

A brilliant flash filled the dance hall, sending another panicked scream through the crowd as people, Rethas included, winced and looked away. I rose to my feet, invigorated by assuming my true form. My scales caught the lights of the dance hall, sending glittering reflections among the suddenly quiet crowd. I stood up, all four claws digging into the flooring and tearing massive gouges into the wood paneling. With a single swipe, I knocked Rethas to the ground, pinning him there.

My tail lashed behind me, and I raised my neck high into the air. Smoke drifted from my nostrils. Opening my jaws wide, I roared, flames dancing across my tongue. The Sidhe struggled in my grip until I dropped my head, narrowing my eyes at him. *"ENOUGH,"* I intoned. Even in the dim light of the dance floor, my golden scales glittered.

He froze. "You- you're... you're—" He choked on his words.

"He's not just any Dragon." Anagen had hopped down off the stage. "I bet you figured you were simply preying on a weak little hatchling, didn't you, you *maláka?*" They put a hand on my flank. "You didn't really think his parents really named him 'Ricky,' did you?" They turned, addressing the crowd. "Before you today stands Fidirikonaz the Gold, the king of the Dragons. And this Fae," they continued, pointing down at Rethas, "in full view of all, has attempted to take the Ra'saar's life – in flagrant violation of the treaty between the Dragons and the Kingdom of Rainbows."

The doors burst open; a cadre of Guardsmen, led by Constable Canmore, filed into the Palace. They were flanked on either side by the club's twin Satyr bouncers. They came up short as they saw me towering over them.

Canmore stepped forward. "Mister Konacsz!" To his credit, his voice didn't even waver, despite having to crane his neck to meet my gaze. "We are here to take the Earl of Elmwood into custody." He nodded to Anagen. "Herald Anagen Nimenos alerted us to your kidnapping. It looks like we arrived just in time." He looked down at Rethas, still halfheartedly struggling against the floor where I had pinned him. "Would you, uh, permit us to do so?"

I craned my neck, bringing my face directly in line with the Sidhe beneath my claws. He froze as I did so, his face growing pale, eyes burning with fury. "Gladly," I rumbled, releasing him from my grip and taking a step back.

Two Trolls dressed in the colors of the Guard came

forward and extricated the Sidhe from the shattered floorboards around him. He glared silently as they hauled him from the wrecked nightclub, several other Guards creating a cordon around him as they did so.

Anagen patted me on the side again and I angled my neck around to look back at her. "Take it easy there, big boy," they said. "You, uh, you wanna shrink back down, Gigantor? You look like shit."

I closed my eyes. Another flash, and I regained my human form. As I did so, I realized two things: one, all the adrenaline that had been coursing through my body was now gone. The pain from getting slashed across the face came back all at once, dropping me to my knees.

The other thing? I was stark naked. In front of Anagen, Neira, the Queen's Guard, and an entire crowd of people. And with that being my final thought, I passed out right on the floor.

EPILOGUE

I eased myself, slowly, into the dining room chair, trying not to groan like a middle-aged dad who had just finished mowing the lawn. "Fuck, I'm still sore, can you believe it?"

Mom set down a full plate of *hangikjöt* down in front of me. The smell of smoked lamb wafted up, making my mouth water. "Well, you did crash through an entire brick wall." She grinned at me. "For a shy kid, you sure know how to make an entrance."

"He's lucky he didn't break his neck!" Dad came into the dining room, carrying a wooden cutting board piled high with freshly sliced homemade rye. He placed it on the table before sitting down himself. "You're gonna have to keep a better eye on him."

Anagen reached out and grabbed a slice. "I can't babysit him. He's gonna get into trouble with or without me." They raised the bread to their face and inhaled. "Damn, this smells amazing. Is it a family recipe?"

"It's *rúgbrauð*," Dags said, not even looking up from her phone. "You're supposed to bake it in a pot that's been buried in the sand next to a hot spring." She grabbed a piece herself, taking a large bite. "Mm, not bad, Mom."

"Not bad? You're outta your mind." Mack speared a few slices of his lamb with a fork and laid them atop his own slice.

"I look forward to this every Thanksgiving." He took an even bigger bite, his eyes rolling up into his sockets. "Goddamn that's good."

"Ah, yes, Thanksgiving. That carnival of lies. 'Oh, yes, the Indians were so *happy* to help!' Was that before or after the colonists started handing out smallpox blankets, Miles Standish?" My sister snorted.

"Hey, not at the table," my father warned. Dags sighed and set her phone face down on the tablecloth.

I looked at Anagen. "Sorry," I said lamely. "Family, right?" I reached for my water glass, taking a sip.

They grinned back at me, pulling a chunk of bread from their slice. "I like it," they said, popping it into their mouth.

My mother sat down, beaming. "I'm so glad you were able to join us," she said. "It's so rare Ricky brings home... friends." Her eyes sparkled mischievously.

I choked on my drink. "Uh, yeah," I coughed out, "about that..."

"Ooooooh, Ricky's got a girrrrrrrrrrrrlfriend," Mack taunted.

Dags tossed her napkin at my brother. "They're not a girl, dingus! How many times to I have to tell you!?"

"Oh, my gods! All right, sorry, jeez!"

Anagen pounded on my back. "Fuck's sake, don't die on me, Ricky."

Waving them off, I managed to clear my lungs. "I'm okay," I said. I sat back up and adjusted my bandage. It had slipped a little while I was trying to clear my throat.

Dad pointed at it. "How's that healing, by the way?"

I shrugged. "Getting there. They say I'll have a nasty scar, but I'll keep my sight. For now I just keep bumping into things."

"It's okay," Mom said, patting the back of my hand. Her phone dinged, and she pulled it out, checking it. "That's Morri, we've got plans to meet up later. The insurance money came through for the damage to the record store. And besides, chicks dig scars. Dudes, too."

"Enbies don't mind them, either," Anagen added, ruffling my hair.

"This is a violation of my rights," I groused, laughing. "I'm invoking the Geneva Convention."

"You're just lucky they seized the Earl's assets to pay for all the damage to the Palace," Anagen said. "Otherwise, you'd be spending your Thanksgiving patching holes in the floor instead of here eating this ridiculously good food."

"Yeah, well that's not over yet," I said, forking a piece of lamb into my mouth. "I have to show up at his tribunal in a couple weeks. Not exactly looking forward to walking into a court filled with fucking Sidhe."

"I'll be right there by your side," Anagen said. "Herald, remember? Plus I'm a witness. Don't worry, Rethas will answer for his bullshit."

I sighed. "Yeah, I just - I mean I'd rather not have to deal with it at all, you know?"

"A little late for that, brother dear." Dags smirked at me. "You're the one who put him through the fucking wall like Conny put Chauncey through the wringer on that Thundercoin nonsense."

"Yeah, I meant to ask you about that – since when did Conny hang out with mortals like that?"

My sister shook her head. "He sold the guy some molly once at the Palace or something."

I wrinkled my nose. "Are you fucking kidding me? I'm, uh, not gonna run into him, am I? I'm shadowing Neira at the club every Saturday night, remember? I still have no idea what it means to 'curate a vibe', or whatever the hell she's talking about."

"You'll get it," my mother said, putting her phone down on the table. "Just don't give up. And no, Conny's on time-out from what I heard. Something about a pump-and-dump gone wrong?"

Mack laughed. "Oh, it couldn't have happened to a nicer Blue. Someone at work told me about this – the majority of the coins in circulation just... 'disappeared.'" He added air quotes.

"I fucking warned him, the idiot!" Dags snorted. "That's what he gets for not using two-factor authentication."

"Well," my mother said, "it takes a smart and humble soul to listen to their significant other. But some Dragons are smarter than others. Right, dear?"

Dad nodded sagely, a small grin playing across his face. "Smarter, or more stubborn? I had given up every time Thorli shut me down when I tried to talk to her—"

Dags and Mack both groaned. "Here we go again," my sister said.

"What?" My father feigned insult. "It's a great story!"

"Yeah, that we've heard dozens of fucking times," Mack said.

The doorbell rang. "Oh, thank Bahamut, saved by the bell." Dags got up and left the room.

"Who the hell would that be?" my mother said. "Chad, are we expecting anyone else tonight?"

My father sounded puzzled. "No, this should be it. Dave said he'd make it for dessert after he closed up the diner."

"You're not gonna believe this." My sister walked back into the dining room, trailed by a stately older woman with steel gray eyes and ramrod-straight posture.

Mack's eyebrows shot up, his expression pleasantly

surprised. "Grandma Jutte? We didn't know you were coming!" He got up hurriedly and went over to her, hugging her warmly.

She returned the hug, giving Mack a brief but genuine smile. "Hello, Mack, everyone. I'm sorry to disturb your dinner, but I'm afraid I'm here on official Council business."

My father shared a glance with Mom. They both stood up as well. "Council business? What's going on, Mom?"

My grandmother looked around the room, her eyes alighting on Anagen. "It's fine, Jutte," my mother said. "They've earned every right to be here. Ricky owes them his life."

"Very well." Jutte pulled her up to her fullest height. "There's been... a development. We're convening the Council at once." She looked over at me. I swallowed. "The entire Council. Including you, Fidirikonaz."

Oh gods, I thought. *She used my full name.* A chill ran down my spine. I shook my head in incomprehension, fear chewing at the back of my mind. "What? What's going on?"

"It's the Ra'keth," my grandmother said. "The Lightning Rod has abdicated. The throne of the Sorcerer King stands empty, and without him, the implications are dire." She locked eyes with me. "We must leave at once. It is time you rose to lead us. Your people need you, my Ra'saar."

ACKNOWLEDGEMENT

This book wouldn't have been possible without the invaluable support of my editors Vaughn R. Demont and Skye Sisk, the rest of the Blackwarren Books staff, and the fantastic community on the Blackwarren Discord server. Likewise our beta readers, Kyrone Rustmore, Chris Shaffer, and Jamie "Reech" Walker, deserve a special shout-out for all their help. Your feedback and guidance made this book possible.

Neither would this have ever happened without the constant encouragement of my family. My parents Bob and Donna, my wife Pamelyn, and my daughter Eleanor have been cheering me on from the sidelines from the very beginning, and for that I am eternally grateful. Ricky's story would never have been told without you!

ABOUT THE AUTHOR

David M. Demar

David M. DeMar holds both a Bachelor of
Arts and a Master of Arts in English from
the State University
of New York at New Paltz. His short stories
have been published in several anthologies.
Certified Gold:
On the Air is his debut novel.
David lives in Queensbury, New York with
his wife, his daughter, and several assorted
wingless miniature
dragons. You might know them better as cats.

BOOKS BY THIS AUTHOR

Samhain Secrets: World Premiere

In the Argent City, where supernatural creatures like dragons, fae, and tricksters live alongside blissfully unaware humanity, Halloween Night remains the craziest night of the year. A dragon who would be king struggles to establish his identity and find his passion in hosting a popular radio show, while the wily Kitsune seek to unmask a conspiracy against the feuding Tricksters of the City, where anyone could be the culprit. Across the City, a pair of Fae entrepreneurs stake their future on cleansing a murder site for the police, but a nosy Brownie can't accept the given cause of death and suspects murder. And finally, a hopeful actress takes a chance at scoring the lead in the reboot of a much-beloved vampire action series, only to find the audition process far more bizarre, and deadly, than even the most committed actor would expect.

Featuring contributions from Chris Shaffer, David DeMar, Vaughn R. Demont, and special guest Sierra Dean, the Argent City is explored through the eyes of the different denizens that call it home, and the one night a year where the brave and curious can discover the secrets lying just beyond the human eye.

www.ingramcontent.com/pod-product-compliance
Lightning Source LLC
Chambersburg PA
CBHW052031240626
47153CB00006B/2040